CRITICS RAVE ABOUT NINA BANGS!

FROM BOARDWALK WITH LOVE

"This is a hilarious, sexy spoof . . . with some sensually sizzling love scenes to create a delightfully amusing romance."

—*Booklist*

"[A] playful romantic romp . . . with lots of teasing, word play, and spoofing, author Nina Bangs creates an eccentric delight readers will adore."

—*The Midwest Book Review*

NIGHT GAMES

"No one combines humor and sex in quite the way author Nina Bangs does. Her ability to take outlandish premises and make them work is a true gift!"

—*Romantic Times*

"Nina Bangs's talent for witty, irreverent eroticism [results in] a tempestuous fantasy with scintillating details."

—*The Midwest Book Review*

THE PLEASURE MASTER

"An irreverent, sexy and hilarious romp . . . Nina Bangs has done a fabulous job of creating a funny, sexy and off-beat romance that time-travel aficionados will absolutely relish."

—*Writers Write*

"Sizzling! . . . Witty eroticism reaches new heights in . . . this erotically intense, wildly imaginative romp."

—*Wordweaving*

"Plenty of laugh-out-loud moments . . . if you're looking for fun and fantasy, you will find it here!"

—*Romantic Times*

MORE PRAISE FOR NINA BANGS!

AN ORIGINAL SIN

"Ms. Bangs has written a fun comedy of people out of time. It is a romp and should be enjoyed in large gulps."

—*CompuServe Romance Reviews*

"If you're looking for a funny, heart-wrenching and truly lovely romance to read, try this one. You won't be disappointed."

—*All About Romance*

"Nina Bangs has come up with a completely new and unique twist on the time-travel theme and has delivered a story that is both humorous and captivating."

—*Romantic Times*

THE POWER OF PLEASURE

"I feel pleasure more strongly than others. And my senses feed that pleasure." He lowered his voice to a husky murmur, calling to all that was elemental in a woman. "The scent of a woman who wants my body stirs me, makes me hard with a need to slide my fingers across her warm flesh, bury myself between her open thighs, taste her breasts, and savor the texture of her mouth, soft and swollen from my kisses."

Her eyes grew even wider. Mayhap he should not have mentioned his need to taste.

"Well, that's really interesting, but I'm sort of tired tonight. I think I'll just call it a day."

He smiled what he knew must be a predatory smile, but he could not help himself. "'Twould take a brave woman to walk with me in the moonlight." He looked away to give her time to think on that. "Ye'll be here only a fortnight. 'Tis not long to try to make one such as me happy. 'Twould be a shame to waste an opportunity."

Darach felt her distress as ripples of worry. "Fine. I'll go. But no stirring need, no sliding of fingers, no *tasting*."

His smile widened. "Ach, lass, the tasting is the best part."

Her gaze narrowed on him. "I just bet it is."

Other *Love Spell* books by Nina Bangs:

FROM BOARDWALK WITH LOVE
NIGHT GAMES
THE PLEASURE MASTER
UNWRAPPED (anthology)
SEDUCTION BY CHOCOLATE (anthology)
AN ORIGINAL SIN
PARADISE (anthology)

Nina Bangs

Master of Ecstasy

LOVE SPELL

NEW YORK CITY

LOVE SPELL®

February 2004

Published by

Dorchester Publishing Co., Inc.
200 Madison Avenue
New York, NY 10016

ISBN 0-505-52557-7

Printed in the United States of America.

Visit us on the web at www.dorchesterpub.com.

To Michelle Brown:
thanks for being the world's best teaching partner.

Master of Ecstasy

Prologue

S+E=X. Seduction plus evil equals x-citement. A winning formula. *Her* formula.

Sparkle Stardust had been perfecting her sex-and-sin act for over a thousand years. A cosmic troublemaker who specialized in creating sexual havoc wherever she went, she was the best at what she did. And what she did was cause sexual trouble. Lots and lots of delicious trouble.

She sat down in the center of the castle's courtyard, wrapped her fluffy white tail around her, and stared up at the tower while feline irritation narrowed her orange eyes. With a small paw, she smoothed down a few errant hairs sticking up on her face and wished she could do the same for her temper. Sparkle was one pissed kitty.

Where the hell was Ganymede? He'd called for her help, asked her to take the form of a white cat . . . Why white? She hated white. It made her look fat. Besides, it was a symbol of good. She hated good. Why couldn't she be black, a true expression of her inner being? And what was with the cat thing? She'd wanted to be in her sexy human form when she met Ganymede again.

Her irritation eased as she thought of Ganymede, of how he'd looked when she'd last seen him. He'd been all golden-haired beauty, a living, breathing invitation to erotic adventure. They'd spent a month exploring every sexual excess, and then he'd left. She'd known it would happen, expected it, but still it had sort of hurt. No other being had ever made her feel regret. Only Ganymede. That was the one reason she'd answered his call. For old times' sake.

Sparkle scanned her surroundings. Nightfall, Scottish Highlands, 1785, old and crumbly castle, quiet looking. There didn't seem to be anything big going down. But whatever was happening must be huge, because Ganymede was the most powerful cosmic troublemaker in the universe. She couldn't imagine him needing help.

Hmm. She sensed a sort of mini-happening in one of those tower rooms. A woman. And she was . . . Sparkle concentrated. The woman was thinking about sex. Just ordinary ho-hum sex. Forget it. Sparkle was looking for something she could sink her teeth into. Figuratively speaking, of course. But wait . . . Now the woman was thinking really dumb thoughts like: nothing could make her get involved in a sexual situation while she was in this castle.

Nothing? Sparkle wrapped her tail more tightly around herself and almost purred with the endless possibilities for irresistible sexual "situations." This woman would be her first work in progress.

Things were looking up.

Suddenly her thoughts scattered. A presence touched her that was so powerful, so *sexual,* it made her whiskers twitch. If she'd been in human form, a lot of other things would have been twitching.

Not Ganymede. This was a sensual presence like none she had ever experienced. It was every dark night filled with the soft moans of erotic fulfillment, every male body slick with sweat as it drove into the female beneath it, every kinky dream of leather, chains, and sex toys.

Sparkle smiled. Or as close as she could get to a smile with her little cat mouth. The being was male, he was in that tower, and she could feel the heated flow of his sensual power.

Yummy. A sexual challenge. Her territory.

Now, what would it take to hook Ms. No-sex-for-me up with all that hot male potential? Sparkle could already feel her creative juices stirring.

Yep, Mr. I-bring-the-heat could just move over, because Sparkle Stardust was in the house.

Chapter One

Darach MacKenzie watched the white cat from his tower window and smiled. The slide of his lips across his fangs stirred familiar hungers: for nourishment, for sexual pleasure. The two needs seemed always entwined. He pushed aside both. He must first know what threatened him. His smile widened, a savage baring of his teeth. He suspected his smile would not be a comforting thing to see.

"Something passing strange creeps in on wee cat paws." His murmur was soft, thoughtful, and meant for no human ears.

His smile faded as he raked his fingers through his hair, then allowed the strands to settle across his shoulders again. Ganymede had brought another of his kind to aid him. It would do him no good, because even their combined powers would not make Darach abandon his duty.

“ ’Tis a mighty nuisance ye’ll be.” He frowned. He knew not what Ganymede and the cat were, but he’d felt their power, a power that was not human. “Mayhap I should know what ye’re thinking.”

He focused his mind on the cat and slipped into her thoughts. It was no hard thing to do. Not only did she do nothing to keep him out, she seemed almost to welcome him.

As his thoughts touched hers, he widened his eyes. He found no plans for death and destruction, only . . .

Sex. Sex in all its conceivable forms. Naked bodies spread and open to every erotic act. An explosion of sensual stimuli, darkness, heat, and insatiable sexual hunger.

Darach stepped away from the window and turned back to his room. She was a strange helpmate for Ganymede, but one that Darach could understand. Both he and the creature masquerading as a cat appreciated the joy of all that was sexual. And with his heightened senses, Darach knew better than most the wonders of sex. He had lost many of his human characteristics when he became vampire, but he had compensated. His smile returned as his gaze touched his bed with its massive posts hewn from native wood, its silken coverings, and its *memories*. Aye, he had compensated.

He strode to the door, then paused. Closing his eyes, he willed his return to human form, breathing out sharply at the smooth disappearance of his fangs like the sheathing of a cat’s claws.

Absently he put his hand over his heart. Even after a hundred years, his heart's beating amazed him.

With his eyes still closed, he searched for *her*, the woman he had sensed but a short time ago. She was there in the room beneath his, all warm female, a temptation to the sensual hunter in him. He had meant to feed this night, but it would do no harm to amuse himself first.

He would meet her, then go down with her to the meal Ganymede had prepared for his guests. It would give him a chance to measure the danger from Ganymede and the cat while they were together. Ganymede would do nothing while all his guests were gathered around him for fear of upsetting them.

His guests. Darach had heard Ganymede speaking to them, people from far distant times who had paid Ganymede for the pleasure of staying in this castle while they sought sensual enjoyment from each other. But the castle belonged to Darach's clan, and Ganymede had not asked permission to use it. Mayhap Ganymede and his guests would experience far more than they had expected.

Darach opened his eyes, settled his plaid across his shoulders, and opened the door. Humor touched him, blunting the hunger still gnawing at him. Ganymede's guests would find much to upset them with their first meal. The vile odor drifting from the castle's kitchen suggested a witch's brew. Darach wondered idly if he would find all of them changed to toads after eating. It would certainly solve his problem. With that cheerful thought, he strode from his room and closed the door behind him.

As he moved silently down the winding stone steps, he wondered about the woman. Was she young or old? Would she meet him with heated welcome or cool disdain? He could touch her thoughts, but he chose instead to savor this small mystery. Though it mattered not. If he wanted her, she would be his. It was always so. He did not question why, only enjoyed what the fates brought him.

Darach reached the bottom of the steps and stopped before her door. He knew his smile was predatory and attempted to rearrange it into something less threatening. He could not do it. Shrugging, he raised his fist to knock.

Blythe turned in a slow circle, studying her room and trying to ignore a sense of something drawing closer, something scary. Which was stupid, because there was absolutely nothing here to threaten her. She was a twenty-fourth-century kind of woman, and by 2300 scientists had determined that all ghost and ghoulie sightings had logical explanations. Besides, she'd booked this trip back to 1785 Scotland through a reputable time-travel agency, and the agency's rep, Ganymede, looked like he could take care of any problems that popped up.

The sudden pounding on her door drove all logical

twenty-fourth-century thoughts from her head. The tiny primitive person who skulked in a dusty corner of her mind but rarely voiced an opinion was whispering gleeful possibilities. *Demon: considers you yummy takeout. Really ugly gargoyle: wants to sleep in your bed.*

Calm down. She was safe behind a locked door. Besides, she'd brought her Freeze-frame. It could paralyze a bull elephant in mid-charge. She doubted any bull elephants were waiting outside her door.

Through force of habit, she tried to touch the emotions of whoever was beyond the door. Nothing. Strange. She could always read emotions. Blythe exhaled sharply. Of course, she couldn't read even a niggiwit's emotions when she was scaring herself silly. She'd just open the door.

Right. She'd just open the door. Visions of childhood nightmares, particularly the ones involving Heeperian mega-headed spiders, kept her hand from the latch.

Her reaction bothered her. She was supposed to be the guru of emotional tranquillity. She wasn't supposed to be moved by vague, unsubstantiated feelings that had no logical foundation. But as night shadows crept across the room, she opted for a closed-door policy.

She leaned close to the massive wooden portal and shouted. "Who's there?"

"Darach MacKenzie. I dwell above ye. Mayhap we could go down to the meal together."

A *human* voice. Instant voice analysis? Dark, sensual, *dangerous,* with an ancient dialect that seemed in tune with this castle. The very humanness of the voice should have calmed her pounding heart. It pounded harder.

"You have the room above me? That's the tower suite. How'd you get it?" *She* was supposed to have had the top suite in the tower. Blythe had requested it because she'd wanted to get as far away as possible from Textron, whose fear of heights kept him on the ground floor. But when they arrived, Ganymede had made some excuse about a mixup in reservations, so she'd ended up in this room.

" 'Twas my room before ye came and will remain so after ye leave."

Blythe bit her lip as she considered this news. Her visitor wasn't with Ganymede's tourist group. And Ganymede hadn't mentioned an owner in residence.

"Ye dinna wish to open the door. Do ye fear me?" His soft laughter mocked her.

"No." *Yes*. She hadn't a clue why, but her instinct's message was clear: Do not open that door. "Uh, I'm not dressed yet. I'll meet you in the great hall . . . Darach." Blythe had no doubt she'd recognize him. A man with that dark slide of sin in his voice would stand out in any crowd. She clamped down on all thoughts of sensual and sinful. No way was she strolling down that path again. She'd learned the hard way that sex was the ultimate booby trap.

She'd just wait a few minutes and give him a head start before going down to dinner. Blythe began to turn away when the latch lifted and the door swung slowly open.

Shock held her frozen. Panicked thoughts bumped into each other as they raced terror-stricken around in her head. Demon! Gargoyle! Giant spiders! *Do something!*

Somewhere between the demon and do-something, a man stepped into her room.

"Ye disappoint me, lass. I thought to find ye without clothing. 'Twould have been a wondrous sight." His amusement mocked her puny lie.

Her survival instinct kicked in. "Get out." A weapon. Her Freeze-frame was still in her purse. Fumbling at the small table beside her, her fingers closed around a heavy vase.

"Dinna destroy the vase. 'Twould take energy ye could well use in a more pleasurable way." His voice was dark smoke and night secrets.

Blythe hesitated for a moment to think about the dark-smoke part and was doomed. He moved close and his fingers wrapped around her hand. She released the vase.

She gazed up at the shadowed face of the man who towered over her. What were her chances in hand-to-hand combat? None. She opened her mouth to scream.

He placed a large palm over her mouth and bent down to whisper in her ear. "Ye're safe with me. 'Tis only that the latch was loose, and the wind blew the door open."

Safe? She didn't think so. The pressure of his warm skin against her lips, his scent of wild dark places and untamed male, and the silky glide of his hair over her cheek muddied her thoughts. Dangerous? You bet. How? She couldn't decide. She'd never been good at multiple-choice questions.

But she couldn't deny that he was human, and since she'd half expected some ancient monster to leap from the darkness, his flesh-and-blood presence steadied her.

He seemed to sense her indecision, because he took his palm from her mouth and moved further into the room. "Ye need light to chase away the night terrors."

"Like how? I didn't bring my Flick-flame, and I never got the hang of rubbing two stones together." She couldn't let him sidetrack her. "And there's no wind." She couldn't let him sidetrack her. "And there's no wind."

Her words were blown away on a sudden cold gust that whipped through the doorway.

"These are old drafty stones, and the wind slips through to play wherever it can find an opening." He didn't turn to look at her as one by one he lit the candles, then crouched in front of the hearth.

How had he done that? She hadn't seen any fire-lighting devices in his hand. When did matches come into use? She couldn't remember. Distractedly, she pushed the door closed before the wind could blow out the candles.

Her complete attention returned to the man. First

impressions? Tall, muscular, and wearing some sort of native . . . She searched her memory of ancient clothing. A kilt. He wore a kilt with a checked pattern of dark green and blue. It didn't quite look like the pictures she'd seen, more like one piece of cloth somehow wrapped around him.

All she could see now was the solid wall of his back and a tangle of long black hair.

She was free to run from the room, but the very fact that she could negated the need. If he meant her harm, he'd had the opportunity.

Wrapping her arms around herself, she moved cautiously toward him. The fire was already blazing in the fireplace, which struck her as odd. She'd never lit a fire in her life, but common sense said it should take time to build to blazing status. And why hadn't she been able to read his emotions? Blythe balanced her suspicions against her need to be warm. Warm won. She moved even closer.

"The room will be comfortable by the time ye return from the meal." He stood, then stared into the fire. "Ye'll want a great pile of covers to keep away the chill when morning comes and the fire dies."

Turn around so I can see your face. She needed to put her unease to rest, give a human face to her fear.

"A man would do as well. Body heat doesna die with the morning."

His suggestion was a rough trail of temptation, raising goose bumps that had nothing to do with the night's chill. *Remember your fear.* But somehow she couldn't whip up the panic she'd felt such a short time ago. That didn't mean she'd heaved out her common sense along with her terror.

"The fire's great. I don't need anything else." She suspected if she spent much time listening to the dark compulsion of his voice, she'd be willing to explore alternate heating sources. But of course she wouldn't, because she had work to do here, and sex wasn't part of her job description.

"We all need something else." With that cryptic comment, he turned.

Blythe stood riveted. If ever the term "terrifying beauty" had meaning, she was looking at it. In her time, body and face molders could give every person the look he chose. But that was only a surface thing. Cosmetic surgery couldn't reveal inner demons.

This man's face hid nothing. Every hard line was elemental male, a face men would fear and women would . . . recognize. He was the hot primitive need that lived in every woman no matter how much she denied it. Blythe's gaze slid across his lips, so sensual that she could almost feel them softening on her mouth. She avoided his eyes. She wasn't ready to go there yet, because she could admire his beauty, like the perfect storm with its wild magnificence, while still recognizing the danger. She didn't need any heightened sensitivity for that analysis.

"Welcome to my time. Ye have not told me your

name." He moved closer, and the room warmed proportionately.

Okay, he knew about the time travel. So why was he accepting it calmly? His clothing screamed primitive. It was 1785, for heaven's sake. Why didn't he run screaming into the night or accuse her of witchcraft? She shivered. Witchcraft. The possibility of becoming a toasted crunchy wasn't a fun thought.

"You don't seem too upset at the time-travel concept."

"I know of things ye could never imagine. So why would I not believe ye've traveled through time?" He sounded sincere.

Things ye could never imagine? That was *not* a comforting answer.

"Ye *do* have a name, do ye not?" He sounded amused.

"Blythe." She supplied her name automatically.

The long, tangled glory of his hair brought the night with it. She couldn't imagine it pulled back and tamed. Blythe knew she should look beyond his hair, beyond the hard lines of his jaw, the full temptation of his lips, to his eyes. She still wasn't that brave yet.

"Blythe? Ye have no other name?" Again he moved closer.

"I'm Blythe number 56-2310 on my birth records. I was the fifty-sixth Blythe born in 2310. But the number is only for official identification." He loomed over her, broad shoulders blocking out the fire's light, moving into her personal space and bringing with him a message that confused her.

She'd spent a lifetime reading other people's emotions and dealing with them. Blythe felt nothing from him but . . . power. Layers of power. Sexual power that tempted and seduced. And a darker power, the one she'd felt drawing closer, the one she'd responded to when he first knocked.

What hid behind all that power? she wondered. Did she really want to know?

" 'Tis a cold name for a woman such as ye."

The wicked slant of his lips suggested he'd like a shot at renaming her. His name would probably be something like Blythe Hot-In-Bed.

Time to shift his attention from her. "How about you? Who are you, Darach?" Her intuition said she'd need a few lifetimes to get an answer to that one.

"I am the MacKenzie. This castle, this land, belongs to my clan. I dinna spend much time here, but this is the home of my youth, and I return to it when I must." He seemed distracted as he reached out to slide a strand of her hair away from her face, then touched the silver Ecstasy charm at her throat.

Blythe checked to make sure the strands weren't smoldering. The rest of her sure was. "The castle looks deserted except for our tour group. Where's the rest of your family?"

Some emotion she couldn't identify tightened his jaw and narrowed his lips. "They dwell . . . elsewhere."

Blythe might not be able to read his emotions, but she understood perfectly that he didn't want her to know much about him. Secrecy. Secrets often spawned stress and unhappiness. Possibilities blossomed. She smiled.

"Sounds like your life is pretty lonely." She should be so lucky. Loneliness was a surefire indicator of unhappiness, and Blythe was all about curing unhappiness.

His gaze was fixed on her lips, and it was as though he'd touched them with his fingertips. She firmed them to discourage touching.

He shrugged. "I need no company but my own." His gaze warmed on her mouth. "Ye should smile often."

She rushed into speech before she lost her breath completely. "So I suppose the travel agency rented the castle from you." She couldn't help it, she backed up.

"They rented nothing from me." A slant of his lips hinted at humor she knew wouldn't reach his eyes, if she had the courage to look into his eyes. "I intend to discuss this with them."

Absently he put his hand over his heart. Maybe she should give that a try to slow down her own heartbeats.

"This was my home before the castle stood, and I willna let Ganymede and his hireling drive me from it." He leaned toward her, and she backed away another step. He smiled his satisfaction.

Before the castle stood? Okay, enough. At this rate, he'd back her out the door and down the tower's winding stone steps. She needed to think about the before-the-castle-stood thing, but she had other worries at the moment.

Blythe searched for her nonexistent spine and stiffened it. A rubbery spine would *not* get the job done. She was letting the castle, the night, and this man play games with her mind. She needed to take control.

"I'll just get my shawl. Remind me to ask Ganymede for some kind of lighter to start a fire so I won't freeze to death here. An Auto-temp-regulator would've been nice, but I guess he didn't think of it." She scuttled sideways away from Darach and refused to consider any comparison to a frightened crab.

"Autotempregulator?"

Her courage increased in direct proportion to his puzzlement. "And I didn't see any bathroom. What do I do if I have to, you know?" She waved her hands to indicate the importance of *you know*. "Anyway, there's only so much authenticity I can stand. I'll discuss life's little necessities with Ganymede over dinner."

"Ye have a chamber pot beneath your bed." Puzzlement gone, amusement back.

"Thanks. I'll remember that." Eeew. Could she hold it for two weeks? Worth a try.

Blythe reached for her shawl, part of the "authentic" wardrobe Ganymede had insisted his time travelers buy so that they would blend in with the locals. She had deviated a little from what was authentic, but hey, it was her trip.

At the same time as she picked up her shawl, she scooped the Freeze-frame from her purse. A three-inch equalizer. Uh-oh, no pocket. Turning her back to Darach, she dropped it down her bra and breathed a hope that she wouldn't have to go fishing for it.

Pasting a bright smile on her face, she turned. "Okay, all ready. Let's go."

Blythe's smile faded as Darach strode across the room, took the shawl from her nerveless fingers, and settled it across her shoulders. It was as though every one of her uncertainties about him lay across her shoulders, weighing her down with unanswered questions. Why couldn't she read his emotions? What had he meant about being here before the castle stood? Why did he make her so uneasy? Why did he make her . . . ? She slid her gaze the length of his hot body. Fine, so she already knew the answer to *that* question.

"Ye've traveled far, and the things ye dinna understand about this place could harm ye. 'Tis foolish ye are to have come here. And Ganymede is not what ye think. Ye would have done better to stay safely at home with your Autotempregulator and bathroom." He shifted a bit closer.

That was it. She refused to retreat another step. In one breath he'd threatened her and insulted her decision-making abilities. Without thinking, she met his gaze.

What a big fat mistake. He had the bluest eyes she'd ever seen. Blythe had once visited a moraine lake that had water exactly that shade, so brilliant that you forgot about its depth, about its bone-chilling iciness born of the glacier that formed it.

Blythe saw it all in his eyes. Depths she couldn't read, didn't think she wanted to read. And unbelievable coldness. Automatically she reached out with her senses, searching for emotion, *any* emotion. Nothing. It was as though he'd closed a door in her face. He must have feelings, everyone did. *Maybe he doesn't.*

Blythe looked away first. She couldn't figure anything out on an empty stomach. "I'm hungry. Let's go down to the great hall." Trying for casual, she walked to the door and hoped he'd leave her room while she tried to secure the stupid latch. Again.

"Ye speak verra strangely." He didn't sound like he was leaving.

"I used the Language Assimilation Program to learn the most ancient dialect available. Unfortunately, the most ancient dialect was from the early twenty-first century." She shrugged. Would he leave now?

Blythe was silently swearing at the latch in Riparian, a language with really great descriptive curses, when she felt him stop behind her. *Felt him.* His body, his heat, his scent, which touched her with something so elemental it made her draw in a deep fortifying breath. Turning, she forgot all about the door.

"Doors never keep out those who truly wish to enter." His soft statement stilled her, took on a meaning she didn't want to examine.

She chose to ignore hidden meanings. "Right. This door wouldn't keep a Kadian sand biddle out."

"Kadian sand biddle?" He smiled. Really smiled. "This sand biddle sounds like a fearsome creature."

Blythe had traveled the galaxy and beyond, and never, absolutely *never,* had she seen a smile like that: dark and wicked, with the promise of nights filled with sinful pleasure.

She blinked. What had he said? "Oh, the sand biddle." She needed to get out of range of that smile before it took her down like a Tomar light missile. "It's pretty harmless." Blythe edged away from him. "It's a small insect. Gets into your clothing, bites you, and leaves a huge purple blotch that takes a week to fade."

Sucking in her breath to make herself as thin as possible, she slid past him and out the door without making body contact.

"Not all things that get into your clothes and bite are harmless." She heard the laughter in his voice as he closed the door behind them and followed her down the castle's dark steps.

Blythe didn't worry about the door being unlatched because she'd brought the danger with her. "Things that bite?" She tried to ignore his presence behind her. Fat chance. "Don't tell me there're wild animals outside." Earth in 2339 didn't have any more wild animals.

"Outside? Mayhap 'tis the one inside ye need worry about."

She could almost feel his warm breath fanning her

neck as he followed close behind her. Blythe shivered. She didn't try to pin down the cause of her shiver.

"If you're trying to scare me, forget it. I don't scare." Lies, lies, and more lies. *He* scared her. Because she didn't understand him, and she always understood people. Because she didn't know how to deal with such a totally sexual animal.

Blythe was so busy thinking about sexual animals and unexpected bites that she missed her footing in the dark. With a squeak of alarm, she reached for the stone wall in an attempt to stop her fall.

Her hand never reached the wall. With a muffled curse, Darach wrapped his arms around her and pulled her against him. "I canna believe Ganymede has not lit the sconces so his guests might see where they step."

"I could've broken my neck." She breathed in short gasps that had nothing to do with her near disaster. Since he was on the step above her and a lot taller than she, when he'd grabbed her he'd settled his hands below her breasts instead of around her waist.

"Aye, and to waste a neck such as yours would be a terrible thing." She felt his soft laughter as he leaned down to murmur in her ear. She had the feeling he was enjoying a joke only he understood. " 'Twould have ruined my whole century for such a thing to happen."

"Century?" One word at a time seemed her limit right now.

"Hmm." His lips touched the hollow of her neck. "Did I say century? Mayhap I meant day." He slid his tongue over the spot his lips had touched.

Blythe's breath caught as his touch sizzled and sparked all the way to her toes. At this moment, the creatures that growled in the night outside the castle seemed no danger at all compared to the sensual threat of the dark Highlander who stood behind her.

She was losing her perspective. This trip was not about enjoying a stranger's mouth on her neck while she fervently hoped he'd slide his hands up to touch her breasts. What did she know about him other than he'd scared her witless? Maybe this was a nightly ritual with him: seduction on the stairs, dinner, then a good night's sleep. She opened her mouth to express her feelings.

He released her before she said anything, and she stood, bereft, on the steps. Chill night air crept inside her open shawl and touched the spot on her neck that was still warm from his lips. Shaking off her inexplicable sense of loss, she continued down the steps, but this time she kept one hand on the stone wall.

"Why have ye come here? The castle offers little comfort, and ye dinna seem overly interested in the 'sensual possibilities' offered by those who brought ye." His voice was cool, as though the heat of a few moments ago never existed.

Sensual possibilities? She frowned. Oh, yeah. The Cosmic Time Travel Agency had promised a sexual adventure, a romantic escape to a distant past when men were men. No kidding.

A sexual adventure was the last thing Blythe wanted. Her last foray into sexual waters had landed her in *hot* water with Ecstasy Inc. When she'd found out that this trip was all about erotic discovery, Blythe had told Textron she didn't want to go. She'd asked him to choose a different tour, but he'd said it would be the perfect test to see if she could focus on the job and ignore the sensual.

Was that what the whole thing on the steps had been about? The thought made her mad, and she didn't have a clue why. "I'm not here for a sexual holiday." She made her voice as cool and uninterested as his. "I work for Ecstasy Incorporated, and my job is making people happy." Absently she fingered the Ecstasy charm that hung from a chain around her neck.

"Ye do it well, lass. I was verra happy while we stood on the steps above." He sounded sincere.

"I don't use sex to make people happy. Sex is short-term. I'm in the long-term happiness business." Amazing that she could talk through clenched teeth. "In my time, scientists have conquered disease and aging. All it takes are a few tiny body implants. I chose to have the implants put in when I was twenty-five, and I'll remain twenty-five unless I'm killed in an accident or the victim of a crime." She was so involved with her explanation that she barely noticed they'd reached the bottom of the steps.

She turned in time to catch his startled expression. Good. His surprise empowered her.

"This has caused unexpected problems. Earth is overpopulated, and living space is scarce and expensive. People have to work throughout their lifetime to support themselves and their families. When people can't look forward to retirement, and they have nothing in their futures but more work for untold years, stress reaches cataclysmic proportions. Some become desperate enough to have their implants removed or even take their own lives."

She paused only long enough to note his intent interest. "My company is dedicated to lessening the effects of stress, to bringing calm and joy into the lives of those teetering on the edge of emotional breakdowns due to overwork. Ecstasy Incorporated doesn't offer sexual solutions, but instead depends on the talents of its well-trained Happiness staff." Blythe frowned. She sounded like one of Ecstasy Inc.'s ads. All cold facts, but no passion. Where had her passion for the job gone?

"Ye should not dismiss the power of sexual solutions." He didn't smile, so she assumed he was serious.

She shook her head. "I use a variety of methods sanctioned by the Intergalactic Association for the Relief of Stress and Depression to make people happy and productive again." Blythe's frown deepened. Why did she feel the need to justify her methods to this primitive who probably solved his unresolved issues by pillaging a few villages? "I can make anyone happy." She'd never felt driven to boast about her power before. Why now? *He makes you feel defensive, that's why.*

His expression suggested he doubted her boast, but he made no comment about it. "I would not wish to live in a world such as ye describe." He guided her toward the glow of candlelight and the murmur of voices coming from the great hall.

Blythe thought about that. "I guess extending people's lifetimes indefinitely does have its down side."

He was silent beside her.

The great hall transported her to another time and place. Okay, so she was already in another time and place. She had no idea how authentic this setup was, but it looked like a passable reenactment of a castle meal in 1785. Candle glow and the hearth fire cast a surrealistic light over the long table and the six people seated around it.

As they paused in the doorway, a man rose from the table and came toward them.

Even though she'd met Ganymede briefly when she first arrived, Blythe still widened her eyes at the total impact of him. He was huge, all mass and muscle, and he had to be close to seven feet tall with wild flame-red hair and a bushy beard. His dark-green-and-blue-checked kilt completed the picture of an ancient Scottish laird.

"Hey, great to see you again, Blythe." He was all booming good cheer, but his glance barely touched her, then shifted away.

She followed his gaze down to where a white cat sat at his feet. The cat studiously ignored her in favor of Darach.

"I want to officially welcome you to Castle Ganymede. For the time you're here, just think of me as Ganymede MacKenzie, the Scottish chieftain who's going to make sure you have a good time. The Cosmic Time Travel Agency always delivers." He clapped her on the shoulder and almost knocked her down.

He sounded a little too jolly, and though he was speaking to her, he'd fixed his gaze on Darach. She took the opportunity to look into his eyes.

And just as quickly looked down. Talk about false pretenses. He might be masquerading as a bluff, good-natured Highlander, but those amber eyes said "predator" loud and clear. His feelings? She'd just take a peek. Blythe reached for his emotions, blinked, then backed away. Wow. Talk about aggression.

"Well, well." Ganymede's smile never wavered, but his gaze grew so cold it made Blythe shiver. "And you are?" His complete attention was on Darach.

"Darach. And no MacKenzie bears the name Ganymede." All of Darach's playful sensuality had disappeared, leaving the same stranger who had scared Blythe witless. "Ye need ask permission before ye bring guests into my clan's home."

Ganymede raised one bushy brow. "Your clan's home? Looked like a crumbling pile of rock to me. Said 'fixer-upper' loud and clear. I claimed it. I restored it. It's mine."

"I dinna think so." Darach's voice was a whisper of menace.

Blythe widened her eyes as the emotion she'd looked for hit her with enough force to drive her back a step. Not the emotion she'd hoped for, though. Anger was a living, breathing force between the two men.

And the power she felt scared her. She didn't know what was going on, didn't *want* to know. Forcing her attention away from the men, she glanced down at the cat. It had deserted Ganymede and was weaving a sinuous pattern around Darach's legs as it gazed up at him with bright, interested eyes.

"At least one of us isn't intimidated, kitty." She smiled at the cat.

Blythe shook her head to clear it of what sounded like a light tinkle of laughter. Great. Now she was hearing things.

"I want your butt out of my castle, bud. You'll upset my guests." Ganymede's voice had risen.

"Ye'll not send me from my home. Ye'll find another place to play your games, or I will cause ye grief." Darach's voice had lowered to a dangerous murmur.

"You and what army of skirt-wearing wimps?" Ganymede was almost shouting now. "Don't count on home court advantage to help you."

Blythe did some mental eye-rolling. She was not going to stand here and listen to this deteriorate into a shouting match. Okay, so Ganymede was doing all the shouting, but she still wanted outta here. But first she would make one attempt to defuse the situation.

"Why don't you come with me, Darach, and have a drink to calm down? Then you and Ganymede can talk business with a little more maturity." She reached out to tug at Darach's arm.

Her tug was like touching a pure power source. He looked at her with the same effect as if she'd been zapped by a few thousand power pulses. The sizzle and burn of his immense anger left her fingers clutching his arm, unable to release him.

Slowly he relaxed and offered her a tight smile. "I might be tempted to have a wee sip, but not tonight." His lips softened, and his eyes promised that the wee sip would be with her. Once again, he absently placed his hand over his heart. "I must return to my room, but be verra careful in this place. 'Tis not always safe for those who do not know it."

Puzzled, Blythe watched him stride from the great hall. She would've sworn his warning was aimed at Ganymede, not her. And why hadn't he stayed to eat? Blythe didn't for a minute think that Ganymede had intimidated him.

Once Darach had left, she turned to look at Ganymede.

His expression was thunderous, and he seemed to have forgotten her. He glared down at the white cat, which was studiously avoiding his stare. "Okay, smart mouth, what do *you* think I should do?"

Fine, so Ganymede talked to his cat. She could live with that. Blythe glanced toward the table, where everyone had stopped eating to avidly follow the exchange between Darach and Ganymede.

"It's like this, little lady." Without warning, Ganymede clasped her arm and propelled her toward the table. "This Darach guy is bad news. I'll work on getting rid of him, but things like this take time."

Ganymede almost pushed her into a seat between Textron and one of the female guests. Both looked startled, but Blythe suspected that their reactions were to Ganymede, not her. She'd just bet that everyone around Ganymede perpetually wore a startled expression.

Textron leaned toward her. "I've found the perfect subject for you."

Great. Just great. The slimy worm wasn't going to give her even one night of down time.

"Now, you enjoy your meal and don't give another thought to that blood-sucking fiend." Seemingly satisfied that he'd offered a perfectly logical explanation for everything, Ganymede strode away with the white cat padding after him.

"Blood-sucking fiend?" Blythe gazed down at her plate of blackened meat and an unidentifiable large rootlike vegetable with what she suspected was a dazed expression. "What was he talking about?"

The woman leaned toward her. "I think he means that your man is a vampire." She smiled at Blythe. "Don't be afraid of the venison. It's tough with a bit too much seasoning, but I suppose it's what people eat in 1785." She frowned. "I don't know about the root thing. Looks weird to me."

Blythe stared at her in wide-eyed horror. "Vampire?"

Oh boy.

Chapter Two

Ganymede knew that if he didn't get out of the great hall he'd do something evil. Right here. Right now. He couldn't afford for that to happen.

He stormed from the castle, past his gape-mouthed guests, and out into the Scottish night. Sparkle padded beside him. He paused in the middle of the courtyard to take a deep gulp of cold air.

I am reformed. I really like being good. Being nice is fun. What a bunch of garbage. He *hated* being good. He wanted to be *bad,* dam . . . darn it. If he didn't think the Big Boss was watching, he'd . . .

Too late for what-ifs. He was a victim of his own success. He'd caused so much trouble during the last few thousand years that the Big Boss had grounded him. Forever. He was stuck with being a nice guy, so he couldn't blow the vampire to bits and scatter his pieces across the universe. No blowing up and scattering allowed by the Big Boss. Ganymede cast a considering glance at Sparkle, who was busy sniffing the night air. That didn't mean someone else couldn't do it. Someone who was totally *unreformed*.

"I love the scent of sex in the night. Rich, full-bodied, sensual. Like licking chocolate syrup off a man's naked—"

Ganymede took a sniff. "All I smell is heather."

"Mmm. The scent of heather. Two hundred years ago, I spent a night in the heather with two exceptionally talented Highlanders. Rolling in heather is prickly, but the sex was great."

"Yeah, yeah. I get the picture." He tugged at his kilt in a vain effort to make it cover more of his legs. Stupid piece of clothing. The cold Highland wind still reached under it with gleeful fingers. If he stood here much longer he'd have icicles hanging from his . . . He shook his head. Icicles were a non-issue right now.

"Why the he . . ." Ganymede drew in a deep breath. He couldn't use that word anymore. He couldn't use *any* of the words that really expressed his feelings. "Why in heaven's name does everything have to be food or sex with you?"

"It's all about happiness, my reformed cosmic troublemaker." She arched her back in a leisurely stretch, then twined her sinuous body around his ankles. "The senses make me happy. I love to roll around in them, coat myself with every luscious experience."

Ganymede pushed away memories of a few specific

"luscious experiences" shared with Sparkle long ago. "Forget all that. You're a cat now. Help me figure out how to get rid of the vampire before he scares my victims . . . I mean my *guests* away." He had to stop thinking like a cosmic troublemaker, but the familiar evil thoughts wouldn't leave him alone.

"I'm in cat *form*. I can still appreciate the finer things in life." Sparkle cast him a sly glance. "And your vampire is very old, very powerful, and very yummy." She licked her mouth with a delicate pink tongue. "Like the smooth slide of brandy warming me all the way down after a night spent celebrating chaos and destruction." Her gaze turned wicked. "Like the moment I wrap my legs around a man who thought he couldn't be seduced, and he realizes—"

"Got the message." Ganymede chose to ignore the tiny stab that was definitely *not* jealousy. "All that stuff's easy for you to say. You don't have Mr. Dark-Evil-and-Deadly living in your castle." Dark. Evil. Deadly. Ganymede had been all of those and more at one time. The numero uno, evilest basta . . . Great. Another word he couldn't use. The evilest not-a-nice-guy in the universe. Was he feeling a little wistful here, a little nostalgic for the bad old days? "I wish I were him."

Ganymede blinked. Oops. He hoped no one important had heard that. "Forget I said that."

Sparkle turned her orange-eyed gaze on him. She

smiled, exposing small sharp white teeth. "We had some great times, didn't we?"

Ganymede exhaled sharply. "Yeah."

Her gaze softened. "I still remember—"

"Don't remember. The old Ganymede is dead. Deal with the new one." Ruthlessly he shoved aside thoughts of dark nights and hot sex with a flame-haired seductress named Sparkle Stardust.

"I liked the old one better." Some elusive emotion appeared in her cat eyes.

He didn't even try to read the emotion. "I don't want to talk about it anymore. Now, here's the deal. I need you to spy on the vampire. If in the course of your spying you have to kill him, hey, that's life. Just don't tell me. And I need you to make my guests fall in lust with each other. Oh, and I want a ghost."

"A ghost?" Her expression said she was not through talking about "it," but that she'd bide her time before pouncing on the subject again.

"Yeah. I promised the guests there'd be a ghost. Makes the castle more authentic. Every castle should have a ghost." His castle would have it all. "I want the ghost of Bonnie Prince Charlie. He was famous for something in Scotland, wasn't he?"

"Maybe you shouldn't—"

"Don't argue. I won't settle for anyone but Bonnie Prince Charlie."

"But he's not dead yet. Sure, I can go into the future

and bring back his ghost, but don't you think it's a little silly when he's still—"

"This isn't negotiable. I want Bonnie Prince Charlie." He started back toward the great hall.

"Okay, okay." She mumbled something under her breath.

Ganymede paused at the door and smiled. It felt great to hear someone curse him again. He was supposed to be good now, but he still got a little zing from annoying her. "Oh, and don't open your mouth and blab to anyone. A talking cat would upset the guests."

"Sure. No blabbing." She slipped past him as he opened the door. "Get this straight, though. I'm helping you because of what you once were, not because of what you've become. You're a major disappointment, Mede." Then she was gone.

Inexplicably, her words really bothered him. Ganymede pushed the door shut, then leaned against it and closed his eyes. He had ultimate evil living in his tower, a viper-tongued assistant giving him flak, and a bunch of horny guests expecting sexual nirvana.

His tummy hurt. He'd have to drink a whole bottle of the pink stuff.

Darach relaxed while he stared into the hearth's flame. Blythe would not be happy to find him resting on her bed when she returned from her meal. He smiled. He hoped she would try to remove him.

The bed was the most comfortable place in the room,

and Darach rarely denied himself things that brought him pleasure. Neither a soft bed nor a beautiful woman.

With half-closed eyes, he touched his world, using senses so sensitive he could hear Blythe's footfall as she began to climb the stone steps toward her room. He savored his anticipation.

While he waited, he enjoyed the faint woman scent still alive in this room, the intense blues and greens of clothing she had flung across a nearby chair, and the crackle and hiss of the fire. And from without the ancient walls, the wind whistled, calling to a need he had denied as long as possible. He would drink tonight, but not from anyone in this castle.

His smile turned mocking. Ganymede would most likely give him eternal indigestion, and Blythe . . . Darach's smile faded. Blythe would tempt him to excess. No, he would go elsewhere tonight.

Patiently he waited while she tried the door, paused when she remembered it wasn't fastened, then pushed it open.

Blythe stood in the doorway, an angry Valkyrie with a fall of golden hair that would tempt a man to barter his soul and trade a score of his years on earth for a chance to slide his fingers through its strands.

Darach had no soul to barter, but he could well afford a score of years. Since he wanted to do much more than run his fingers through her hair, he suspected a score of years would not be nearly enough.

With hands on hips, she strode into the room, fearless in her anger. "This place is wacko. Textron has picked you as my test subject, Ganymede talks to his cat, and you wouldn't believe the woman who sat next to me." She flung off her shawl and sat down on the chair he'd rejected.

Test subject? "Ye would do well to stay away from Ganymede. He is not what he seems." Darach recognized the irony of his words.

"That's what Ganymede said about you." She paused in her tirade long enough to register that he was resting on her bed. "What's with you? Are you directionally challenged? This is *my* room. Get off my bed. Go sprawl all over your own bed."

"Ye must tell me about this Textron first. 'Tis a strange name." *Come lie beside me. Remove your gown, and let me touch your breasts with my lips, taste the smooth skin of your stomach, bury myself in your heat, and share the life flowing through ye.*

Her gaze grew unfocused for a moment, then cleared. "Okay, I tell you about Textron and you leave."

Darach blinked. She had not answered his call. He had rarely resorted to drawing a woman to him with his mind, but when he had, they had come to him. Was his power diminished because he had gone so long without nourishment?

Distracted, he put his hand over his heart. Still beating. When uncertainty touched him, the miracle of his beating heart steadied him, renewed his confidence in his power.

"His father invented a fabric called Textron. It's completely indestructible but abrasive next to the skin. He named his son after the fabric. The name fits. Textron is a real pain, and nothing gets rid of him."

Darach did not wish to know about Textron, but he enjoyed watching Blythe speak of him. Her emotion shone from eyes that were a golden brown. Warm eyes. Eyes that hid nothing. "What did Textron say that fashes ye so?"

She bit her lip, and he knew she was wondering how much to tell him. He cared not what she said, because his attention was fixed on her lip: moist, full, and vulnerable. It spoke to the predator in him. Darach pushed himself to a sitting position, then leaned against the carved headboard. He bent his knee to ease his growing . . . interest.

"I guess you have a right to know. Textron is my supervisor, and he scanned the emotions of everyone in the great hall. No one was unhappy enough to suit him, so he chose you. He doesn't know squat about you, but he said you were seriously depressed." Her gaze narrowed at the thought of Textron. "Anal retentive liar. He can't read your emotions any more than I can. He's setting me up for failure."

Anal retentive? "I dinna understand. Why must I be your test subject, and why would he think me depressed?" Darach could easily read her thoughts to find the answers to his questions, but the pleasure of watching her speak was not to be denied.

Blythe stared at him, and he sensed her pulling apart the truth, deciding which parts she would tell him and which she would keep secret. He smiled. Women could not keep secrets from him. Few tried.

"My position at Ecstasy is unstable right now." She drew in a deep breath. "If you're on an assignment for the company, no matter what it is, you're in a no-sex zone until you finish the job. Ecstasy thinks that sex is a distraction, and nothing should interfere with an employee's work. Textron's job is to monitor my performance, and my job is to make you happy. So company policy says no sex for either one of us until the job is finished."

Her gaze slid away from him, and he recognized her reluctance to tell him the rest. "I got a little too personally involved with my last client. Textron somehow found out and reported me. His report earned me a giant red X on my evaluation form next to: always maintains a professional relationship with customers." She crossed her legs and stared down at her lap while she folded and unfolded her hands.

"Ye tried the forbidden sexual solution? Did it work?" He wondered about her legs. They would be long and smooth, rubbing against his thighs as he lifted her to meet his thrust, then wrapping around him as he plunged—

"I don't know. The company reassigned me to their Casper, Wyoming, office. Someone else took over the client." He read her regret in her lowered lids, her deep sigh. "Do you know how much unhappiness there is in Casper, Wyoming?" She didn't wait for his reply. "None. A little angst, a few emotional potholes. You don't know the true meaning of boredom until you've tried to find sad people in Casper, Wyoming."

He tried to focus on Casperwyoming. "Why would ye stay with this Ecstasy Incorporated when it does not allow ye to use all your skills? Ye could have found another place to work."

She shook her head, and strands of her long, gleaming hair framed her face and slid across the swell of her breasts. He forgot about Casperwyoming. How would that hair feel gliding across his bare stomach, his sex?

"Not an option." She frowned. "Besides, the company was right and I was wrong. I'd convinced myself that since I already had the relationship thing going on with my client, it was okay to supplement my work-related skills with sex. It seemed the right thing to do at the time." She avoided meeting his gaze. "A weakness. I enjoy the sensual in life more than an Ecstasy employee should."

Darach didn't show his surprise. He knew few women who would speak so openly. His interest in her as a person increased almost to the level of his interest in her body. Almost. "I still dinna understand why ye wouldna work elsewhere."

Blythe finally smiled. "Loyalty. My strength and my curse. My parents worked for Ecstasy. My grandparents worked for Ecstasy. My great-grandparents. . . .

Well, you get the idea." Her smile faded. "I was my family's shining hope. My parents sensed my special power from the moment I was born. That's why they named me Blythe. They believed that my gift would take me to the top in the company. They counted on it."

"Ye canna always live your parents' dreams." *Sometimes ye couldna even live your own.*

She finally met his gaze, and he didn't mistake the determination he saw there. "My family is dead." Her gaze shifted to the fire. "I'm the only one left to carry on the family tradition, and I won't stop until I reach the top. To get out of Casper, I have to prove to Textron that I can be successful with a difficult subject." She sighed. "The lousy jerk wants me to fail. He thinks I'll take his job." Her expression hardened. "And I will."

Darach did not think she had told him everything, but right now all his focus was on one thing. "Ye willna try any more sensual solutions?"

Her gaze was direct. "I will *never* again involve myself sexually with a subject. You're my subject." She paused to make sure he understood the implication. "I can usually read people's emotions, but for some reason I can't touch yours. So you'll have to tell me what makes you sad."

He smiled at her determination. "Never may seem overlong when the temptation is great." She did not know it, but she had challenged him. And no woman had challenged him in a very long time. "And ye canna make me happy because I am not sad." He shrugged to emphasize the futility of her effort.

Blythe narrowed her gaze. "I don't believe it. Everyone is sad about something." She paused. "Except in Casper, Wyoming." She smiled, a smile that held little sincerity. "Work with me here, Darach. I need a few repressed memories, some emotional trauma. Do you understand duty? I take my duty seriously."

For the first time, she did not amuse him. "I understand duty verra well." He must change the subject before he blurted out a few repressed memories that would send her scurrying back to her own time. "Tell me of this woman who sat next to you."

He watched her consider his desire for a change of topic and decide to allow it. "First off, she said you were a vampire. Can you believe it?" Blythe flung her arms wide to indicate the scope of the woman's stupidity. "When I asked her how she knew, she said that in 2002 she watched *Buffy the Vampire Slayer* all the time. She said that vampires take a beautiful form, but when they change they're really yuck. She was sure you were a vampire because you didn't have an aura. She also said she believed in time travel because aliens had kidnapped her, and if that could happen, so could time travel. She didn't tell me her name, and I don't want to know it."

Blythe frowned. "I figured with delusions like vampires and alien kidnappings, she must be one unhappy woman. So I checked her out." She shook her head.

"No serious sadness. I guess her delusions keep her satisfied. But I think Ganymede's going to have trouble hooking her up with any of the three guys. Unless one of them is a vampire or alien."

Ganymede's problems did not interest Darach. "Ye dinna believe in vampires?"

"No." She was very emphatic about that. "And I don't believe in ghosts, werewolves, or other manifestations of primitive minds." Her smile softened her pronouncement. "I know, I'm being closed-minded. But those things aren't real. Scientists have done extensive studies over time, but have never found definitive proof that any of those things exist."

Any of those things. She had defined his existence with those words. He knew his smile was cold. "Mayhap I should leave ye to your comfortable certainties. I have things to do this night before I rest."

He knew his anger was unreasonable. Why should she believe in things she had never seen? Besides, it would serve his purpose well if she did not believe in vampires. He needed a friend in the castle.

Even though Darach had long ago found that human thoughts were rarely entertaining, he could read them if need be. But he could not touch Ganymede's thoughts. Ganymede might not have the power to defeat him in open combat, but Darach did not want to be caught unaware.

Darach could place a protective force that none could breach across his door while he slept, so Ganymede could not destroy him in his bed. But Ganymede would try to find another way to kill him. He needed Blythe to watch during the day and report if she discovered Ganymede plotting against him.

But Blythe would not offer friendship to one she considered a "yuck." Distracted, he placed his hand over his heart.

"Do you have a heart problem?" Her voice was quietly concerned. "I've noticed how often you put your hand on your chest. And you're mad. Why?"

" 'Tis only a habit. I will live a long life." Truer than she knew. And he'd grown careless. He had allowed his enjoyment of his beating heart to become an unconscious action. "I am not . . . mad." He suspected her use of *mad* meant angry, but he used it in the truer sense. She would surely doubt his sanity if he told her what he really was.

"I'd like you to stay a little longer, Darach, and tell me more about the castle, your life. History has always interested me, but I've never traveled this far back in time." She offered him a tentative smile.

Darach could tell her that she must practice long before lying to him. The untruth glimmered in those clear brown eyes, in the nervous way she clasped the metal talisman at her throat, and the shift of her gaze from his face to his raised leg. He knew the exact moment her glance moved higher on his thigh and became sexual. Darach intended to make it very difficult for her to forget his sexual nature.

When she had first entered her room, she had wanted him gone. Until she remembered that he was her "subject." Now she wanted him to stay so that she might use him. The knowledge did not bother him, because he intended to use her as well. He shifted on the bed, offering more of his body for her viewing, and watched her swallow hard.

"Mayhap I can stay a while longer." He smiled at her. Darach suspected his smile would frighten small children and foolish women. He would enjoy telling Blythe, who thought she knew all, of the things that lived in darkness. He shook his head. Lack of nourishment must be affecting his judgment, because there was no sane reason for him to tell her anything.

A faint meow from the other side of the door shifted her attention away from him. "A cat?"

" 'Tis most likely Ganymede's cat. Leave it without." He trusted nothing connected with Ganymede.

"I can't. I love cats. I love all small helpless animals." Her glance suggested that he would never fit in that category.

He could tell her that Ganymede's cat would not fit either. She rose and opened the door. The cat slipped past her, leaped onto the bed beside Darach, sat down, and wrapped its fluffy white tail around itself.

Blythe studied the cat. The cat studied Darach. If her bed got any more crowded, she'd have to sleep on the floor. But at least the cat provided a brief distraction so she could think.

When she'd first suggested this trip to Ecstasy Inc. as a way to prove that she could interact with a client on a totally impersonal level, it had seemed like a great idea. Blythe loved the past. She loved its uncluttered reaches, its simplicity. And of course she had complete faith in her abilities. Everything had been fine until she learned about the sexual vacation part, and that Textron would be going along to monitor her progress and report back to the main office.

Fine, so she was bitter. All those years spent busting her buns for Ecstasy, and they wouldn't even trust her to record her results and present them when she returned. They had to send Super Snoop along.

Textron thought he was so clever choosing Darach as her subject. But maybe she could make this work. She still got no emotional reading from Darach, but a happy person would feel no need to hide his feelings. Ergo, he must be unhappy. Blythe knew her logic was flawed, but the bottom line? She *wanted* to work on Darach. So much for professional objectivity. Besides, her triumph would be even greater if before making him happy she had to pry open the door to his emotions and drag them growling into the light.

"Once ye let a cat in, 'tis often hard to get rid of it." Darach frowned at the cat.

"The same could be said of some Highlanders." She smiled sweetly at him.

"Ye asked me to remain, lass." He *didn't* smile at her.

"Sure." She needed to kill a few seconds while she

chose a meaningful question. A question that would encourage him to open up about his feelings.

Distracted, she watched the cat lean into Darach and rub its head against his bare leg. She tried not to follow the bare-skin temptation of that leg to its obvious conclusion. Disaster lay along the imagined path of his inner thigh.

She dragged her attention away from the siren call of his body and focused on the cat. "What brings you here, kitty?" Now, *that* was a meaningful question.

Boredom. I need some girl talk. Oh, I love your dress. Green is you. And I'm seriously jealous. You haven't been here a day, and you already have a hot man in your bed.

Blythe blinked and stared. She had clearly heard the cat answer her question in her mind. Which was absolutely impossible. "What are you?" Great. Now she was talking to voices in her head. Blythe glanced at Darach, but his gaze was fixed on the cat. He didn't seem to notice that she was talking to herself.

"You mean 'who,' of course. 'What' is so impersonal. Sparkle Stardust. I'm sort of Mede's assistant. Mede insisted on the cat form. I think it sucks." The cat's gaze turned sly. *"He told me I couldn't open my mouth to talk to any of the guests. So I'm not opening my mouth. There's more than one way to skin a cat. Oops. That was insensitive to cats. Mede says I have to be sensitive to the feelings of others. Want to know*

something? I don't give a damn about anyone's feelings. That's just me, though."

Darach smiled. Okay, what was so funny? He reached down and stroked the cat's head and back.

Sparkle pushed into his hand and began a rumbling purr. *"If I were in my real form, I wouldn't be just getting a few strokes. There isn't a more sensual animal anywhere than a very old, very evil vampire."*

"Old, evil vampire?" Blythe's voice was an alarmed squeak.

"Mmm. Too bad Mede will have to off him. What a waste."

Darach stilled, a quietness that spoke of danger.

"What are you?" Blythe wasn't sure which weirdness she was addressing.

Sparkle offered an exaggerated sigh. *"Back to that again, huh? Mede and I are cosmic troublemakers. We disrupt the universe, cause chaos wherever we can. It's what we do. It's a great life."* She leaped from the bed and padded to the door. *"Except when you're in cat form and can't open a frickin' door."*

As if in a dream, Blythe rose to let the cat out. She could feel the darkness of secrets she wanted no part of waiting silently behind her. Frantically she sought to prolong the moment with Sparkle Stardust. A telepathic cat was way easier for her to deal with than what watched from her bed.

"So you just came for some small talk? Nothing else?" Blythe did some mental arm pinching. She was talking to a cat. A small, furry, white *cat.*

"I think nothing she will tell ye will be *small.*" There was no humor in the voice of the . . . man behind her.

Sparkle slipped out the open door, then paused. *"Uh-oh. I forgot. I'm looking for my ghosts. Mede insisted I get Bonnie Prince Charlie, but I didn't."* Her laughter was light with an underlying sly triumph. *"Mede has turned into such a self-righteous butthead that I love yanking his chain. I'll tell him that good old Charlie was on another job, so I got Bonny and Charley Prince, a sixties couple from Bottleneck, New Jersey. They're perfect. They were sightseeing here in 1967 and decided to have exploratory sex on the battlements. Bought it when they fell off. What a way to go. Anyway, they're here somewhere. If you see them, give a yell."*

A yell would be easy. Blythe watched Sparkle disappear into the darkness. Okay, how long could she stand here before she'd have to turn around and face whatever was lying on her bed? *How long before she'd wake up from this nightmare of cosmic troublemakers and vampires?*

"Ye fear me now." His voice was calm, emotionless. No anger, no regret. " 'Tis too bad that Ganymede's minion could not keep her wee thoughts to herself."

"You read our minds?" Blythe turned slowly, all her pent-up fear, disbelief, and horror focused on the invasion of her thoughts.

He shrugged. " 'Tis rarely worth my effort, but I couldna resist the cat's thoughts. She amused me, ye ken." His expression said his explanation should calm her. " 'Tis too bad I canna enter the thoughts of Ganymede, but he is more powerful than the cat." Darach's eyes grew colder, if possible. "I dinna need to read his thoughts to find a way to destroy him."

Blythe forced herself to meet his gaze and reach once more for his emotions. Nothing.

His smile was a slow slide of mockery. "Ye waste your time. Ye'll discover nothing about me that I dinna wish ye to know."

This was not some horrible dream. She never dreamed of demons and darkness, would never come up with this kind of horror even in her subconscious. Blythe was perfectly centered in her personal universe. Her work demanded this. Ecstasy Inc. put its employees through psychological testing on a regular basis to ensure mental and emotional stability.

She was sane, she was awake, and this was real. She would accept the reality and deal with it. *Right after she had a screaming fit of hysterics.*

His smile widened and for the first time touched his eyes with real amusement. "I dinna usually drive beautiful women to hysterics."

"Get out of my mind." Anger. Good. Maybe the anger would hold back the wave of fear threatening to wash away all reason. "And get off my bed."

"Ye challenge me. I like that." He patted the covers beside him. "Join me so that I may tell ye what I am."

"No." Blythe's world might be spinning out of control, but she still retained enough common sense to know that climbing onto that bed with Darach-the-demon would be the biggest mistake of her life.

His gaze darkened, and Blythe felt the threat all the way to the core of her terrified soul.

"Come to me, Blythe." The soft, husky murmur of his voice wrapped around her, pulled her to her feet, and propelled her to the bed.

Shocked, she stared down at him. Close up, his pure physical presence caught at her, made her legs shake, and forced her to cling to the bed's poster for strength. "How did you do that?"

He reached out and pulled her down beside him. "I can do many things. Let me show ye."

She perched on the edge of the bed, every tensed muscle poised to attempt escape at his first move toward her neck. Her voice of reason was in I-told-you-so mode. *I told you to find a subject at home, but oh no, you had to search for some exotic challenge in the past. Hey, you found him, stupid. Now what're you going to do with him?*

"If ye need help deciding, mayhap I have a few ideas." His soft chuckle promised a thousand nights filled with new sensual experiences.

He must be growing more arrogant, because for the first time she could feel the touch of his mind on hers. Or maybe she was just growing more sensitive to his alien presence. "You're still in my head. I hate that."

She felt him touching her mind, trying to soothe her from the inside out. It wouldn't work.

Unexpectedly, her mind was free of his presence.

"Thank you." Now she could ask the really tough question. The question that ideally she should ask from across the room. No, from the other side of the closed door. Uh-uh, not far enough. It was a question asked safely from her own time with 554 years between them.

"Your question is written in your eyes, Blythe-with-no-other-name. Ask it." His voice was dark arrogance. He'd probably use the same tone as he murmured carnal intentions against her bared neck.

"Okay, here it goes. Are you a vampire?" Her voice was a whisper of sound. Obviously, if he couldn't hear her he couldn't answer. She could live with a non-answer right now.

"Aye."

His voice was just as soft, but it was loud enough for her to hear. Loud enough to make her clench her hands into fists to keep them from shaking. Loud enough to make her heart skip a few beats and her whole body tense for a fight-or-flight adrenaline rush.

"Oh." Was she articulate or what? You'd think that during one of her life's most momentous events she could come up with a more enduring quote. Something posterity could remember fondly after the vampire sucked her dry.

"Ye need not fear me. I dinna desire your blood."

Hah! She'd just bet he didn't.

He slid his fingers the length of her bare arm, a warm glide of what she supposed he thought was a calming gesture. She could tell him that his touch could *never* calm her. He wisely kept his fingers away from her neck.

"Right. No fear. No teeth in neck. I believe you." She didn't believe him. If he was a vampire, and she was too terrified to make that judgment, then she didn't think her neck was safe.

Darach sensed her tension, her terror. He would feel regret if he had not long ago banished that emotion from his . . . heart? The thought of his beating heart soothed him, as it always did. Absently he placed his palm over it, then jerked his hand away as he realized what he was doing. He must break that habit. Enemies looked for weaknesses, and his heart was a human weakness.

He must calm her or she would be lost to him. If she feared him, she would not spy on Ganymede during the daylight while Darach slept. He searched beneath this first reason and found another. If she feared him, she would not talk with him, would not share her body with him. And he knew that he wanted both.

"Ye fear what ye dinna understand." He clasped his hands behind his head and leaned back against the headboard. Blythe would be less fearful if she thought his hands could not easily reach her.

She nodded, her gaze uncertain. Darach watched her glance slide from his clasped hands down the length of his arms and skitter across the patch of bare skin where his shirt gaped open. He smiled. He would join with this woman, but first he would gain her trust.

"So exactly how old and how evil are you?" She swallowed hard, as though forcing the words from her mouth had taken much effort.

He would tell her as much of the truth as he wished her to know. "I was born in the year one thousand two hundred fifty."

"Twelve fifty?" She winced as though the number was a physical blow. "That makes you . . ."

"Aye. I am five hundred thirty-five years old." Darach forged on before she could think too long about his age. "I was born human, as are all of my race. I changed when I reached thirty years."

"Changed?" He noted that her hands had stopped shaking. "You make it sound like part of the maturing process. I thought a vampire jumped on you, bit you, and then you became a vampire."

It was Darach's turn to wince at her simple view of his clan. "If ye judge all who need blood to survive and shun the light as one race, ye would be wrong. All who belong to my clan change when they become fully adult. It is a change we celebrate with great joy."

He felt more of her tension uncoil as she unclenched her hands. "Why?"

Darach shifted his gaze to the blazing hearth, where each leap and dying of a flame mirrored the extremes of his life. "Who would not choose to be immortal?

Who would not choose heightened senses that make even the smallest pleasure a wondrous experience?" He turned his attention back to Blythe and held her gaze. "Who would not choose the power?"

"The power." Blythe's expression said that she would know more about his power later. "What happens when you change?" She bit her lip before asking her last question. "Are you . . . dead?"

Darach leaned closer, but she did not move away. He silently applauded her bravery. A smile touched his lips. "Look at me, lass. Do I look dead?"

Her eyes widened, and panic showed in them as he leaned even closer. She shook her head.

He should be reassuring her, speaking lies that would soothe her fears, but it seemed a demon drove him. "Touch me, Blythe. Feel the warmth of my flesh." Darach thought she would refuse. She surprised him.

She laid her hand on his bare thigh, and at least one part of his body rose to proclaim, "I live."

Blythe smiled weakly. "You've wanted me to do that from the first moment I entered the room. You're not very subtle, MacKenzie." Her smile widened, and she seemed to gain strength from it. "You're right. Nothing cold, clammy, or undead here."

If she left her hand on his thigh much longer, she would gain further proof of how truly alive he was. "I am not dead, only changed. I gave up certain human characteristics, but gained much more." He listened to his heartbeat and gloried in the one human characteristic he had won back. Soon he would have another.

She nodded her understanding. "Sort of like a computer upgrade."

"Computer?" What was this thing called a computer? She was as strange to his world as he was to hers. He looked forward with pleasure to finding out more about all that touched her.

She shook her head. "Never mind." Blythe moved her hand from his thigh, and he mourned the loss. "I want to know everything about you, but I think I've reached my shock limit for right now. After a good night's sleep I'll be ready for the rest."

He nodded. *The rest*. Would she be ready to know what he had been before he was Darach MacKenzie? Would she be ready to know about those he hunted and those who hunted him? And would she be ready to accept that only a sensual solution might unlock his emotions?

"Aye. Sleep well, lass." He offered her what he hoped looked like an open and boyish smile.

The flare of alarm in her eyes suggested that his smile had been less than open and boyish. "Why have you told me so much about yourself? Should I be afraid of you? I never got to the evil-vampire part of my questioning."

"I want something from ye." He smiled as she placed a protective hand to her neck. "No, not that. Although the thought is tempting."

He could not deny the truth of his words. She

tempted him in every way. "I was but joking. I would have ye watch Ganymede while I sleep during the daylight hours. Ye need understand that Ganymede is a danger to ye. More so because he wears a friendly mask. He wishes to destroy me, and I may be the only one who can protect ye from him."

"And who will protect me from you, Darach MacKenzie?"

Her question hung between them, a wall that would forever separate them. She would never trust him fully, never understand that he could not harm her without destroying himself. He accepted her distrust and simply shrugged.

Darach could sense her weighing the threat he posed against the thing that she wanted from him. He could enter her mind, but he chose to wait until she told him herself.

Her sigh indicated she had made her decision. "All right, here's the deal. I'll keep an eye on Ganymede if you'll do something for me."

He waited, his gaze never wavering from her face.

"I don't have to be a galactic wizard to know there's a lot you haven't told me about yourself. You didn't tell me much about your family, and you keep avoiding letting me in on the evil part of your nature." She tapped her finger on her knee. "So I've concluded that you're not a happy . . . vampire. Despite what you say, being a vampire has to be the pits. You can't eat solid food. You have to drink blood to survive. You can't go out into the sunlight. You have to avoid wooden stakes, garlic, crosses, and holy water. And you can't see your reflection in a mirror."

She held up her hand as he opened his mouth to respond. "Don't interrupt. I'm on a roll. If you can't see your reflection, how do you know what you look like when you go out? Your hair could be standing on end, or you could have spinach between your teeth." She frowned. "No, I guess the spinach thing would never happen."

"Cease, and tell me what ye want." She amused him mightily, but the night and his increasing need called to him. If he stayed much longer, he would be tempted to still her warm lips with his mouth. From there he could easily move to the smooth flesh of her neck. He had survived over five hundred years because he had learned how to deny himself.

"You're right." She drew in a deep breath. "I want you to at least give me a shot at your emotions. I figure that you've had five hundred years to pile up a lot of unhappiness."

"Mayhap ye will touch my emotions." He shrugged. She would *never* touch his feelings, other than those that were sexual. "But ye will find little sadness."

Her gaze narrowed. "I don't believe you. No one could be happy as a vampire." Her challenge was clear.

"Ye may try to make me happy another day." He glanced at the door. His hunger grew with each moment. "I must leave ye."

Her expression said she knew why he must leave and did not approve. He rose from her bed and walked to the door. She remained sitting on the bed staring at him. He had given her much to think on tonight.

He stepped out into the darkness and closed the door on her silent conjectures. Leaning against the closed door, he felt the change, the smooth slide of fangs preparing him for the night, for the *hunt.*

He knew not the meaning of "yuck," but it must be a vile thing. If Blythe were to open the door now, would she scream "Yuck!" and slam the door shut on the horror of him?

Darach knew what he looked like in his human form because he had given a man gold to paint his likeness, but he knew nothing of what he was when he hunted. He must know. *Because Blythe thinks ye would be yuck?* There was no end to his foolishness tonight, but he knew he would use the power he had been hoarding for over a hundred years to fashion his reflection in a mirror.

As he swept down the winding stairs on a sudden gust of spiraling wind, he knew that those who hunted him would not find him tonight. They needed to gather in greater numbers before they could harm him. He would be gone before that happened. And Ganymede? He knew not what a cosmic troublemaker was, but he recognized power almost as strong as his own. Almost. Ganymede could not best him.

Once outside, he paused to rid his mind of those who

dwelled in his castle. He stared out at the dark waters of the loch surrounding the small island on which the castle stood, then shifted his attention to the stone footbridge that connected the island to the mainland. He turned toward the stable. A swift gallop would clear his thoughts. Tonight he would hunt with Arnora.

A short time later, he rode Arnora across the footbridge. His last thought? What exactly was a *Buffy?*

Chapter Three

Blythe felt really cranky. She'd spent the second day of her working vacation sneaking around after Ganymede and avoiding Textron with his demands for hourly updates on her progress. She also had to add Clara Thomas, the *Buffy the Vampire Slayer* fan, to her growing list of people to avoid. Clara was fixated on meeting Darach, her first real-life vampire. Blythe wasn't in the mood to wrestle a wooden stake from Clara's determined hands as the woman made her move to become a vampire-slayer-in-training.

Over breakfast, Clara confided that vampires had to sink their teeth into your neck to fully enjoy the sexual experience. This was not a tidbit of vampire folklore that Blythe needed to hear with her morning tea. And where was her coffee? Tea didn't do it for her when she had to face a day of spying on Ganymede-the-elusive.

Blythe sighed as she stared at her dinner, another unique offering of unidentifiable authentic cuisine. But even the thought of imminent food poisoning couldn't distract her from worrying about how she was going to make Darach happy while dodging his powerful sensual pull.

The sun had set, and soon she'd be able to talk to Darach. She'd had a whole day to try to come to terms with what he said he was. Did she believe that he was a vampire? Blythe was leaning toward a yes on that. How could she deny the possibility of vampires existing when she was sitting at dinner listening to a cosmic troublemaker in cat form whine about the ghosts of a Bonny and Charley Prince?

"Those ghosts are real pieces of work. It took me five hours to find them, and when I finally tracked them down, do you know what they were doing?"

Blythe cast wary glances at Sparkle Stardust, who'd planted herself next to Blythe's chair and settled in for some serious dinner chatter.

"No, don't answer. I'll tell you what they were doing. They were having sex on the battlements. A couple of cheap exhibitionists. Sure, I admire their commitment to the sensual lifestyle, but you'd think after falling from the castle once, they'd have learned to keep their action in the bedroom." She paused for thought. *"Of course, since they didn't technically die until 1967, you could argue that they haven't learned any lesson at all yet. Hmm. I hadn't considered the possibility that this*

could cause problems with the future. What if they change something now so that they don't fall from the castle in 1967? What if they live on to litter the universe with their offspring? My eyes are crossing. Time travel drives me nuts." Sparkle remained quiet for the second necessary to think about the vagaries of time travel. *"Anyway, they agreed to start work tonight. Nothing really scary, just enough haunting to add ambiance to the old pile of rock. Throw me down a piece of meat."*

Blythe offered a piece of her meat in the hope that the chewing process would shut Sparkle up for a few minutes.

"You shouldn't feed pets from the table. It spoils them."

The woman next to her interrupted Blythe's attempt to focus on the sex habits of vampires and how she would approach making one happy.

"Bitch." The pet in question offered her opinion as she swallowed Blythe's offering and waited for more.

"I'm Sandy Blake." The woman smiled at Blythe. "From 2216." She watched Blythe offer another piece of meat to Sparkle. "I noticed that great-looking man you were with last night."

Sparkle burped daintily, then padded back to Ganymede, who was expounding on the sexual prowess of Highlanders. He offered the opinion that it was something in the air, so everyone should breathe deeply, then have sensational sex. Ganymede wasn't subtle.

"Your man could use my product." Sandy leaned closer.

"Product?" Blythe finally turned her full attention to what Sandy was saying.

Sandy's smile widened. "Ganymede thinks I'm on vacation, but this is a business trip for me. When I found out we were scheduled to visit ancient Scotland, I immediately saw the possibilities. I'm a visionary, always searching out new markets. That's why I'm tops in my sales department."

"What do you sell?" Blythe's attention drifted as she peered around one of Ganymede's new serving staff to note that Sandy's great-looking man had just entered the hall.

"Men's underwear. We offer a full range of body-molding briefs that hug firm round buttocks and cradle even the largest male packages in soft, comfortable fabrics." Sandy's attention had also gravitated to Darach. "For really spectacular male sexual displays, we carry transparent briefs."

Sighing, she returned her gaze to Blythe. "I knew it'd be cold in Scotland, so I brought a lot of our heated products. Unfortunately, the heat cuts down on sperm count, but there're so many of the little sweethearts swimming around that a few less is no big deal. Oh, and just in case, I brought samples of our padded briefs for those who feel cheated by the gods of sexual equipment."

As though unable to help herself, Sandy glanced

back to Darach. "Of course, there are some men who would better serve womankind by ignoring our briefs. They were born to hang full, jut hard and long. Their sexual equipment was meant to live life wild and free." Sandy's eyes were glazing over as she fixed Darach with her unblinking stare.

Blythe controlled a snort of disbelief. Any minute now drool would drip from Sandy's gaping lips. Blythe never could understand women who couldn't . . . Hmm, she seemed to remember something from her study of ancient societies. Highlanders didn't wear anything under their kilts. She firmed her lips. Okay, no drooling, no mental imaging, no eye-glazing. Blythe stuffed a piece of meat into her mouth in the mistaken belief that she couldn't chew and generate erotic scenarios at the same time.

Darach strode to the table and sat down beside her. At the end of the table, Ganymede grew still.

"I don't think Ganymede's happy about you joining us for dinner." That was an understatement. Blythe had to look away from Ganymede's furious amber stare. She didn't think Ecstasy Inc.'s entire Happiness staff could make a dent in the emotional volcano Blythe saw building in Ganymede's eyes.

"His feelings dinna bother me." Darach slanted an amused glance in Ganymede's direction.

Their gazes met and held. Blythe felt the air move, shift, and shimmer with the force of their wills. The tense stares of everyone around her said that the others felt it, too.

The sudden explosion of power between Darach and Ganymede was like a physical blow. Sandy's chair tipped over, carrying her screeching with it. Glasses shattered, and dishes skated across the table, only to tip over the table's edge and crash to the floor. It felt as if the great hall had sucked in its breath at this display of power, leaving no air for anyone to breathe.

Sparkle Stardust crouched close to the floor and screamed in feline terror. Blythe was sure she expressed the feelings of all those at the table who were unable to utter a sound.

Without warning, it was over. Released from the horror of bearing unwilling witness to the power of Ganymede and Darach, five of Ganymede's six guests rose and stumbled from the great hall.

Ganymede stood. His normally ruddy complexion was chalk white. "Now look what you've done. How the hell . . . I mean, how the heck am I supposed to get them to think about sex when you've scared the crap out of them?" He glared down at a shaking Sparkle. "Fat lot of help you were." He speared Darach with an accusing stare. "You've upset my tummy. I have to go to my room and drink a whole bottle of the pink stuff."

Blythe watched Ganymede totter from the great hall with Sparkle slinking behind him. Blythe turned to Darach. "Well, you cleared the hall nicely." Fine, so she was feeling bitchy, but she didn't know how else to react to what she'd just experienced. Either she attacked or she ran screaming from the room like everyone else.

"Ye stayed." He rewarded her for her courage, or maybe stupidity, with a smile that promised her a sensual reward of untold value for staying.

Blythe didn't think she'd have the courage to collect her reward. Sex with Darach would most likely kill her. Literally. "You're my job. I had to stay." That wasn't exactly true, but it calmed her common sense, which thought she should go home *right now*.

" 'Tis a shame I ruined your meal, but Ganymede challenged me. He would see it as weakness if I refused to test his power." Darach didn't look very sad about the whole thing.

"What is it about men and their egos?" Okay, not technically *men*. Blythe couldn't think about something this deep sitting down. She couldn't think about *anything* this close to Darach. To encourage deep thinking, she pushed her chair away from the table, then wandered over to the massive wooden doors leading to the courtyard. If she were smart, she'd pull open the doors and run far, far away. She thought about her job. Nope, no running tonight. "Why can't men walk away from stupid chest-pounding challenges?" Hmm. The doors seemed to be vibrating. The wind? Not unless it was a tornado.

"The same way that ye are walking away from Textron's foolish challenge?" His soft laughter assured her that it was foolish as well as useless.

"That's different." It was different because . . . Okay, give her a minute and she'd think of a reason. But she couldn't pull her thoughts together as she narrowed her gaze on the doors, which were now shaking. What the . . . She couldn't hear any sounds beyond the door.

She sensed Darach's sudden stillness. Blythe started to back away while the doors shuddered as if from massive blows. There were still no sounds to accompany the attack.

"Return to your room and fasten your door." Darach's tone allowed for no disobedience.

"I don't—" She backed further from the door.

"Dinna argue with me, woman." His command sounded urgent, and she could hear him striding toward her. "I didna come down to challenge Ganymede. There is something without I must destroy."

Blythe decided that Darach could deal alone with whatever was outside, because she was outta here. But before she could turn and run, the doors burst open.

The thing that rushed into the room and hurled itself at her made Blythe cover her mouth to stifle a cry of horror. She would've covered her eyes as well, but her other hand was busy clutching her heart. The creature looked as though it had been caught somewhere between a change from human to beast. She couldn't specifically identify the beast, but whatever it was had fangs that seemed to take up its whole face. Which was a good thing, because what she could see of the face beyond its fangs wasn't a pretty sight.

Years of Ecstasy Inc. training made looking into the creature's eyes automatic. Blythe looked. And wished she hadn't. If Darach's eyes revealed no emotion, this creature's told everything about its soul. Hate, ravenous hunger, and madness shone in eyes the same shade of blue as Darach's.

Blythe now understood the true meaning of the phrase "frozen by fear." Her brain was frantically sending messages for appropriate body parts to initiate evasive action, but said body parts were ignoring orders from the top in favor of turning to jelly as disaster approached at warp speed. She was doomed. Darach wouldn't reach her in time to stop the creature from leaping on her.

A booming voice suddenly echoed around the great hall. Blythe didn't understand the words the voice shouted, but she recognized the tone. Anger.

The creature did, too. It stopped in mid-charge to turn toward the voice. Blythe followed its gaze.

A man stood in the darkened doorway. Massive, with huge muscled shoulders and tree-trunk legs, he held a wooden shield in one hand and brandished a deadly looking ax in the other.

As he strode toward the creature and her, Blythe registered mini-impressions between waves of terror. Wild mane of blond hair. Full beard. Metal helmet. Long cloak. Short tunic. Chain mail. Where had she seen . . . ? *A Viking.* He looked like images she'd seen of ancient Viking warriors.

Blythe had no more time for thought as the Viking drew closer. He shouted in the strange language, and the creature cowered and gibbered.

Since no one seemed to remember her, she forced her frozen feet to edge away from the creature, but not far enough to avoid a close encounter of the scary kind with the Viking. Intent on the creature, he strode past her. Blythe sucked in her breath as his cloak slid across her arm and his shield brushed her hip.

Suddenly an arm wrapped around her waist and lifted her off her feet. Her intended scream of terror emerged as a frightened squeak.

Her struggle died almost immediately as she recognized Darach: his scent, the press of his body against her back.

He set her down well away from the danger. "Leave." His harsh whisper brooked no defiance.

Good advice. Blythe ran from the great hall. She had her foot on the bottom step that would lead to the semi-safety of her room when she paused.

The voice of caution said there was nothing she could do to help Darach. *You have your Freeze-frame. Remember?* She didn't want to remember. She'd be stupid to go back into that room. Drawing in a deep breath, she surrendered to her stupidity.

Her gene that regulated idiotic acts was obviously faulty. The same need to do her job no matter the personal cost now insisted that she try to help. Dumb. Dumb. Dumb. Besides, she had to watch anyway, because if she ever hoped to reach Darach's emotions, she had to understand what he was.

She crouched in the doorway while she fumbled in her bra for her weapon. With his back to her, Darach moved behind the cowering creature, whose attention was fixed on the Viking menacing him with raised ax.

Some primitive instinct for self-preservation must have warned the creature, because it turned and with a shriek of fury flung itself at Darach.

With an exclamation of triumph, Blythe pulled the Freeze-frame from her bra. But as Darach met the creature's assault, a black cloud formed around the three combatants. The cloud moved and changed shape, turning from black to a fiery red as the battle raged silently.

No, this was *not* happening. She was not watching a vampire, a Viking, and an unidentified terrifying entity struggle to kill each other while the hearth blazed cheerily as though this were a perfectly normal occurrence.

Blythe rethought her decision to stay. She couldn't help Darach if she wasn't able to see him, and she wouldn't be able to touch Darach's emotions if her own emotions were in tatters. This was beyond not only her own experience, but beyond her most terrifying imaginings. Just as she prepared to race up the stairs to the dubious protection of her room, the battle ended.

There was a brilliant blue flash like the superheated center of a flame, and the cloud disappeared, leaving Darach standing alone. If it wasn't for the bleeding gash across the part of his chest exposed by his shirt, Blythe could have believed the battle had never happened.

"Did ye enjoy watching the destruction of a life?" Darach knew she didn't, but as always happened when he was forced to destroy, he felt the need to lash out at someone, something.

"Me? No, I . . ." She trailed off, her eyes wide as he strode over to her.

"Do ye have your proof of what I am? Do ye fear me now?" He leaned close and watched with satisfaction as she backed up a step.

"I didn't actually see much."

She swallowed hard, her attempt to clear her throat of the fear that clogged it drawing his gaze to the smooth, warm flesh of her neck. It would be so easy now. He could bend his head and touch her skin with his lips, his teeth, and feel her life force flowing into him, renewing him, driving out the demons that rode him after a kill.

Darach wrapped his willpower around his desire, holding it where it was, not allowing it to run free. As he had so many times in the hundreds of years of his existence, he defeated the temptation.

"Ye didna see because I drew the cloud around us

when I sensed ye watching." If only he could draw the same cloud around his memories.

She offered him a tentative smile. "It was kind of you to shield me from seeing that kind of violence."

"I wasna trying to shield ye, but rather keeping ye from viewing Ian's last moments."

"Ian?" She blinked as though it had never occurred to her that what he had fought could bear a human name.

He nodded. "Ian MacKenzie, my nephew." Darach waited for her cry of disbelief and disgust. Surprisingly, she just stared at him.

"Ian? He was the creature? Who was the Viking? What happened to Ian? Could that happen to you?" Emotion flooded her eyes. "Tell me that couldn't happen to you."

He chose to answer only one of her questions. "The Northman?" His smile was no smile at all. "Ye speak of Jorund. He was Ian's greatest fear."

She blinked. "I don't understand."

"Ye'll come to my room, and I will tell ye about Ian." He knew his smile was little better than a baring of teeth. But at least they were now human teeth. He had lied to her about the cloud. He had wanted to protect Ian's last moments, but he also had wanted to protect himself. He still did not want her to see him in his vampire form, still did not want her to utter the dreaded word "yuck."

"Is this visit to your room negotiable?"

For all her brave front, he saw that her hands shook and her breaths came quickly. "Ye have no choice. Now that ye have seen what ye shouldna have seen, I would have ye understand what Ian was." He must also persuade her to choose another to make happy while still watching Ganymede for him. Darach needed no woman trying to pry open doors best left locked.

Instead of arguing as most women would, she simply turned from him and started up the darkened steps. When she reached the top of the stairs, she stepped aside for him to open his door. Darach needed no fastening other than his will to keep unwanted visitors from his room. He pushed open the door, then lit the candles while Blythe hovered in his doorway. The room was already warmed from the fire he had left blazing in the fireplace.

"Legends say that vampires sleep in coffins. Humans don't use coffins for burial anymore because Earth is too crowded. If you sleep in a coffin, it'll really creep me out." She scanned the room for coffins.

Even though her voice was a mere whisper of sound, she still stood in his doorway rather than running back to her room. Brave woman. *Foolish woman.*

"Ye fear to be alone with me, yet ye stay. Why?" He usually did not care what drove human behavior, but he found that he had an uncommon curiosity about this woman.

Deliberately she moved into the room and seated herself in a chair close to the fire. Taking a deep breath, she met his gaze. "You scare me more than any man I've ever known." She offered him a weak smile. "Okay, so maybe my first date with Caekal, the space-bus driver from Sovarn, was a little scary. Sovarnians have three hands, and Caekal was unstoppable when all three were in motion." Her smile disappeared. "There's only one reason why I'm not pounding on Ganymede's door demanding a refund and immediate transport out of here. My job is more important to me than anything else I can think of. Right now, you're my job, so I stay."

Darach willed the door shut, then sat on his bed.

"If you don't mind, I'd like to sit here." Her expression said that if he called her to his bed, he could risk injury to sensitive parts of his immortal body.

"Ye need only listen." It was a lie, but she would find out too late.

Blythe nodded as though his words made perfect sense. She reached up to finger the metal talisman lying against her throat. It spelled "Ecstasy," a constant reminder of her purpose. "The need to talk about a tragic event is the first step toward healing."

He felt her try to touch his feelings, a soothing slide of power meant to coat his emotions, make him *happy* again. He would not let her in, would not accept what she offered. Absently he put his hand over his heart, then jerked it away as soon as he realized what he was doing.

"I wish ye to know what happened to Ian so ye will understand why ye're safe with me." Why her *neck* was safe with him. He made no promise about other parts of her body. "But first I would make myself more comfortable." Removing his plaid and leaving only his shirt, he propped himself up against the headboard. When the silence dragged on, he raised his gaze to meet hers. "Ye may remove anything ye feel makes ye uncomfortable."

"If I could, then you'd be gone. And not one piece of clothing leaves my body." Blythe stared at his chest where his shirt gaped open, her gaze touching his flesh with the same result as if she had slid her fingertips across his skin. His body acknowledged her power to distract him from what he did not want to remember.

"That gash on your chest is almost healed." She shifted her gaze to the fire. "So I suppose regeneration is one of your powers."

"Aye." Darach smiled. Staring at his body made her uneasy, but she could not watch the fire all night. "Only the most serious injuries dinna heal quickly."

Her gaze strayed from the fire and shifted to the sword he had propped in a corner. "You're a violent man, Darach MacKenzie."

"Ye've come to a violent time."

Sighing, she finally looked back at him, but kept her gaze safely above his neck. "Okay, tell me about Ian."

Curiosity tugged at him. "Are *ye* happy, Blythe?"

Her eyes widened, and he realized that no one had ever asked her that before.

"I'm perfectly happy. Why wouldn't I be?"

Was her answer a wee bit too definite? "Aye, why would ye not?" He would pursue the question of her happiness later. "Ye would know about Ian."

He willed his attention away from her as he forced himself to tell Ian's story.

"When we first become vampire, we are powerful with undiluted blood. We are meant to stay that way. We dinna feed often, because too much human blood weakens us, makes the blood lust too strong to resist. Humans are the greatest danger to our control. If we kill, the blood lust rises. Those who are weak surrender to it. They become like Ian, mad with the need for more and more blood. Eventually their vampire blood is so infected with human blood that they must be destroyed to stop their killing frenzy." He hoped her disgust would keep her from asking for more, and yet the thought of her disgust bothered him in a way he didn't want to examine.

"Are there any other things that can send you over the edge?" She leaned forward in her chair.

"Send me over the edge?" Every time she used words he did not understand, she reminded him of how different they were. Except in the matter of sexual desire. The need to join knew no boundaries of time.

"Make you lose control." Her intent stare allowed for no lies.

Darach considered lying anyway, but then discarded the thought. She had not run from the battle in the great hall, so this small truth would not send her screaming from his room.

"Sexual desire is entwined with the need to feed." He watched her carefully to see the effect of his words.

"Oh." She frowned. "So what happens when you're really hungry?"

"I feed from verra ugly men."

The corners of her lips tipped up in her first attempt at a sincere smile he had seen this night. "How about when you're with a 'verra' beautiful woman?"

"I make certain I have already fed. I am verra good at resisting temptation." She would never know how good.

"So you're like on a permanent diet?" A line formed between her brows, signaling her attempt to understand what he had told her.

He nodded. "I survive because I am strong, have stayed strong over the centuries, and gained power because of it. I would never risk what I have gained."

"That means I'm safe with you?" She looked uncertain.

He allowed himself a real smile. "Aye. Your life is safe. But ye might want to guard other things."

"Right." She looked away. "What happened to Ian? Was he just weak-natured? And why did he show up here?"

"Ian was not weak." His gaze shifted to the hearth's flames, and within their dancing brilliance saw the Ian he remembered. Laughing, strong, vital. "I believe that he was captured by a group of women who keep their identities secret and harbor dark obsessions. Their wealth allows them freedom to stalk us."

Blythe leaned forward, her unease evidently forgotten in her fascination with his tale. "Women? What would a woman want with a vampire? And how would these women even find one?"

He watched her flush as she realized what she'd said, and he knew his smile was bitter. "Gold can achieve much during any age. And indeed, what *would* a woman want with a vampire?"

Blythe leaned back, her eyes troubled. She hid none of her emotions from him. What would it feel like to open his emotions to others? After so many years of guarding himself, he doubted he would know how.

"These women desire but one thing: immortal life. They believe they can attain this by mating with a vampire." He felt the familiar rage building along with his need to destroy.

"That's crazy. I don't understand how—"

"They use bog myrtle to sedate a vampire until they can strip and bind him." Darach's heart beat faster at the horror of being helpless. It was what he feared most.

"Bog myrtle?" Blythe's confusion washed over him.

"Bog myrtle is used by the Northmen to increase their bravery before battle. It has the opposite effect with us. We are unable to defend ourselves when under its power." He forgot that Blythe was listening and lost himself in his tale. "Ian was strong-willed and wouldna have done this to himself. These women must have captured Ian, then cut him so that he bled. We can heal one wound quickly, but many wounds that cause great loss of blood take much longer to heal. This is their way to weaken us further. Then they each would have used him."

Hate was a living, breathing part of him now. "He must have managed to escape, but by that time he would have lost much blood and been forced to replenish it by taking from humans. He should have hidden himself and regained his strength slowly, but no doubt his need was so great that he took too much at one time. He would have done better to let himself bleed, because he was dead the moment he tried to replace his lost blood at one feeding. He became what you saw in the great hall, a mindless thing that lived only to kill." It was fortunate that Blythe was not probing his emotions now, for he doubted he could mask all he felt.

"Is that why you came here? To meet Ian?"

"I came here to meet *any* who returned." Darach gazed back to the fireplace's leaping flames. "Even though none of my clansmen live here now, the clan memory of our ancestral home is imbedded deeply in each of us. Like many animals, our instincts draw us here when we sense our time to die drawing near. This is true even of those who were born in distant lands. They all come home. 'Tis a compulsion we canna resist.

Even in his madness, Ian knew he must return." Darach allowed the flames to soothe him. "Once every twenty years, 'tis my duty to stay here for one full cycle of the moon, waiting for those who seek their final release."

"And when your month is up?" Blythe's soft question didn't contain the horrified curiosity he would reject, but rather a sincere desire to know, to understand.

"Another member of my clan arrives to continue our duty."

"How can you say you're happy when you have to face *this*?"

"In five hundred years, I have learned to mourn, but then to put the sadness aside and celebrate life, the joys it can bring. I willna forget Ian, but I will choose to remember only the good things about him."

"Sounds great in theory, but I don't believe you can neatly compartmentalize something like this and forget it. The residue of all the violence you've seen must eventually seep out. I think that's why you're hiding your emotions from me. They're a weakness, aren't they?" She studied him intently. "Who was the Viking? You called him Jorund. Did you destroy him, too?"

"You judge me by your own emotions. I choose to control what I feel, control *everything* that touches my life." Darach frowned as he remembered Ganymede and the troublesome cat. He must deal with them soon. "I would speak of Jorund at another time." Another time when she was not so burdened down with what he had just told her.

She said nothing. Asked no more questions. He felt her reluctant acceptance of what he had said, of his wish to tell her nothing more tonight.

Darach drew in a deep breath, then tried to push aside the darkness that had settled around him. "I need to walk in the hills tonight. Come with me so that I may show ye my land." Mayhap he should use a temptation she could not resist. "I do feel a wee bit unhappy. Ye could help me banish the sadness." She would not know that even an army of those from her Ecstasy Incorporated could not dispel his demons tonight.

Her laughter shook even as it mocked. "A wee bit unhappy? You're kidding, right? How about full-blown depression? I can't believe you told me you were happy."

He drew his outer garment around him, belted it, then rose from his bed. "I have lived five hundred years. 'Tis not possible to exist so long without sorrow, but the sadness makes the times of happiness more intense." Darach smiled at her. "I would not change what I am. I live to feel pleasure."

Something in his voice must have warned her, because her eyes grew large, her breath quickened. Need moved in him, pushing back his memories of Ian. He welcomed the need.

"I feel pleasure more strongly than others. And my senses feed that pleasure." He lowered his voice to a husky murmur, calling to all that was elemental in a woman. "The scent of a woman who wants my body stirs me, makes me hard with a need to slide my fingers across her warm flesh, bury myself between her open thighs, taste her breasts, and savor the texture of her mouth, soft and swollen from my kisses."

Her eyes grew even wider. Mayhap he should not have mentioned his need to taste.

"Well, that's really interesting, but I'm sort of tired tonight. I think I'll just call it a day. I didn't find out anything from Ganymede today, but I'll tag around after him tomorrow." She rose so quickly from her chair that she almost knocked it over.

He smiled what he knew must be a predatory smile, but he could not help himself. " 'Twould take a brave woman to walk with me in the moonlight." He looked away to give her time to think on that. "Ye'll be here only a fortnight. 'Tis not long to try to make one such as me happy. 'Twould be a shame to waste an opportunity."

Darach felt her distress as ripples of worry. "Fine. I'll go. But no stirring need, no sliding of fingers, no *tasting*."

His smile widened. "Ach, lass, the tasting is the best part."

Her gaze narrowed on him. "I just bet it is."

She put on her shawl, flung open the door, and almost ran down the steps. "Let's get this walk over with."

Bemused, he followed her out into the Highland night.

"It's so . . . dark out here. So empty." She glanced up at the evening sky. "Earth is overpopulated in 2339. If I looked up at night, the sky would be lit by millions of mobile sky homes." Even as she commented on the dark emptiness of the sky, she strode across the stone walkway connecting the island on which the castle stood with the mainland, determination to walk and be done with it evident in every step she took. "Don't we have to worry about wild animals? What about bandits? How many dangers are out here?"

He knew he shouldn't chance that she would turn and race back to the castle, but the need to tease pushed at him. How many hundreds of years had it been since he had felt a desire to tease a woman? He could not remember.

Purposely he moved close, not allowing her to back away from him. Her body almost touched his as she looked up at him with eyes that shone in the moonlight. He leaned toward her. Her parted lips were a mighty distraction.

"Ye need have no worries about wild beasties in the night." He allowed his smile to tell her all he wished to do with her. "Because the greatest danger walks beside ye tonight, lass."

She blinked those wondrous eyes at him. "I feel much better knowing that."

Chapter Four

"You did *what*?" Ganymede paused in the process of chugging another gulp of the pink stuff straight from the bottle. At the rate he was knocking it down, he'd have a stomach permanently coated in pink by the time he got rid of the vampire.

"I hooked up two of the men from your group." Sparkle offered him her sly sexy look, the one that had driven him crazy with lust when she was in human form. Now it just scared him.

"Hey, that's great. With two men paired with two of the women, I only have one more couple to worry about." Maybe he'd misjudged Sparkle's expression. Restlessly he paced his room, stopping to glance out the narrow slit that passed for a window.

"Did I say that? I don't think I said that." Sparkle tried on a cute pout, but it didn't come off in a face with whiskers. "I hooked up two of the men"—she paused for effect—"with each other. I helped them understand that their full sexual potential would only be realized together. It was a beautiful moment."

Ganymede didn't reply; he just gulped down the rest of the bottle. He'd worked alone for thousands of years, wreaking havoc on the universe, and been a poster boy for great mental health. Two days with an assistant and he was ready for a shrink and some Prozac.

"I know, I know. You wanted the boy-girl thing. But your way isn't the only way." She seemed to lose interest as she sat down and peered at her rump. "Does my butt look fat? White sucks. Why'd you choose white?"

"Great. I have three women and one man left. Now what do I do, smart-ass?" For one out-of-control moment, he allowed an evil thought to take charge. How satisfying would it be to squeeze Sparkle through that stupid excuse for a window, then watch her fat, furry rump bounce off the courtyard surface? "And your butt looks huge." That was mean and small, but gratifying.

Instead of an angry retort, she smiled a smug cat smile. "Very good. See, you can still think evil thoughts. And I wouldn't bounce. Cats always land on their feet." Her smile faded. "Why'd you check out of the game, Mede? You were the baddest of the bad. You were my *hero*."

"I wanted to." He offered her a glare that at one time would have signaled the end of whole planetary systems.

"Admit it, the Big Boss *made* you." She washed her face with one small paw.

"It was *my* choice." A lie. Thank heavens no one was monitoring his lies. "Maybe you should get with the program and learn the joy of doing good." The lies just kept on a-coming.

Her snort was a puff of defiance. "Forget it. I love what I do. Anyone ever tries to turn me into a cosmic do-gooder, I'll rip his nonexistent heart from his chest." She cast Ganymede a pointed glare.

"Look, this argument isn't getting us anywhere." Translation: Ganymede was losing. "This Darach needs some encouragement to leave. I want you to mess with his room, make things a little uncomfortable for him."

"Why can't *you* mess with his room?" She was now in sulky mode. "Oh, I forgot. You're *good* now. Can't dirty your hands with evil doings." She slid him a narrow-eyed warning. "You have no idea how mad it makes me to know you brought me here just to do your dirty work." Turning her back on him, she padded to the door and waited with regal dignity while he opened it.

Ganymede swallowed hard. A pissed Sparkle was not to be taken lightly. As soon as she slipped from his room he closed the door, then slumped against it. Five minutes of being good took more energy than five thousand years of being bad.

Sparkle's light trill of laughter echoed in his mind. *"If you ever decide to try bad again, show me your golden-god form and I'll show you all the things one woman can do to one man."*

Her sensual temptation dragged a groan from him. Angrily he strode across his room and brought his fist down on a cherub figurine smiling benignly from his bedside table. A white figurine. He swept the shattered pieces onto the floor. He felt better now.

Darach walked beside Blythe along the dark, winding path. She drew closer to him at the thought of other creatures like Ian lurking within the shadows of objects made unfamiliar by a night washed in pale moonlight. She leaned into him, so close that his hip touched her side as he skirted a large boulder in the path.

Her awareness of him grew with every step. His heat, his pure physicality, his clean male scent. If he stopped, turned to her, then drew her down with him beneath one of those dark shadows, she might make a token murmur, but that's all. He would cover her, the warmth of his large body driving away all demons, those that roamed the Scottish night and those that lived in her. *And her job would be toast.*

"Ye're quiet." He didn't break stride, only put his arm across her shoulders and pulled her closer against his side. "We dinna have much farther to walk."

"Where're we going?" Blythe wasn't sure she wanted to go anywhere in particular. The crisp Highland air, Darach's heat warming her, and the hard, muscular shift of his body as he strode through the dark were pleasures in themselves. Who needed a destination?

"Look." He pointed down the small hill they'd just crested. "An inn rests at the edge of yon village. I thought ye might enjoy meeting others besides the ones ye came with."

Village? Talk about culture shock. All she could make out were what looked like a few cottages, a slightly larger building, and a rutted dirt road that wound past them. The cottages were dark, but the one window of the larger building shone with a soft glow that didn't have the harsh glare of the light she was used to in her time.

They descended the hill and Darach pushed open the inn's door. The only two people in the dimly lit room stopped to stare.

The larger of the two men lumbered to meet them. " 'Tis late ye be traveling. Do ye wish lodging?" While he spoke, his dark gaze swept over Blythe. " 'Tis a plague of women we've seen these past days. I dinna know where they come from, but they shouldna be traveling the roads like men. They should stay home doing the work of women."

Whoa, Cro-Magnon man lived. What a comfort to know that jerks existed in every age. Blythe opened her mouth to verbally unman him, then caught Darach's warning glance. Reluctantly she settled for a glare that should have left a smoking hole where his heart had been.

"I dinna understand." Darach's voice was casual, but Blythe sensed tension beneath it.

The man shrugged massive shoulders as he shifted his attention to Darach. "Two passed through today, four yesterday. They asked about work at the castle. Women are daft to travel alone." He paused to consider the foolishness of all women. " 'Tis strange the laird doesna have women from the village to serve him. 'Tis for the best, though, because there be strange things happening at the castle. Our lasses wouldna wish to work there." His expression said that he could tell many stories about the strangeness of the castle if he so chose.

Darach nodded, but he seemed distracted. "We but wish to rest a bit." He handed the innkeeper payment that brought the first smile to the man's florid face.

"I'll get ye something to drink."

As the innkeeper moved off, Darach steered Blythe toward an old man seated at a table near the fire. He sat down next to the man, pulled Blythe down beside him, then nodded a greeting. " 'Tis a fine night."

"Aye." The old man studied him with bleary eyes. "I met a man many years ago who looked as ye look. Strangers dinna visit often, so I remembered him."

"Ye must have met my father. We look much alike." He acknowledged the innkeeper, who plunked down a mug in front of him and one in front of Blythe.

Blythe took a sip of the drink, then grimaced. Gross. Strong enough to grow hair not only on your chest but also on a variety of other body parts. Definitely a drink for this time period, a hairy man's drink.

Darach raised the mug to his lips but didn't drink. He gazed at Blythe over the rim of his mug, and his eyes laughed at her. She drew in her breath at the pure beauty of this . . . man? Yes, no matter what he called himself, he was a man to her.

"Do ye find the ale to your liking, wife?"

Wife? "It tastes fine." It tasted like Carpian sludge. No, it tasted worse. *Wife?*

The old man nodded. "Sharing Jamie's ale is a fine way to spend a spring night. Do ye go to the castle?"

"Spring?" Spring nights were never this cold. In her time, the temperature-regulating satellites kept Earth's nights at a balmy seventy-three degrees during the spring.

"Aye." Darach paused long enough to place his hand on Blythe's thigh. "My father told me of the MacKenzie stronghold, and I would see it." He slid his hand the length of her thigh.

Blythe had opened her mouth to say something, but the sizzling path of his hand erased all coherent thought. Except for one. *Wife?*

" 'Tis a wondrous sight, even though no one understands how the MacKenzies rebuilt it so quickly without help from the villagers. Only the tower has stood since before my lifetime." The old man's gaze grew distant. " 'Tis how it must have looked when 'twas built five hundred years ago to protect this land against the Northmen."

"Northmen?" The old man's comment reminded Blythe of the Viking who had put such fear into Ian. Okay, so he'd scared *her* a little, too. Fine, so he'd scared her a lot. Darach had never explained the Viking's presence.

The old man turned to Blythe, his eyes alight with the pleasure of telling his tale to this new audience. "Five hundred years ago Black Varin Kylandsson was the scourge of this part of Scotland. Most of his evil brethren had pale hair, but his was as black as his demon heart. The devil's own slaughtered and pillaged up and down the coast. May his evil soul and the souls of his accursed followers roast in hell." He smiled, evidently pleased with his mental picture of roasting Vikings.

"He may have found Valhalla in spite of your wishes, old man." Darach frowned. "Ye believe that good is rewarded when ye die. The Northmen believe rewards after death come to those who die fighting bravely."

"Did he die bravely?" Something about Darach's response niggled at Blythe, but she couldn't put a finger on what was bothering her.

The old man spat on the floor. "No one knows. Stories passed down swear that on stormy nights ye may still hear his battle cry and see his phantom ship sailing in from the sea." He leaned forward to peer at her. "I could tell ye of how Black Varin butchered all—"

“ ’Tis past time we left.” Without warning, Darach stood.

“Ye would do well to stay here.” The innkeeper looked stricken at losing such a generous customer.

“We are expected elsewhere this night.” With no other explanation, he guided Blythe to the door.

Her last view of the inn was of the surprised expressions on both the innkeeper’s and the old man’s faces.

“I was just starting to enjoy the conversation,” Blythe complained to Darach’s broad back as he strode ahead of her. “I never even got a chance to scan the old man’s emotions. They must be pretty twisted to get such a kick out of what some murderous barbarian did five hundred years ago.”

“Ye never forget your job. ’Tis not healthy. And mayhap the ‘murderous barbarian’ didna do all the old man said. Stories grow with the years.” He sounded angry.

“My job is my life, so I’m always interested in emotions.” Why was he angry? “What was the ‘wife’ thing about, and why did we have to leave so soon?”

“I grew tired of the old man’s blather.” Impatiently he stopped so that she could catch up. “And ye needed to be my wife to avoid questions ye might not wish to answer.”

Blythe couldn’t help smiling. “Right. I might have told him that we weren’t married because vampires and women from 2339 don’t share a common life vision. That would’ve livened up the conversation.”

“Hmmmph.” His grunt still sounded angry.

Blythe walked beside him as they retraced their steps to the castle. She allowed herself a fleeting regret that he didn't put his arm across her shoulders again.

"The old man's story bothered you. Why?" She tried to touch his emotions, but as usual came up empty. His heavy fall of black hair shifted across his broad shoulders as he turned his head to look at her.

"The tale didna bother me." His stride lengthened.

"You know a lot about the Northmen."

"I dinna know more than others." He walked faster.

"You were around at the same time as this Black Varin. Did you know him?" She was breathing hard in her attempt to keep up with him.

"Aye." With every word he said, his step quickened.

Enough. Blythe would have to run to keep up with him. She stopped in the middle of the path. The castle was in sight, so if he didn't come back for her, she would have no trouble getting home even though the dark emptiness of the Highlands scared her. She reached into the pocket of her dress to assure herself the Freeze-frame was still there.

He had already rounded a curve in the path and disappeared from sight before he realized she wasn't walking beside him. She heard his steps returning. Angry steps. She smiled.

Darach strode toward Blythe, and it was like that first time in her room when he'd turned to look at her. His long dark hair swept away from a face so beautiful, so *strong,* that it took her breath away. His clothing, primitive or not, showcased a body any woman would want to touch, to strip down to bare flesh, to—

"Are ye daft, woman? Why are ye standing here when we need return to the castle?" Even in anger his voice was a husky temptation to any female.

"Tell me about him." Every instinct Blythe possessed said that it was important to know more about Black Varin. Absently she fingered the Ecstasy charm at her throat. Should she set the charm to record this conversation? At the end of two weeks, Textron would demand recorded proof that she'd made Darach happy. She dropped her hand to her side. No, nothing really essential to her assignment would likely come from this.

"Not here."

Hands clenched into fists, he loomed over Blythe. And for the first time, she sensed a crack in the wall he'd thrown up between them. Worry. A worry strong enough to seep under his emotional guard. This wasn't a surface emotion like the anger he had just displayed, but the deeper kind she'd wanted to find.

"Here. Now." Strong worry went hand in hand with emotional distress, and emotional distress was her specialty. Was he worried about her questioning, or something else? Whatever it was, she had to convince him that she could help him approach his problems in a more positive frame of mind. And she had to do it without Textron peering over her shoulder.

Blythe watched him slowly unclench his fists and knew she'd won.

"Varin killed, but only those men who fought him. He didna slaughter innocents. He and his men wished to gain land so they could settle here. 'Twould not be wise to kill those he might need." His expression said he hoped this information would satisfy her.

He hadn't told her nearly enough. "What about the women? Did he rape and pillage?" Her hands had no self-control. They refused to stay at her side when Darach was in touching distance. And they had absolutely no understanding of Ecstasy Inc.'s company policy. This was a disturbing discovery.

She reached out to run her finger down the center of his chest and sighed at the layers of cloth separating her fingers from his skin.

His eyes lit with laughter at the same time as Blythe sensed his worry changing to something else entirely. Something that widened her eyes and quickened her heartbeat.

"Varin pillaged. 'Twas the way of all Northmen. He didna rape." Darach grasped her hand where it still rested against his chest. "Would ye like to know what happened when Varin met with an unwilling lass from a village he had just raided?"

Blythe shook her head no. Her brain applauded her strength of character, but the rest of her body thought she was a big fat wuss.

The glitter in his blue eyes had nothing to do with

remembered sadness and everything to do with sexual excitement. She'd been down the path of sensual temptation once, and look what she had reaped. Textron.

He moved close, and suddenly his playfulness was gone. He slid his hands across her shoulders and down her arms, a light skimming that made her shiver with anticipation. But when he tried to slide her shawl from her shoulders, she clung to it with the tenacity of a Voviar leech.

His soft chuckle mocked her. "The turtle thinks itself safe within its shell. The fox could tell it differently."

Blythe had no trouble identifying the fox and turtle in his little fable. But she had no time to search for the moral as he pulled her to him and lowered his head.

The unexpected explosion of need she felt as his warm lips touched hers shattered Blythe's belief in her own self-control. She was a ravenous beast intent only on his body and her desire. She opened her mouth to him, tangled her tongue with his, tasted everything that was elemental male in him, and whimpered at the clenching hunger thrumming through her.

In a tiny corner of her mind where reason had taken refuge, she knew this wasn't her, could *never* be her. She didn't feel like this, *need* like this. Passion was pleasure. This was want so strong it was almost pain. He must be manipulating her, but she couldn't stop him. Blythe suspected that if she moved away from him she'd die of sexual deprivation.

Darach abandoned her mouth to kiss a path down

her neck. He paused with his mouth on the pulse-point at the base of her throat. The slow, heated slide of his tongue against her throat weakened her knees. She clung to his shoulders as she searched every hiding place in her soul where mortal fear could be lurking. Where was it? The fear should be there front and center. A vampire had his mouth on her neck. Could a bite be far behind?

"Do ye know how much ye tempt me, woman from another time?" The heat of his words touched her with a promise of carnal bliss. "Ye need beg me stop before ye learn what I truly am."

"Please." She *wasn't* begging him to stop. Where was the fear? She needed it. *Come out, come out, wherever you are.* Nope, no fear.

"Ye should not tempt the darkness."

Before she could consider what tempting the darkness entailed, he pulled her into the shadow of a massive boulder. Sitting down with his back propped against the rock, he urged her down to kneel between his spread legs.

"What are you—"

He placed a finger against her parted lips. "Shush. Ye talk too much, woman."

"I certainly do not talk too much."

His soft expulsion of breath was pure male impatience. Without answering her, he reached beneath her shawl to unbutton her dress.

"No." She wanted to say yes, but yes wasn't an option

with Darach. Not with her job on the line. Even as she knelt here, Textron was probably skulking around hoping to catch her using a sensual solution.

Luckily, she'd worn a dress that buttoned right up to her throat. Logically, any man who had to unbutton buttons to the power of ten would be so tired by the time he finished that he wouldn't remember why he'd started. Okay, so Darach would remember.

He didn't have any buttons. Ecstasy Inc. had a very specific "naked" policy. It only demanded that employees keep *their* clothes on. Blythe felt absolutely righteous as she unbuckled his belt, then pushed his plaid aside. Darach paused to help her by pulling his shirt over his head.

There were few things in life that could take Blythe's breath away. Darach's bared body was one.

She hardly noticed when her buttons exploded from her dress. She didn't care that the tiny buttons flew in every direction like a miniature fireworks display. She wasn't tuned in to his angry exclamation.

"Ye must have a thousand fastenings. 'Tis enough to drive a man mad."

His body. Blythe didn't think of herself as someone who was only into the physical aspect of sex, but great superheated stars, this man's body was incredible.

Vampire. Not a man's body. Remember. Her little sticky-note reminders to her brain weren't working.

It looked like a man's body . . . broad, muscular shoulders, smoothly muscled chest tapering down to flat, ridged stomach, hard thighs and long, strong-looking legs. She slid the tip of her tongue across her lower lip to moisten it. Okay, she'd saved the best for last. Call her shallow, but she'd wanted to see this since . . . She looked between his spread thighs and forgot to breathe. The men in her past disappeared in a poof of inadequacy. She could spout sanctimonious litanies about how size didn't matter, but when faced with Darach's overwhelming maleness, she could only gasp and gape.

"Your fastenings are devices of the devil. What are these metal teeth?"

"A zipper." She'd forgotten that the zipper took over where the buttons ended. And she hadn't checked to see when zippers were invented. Zippers had been used in her time for hundreds of years, so she'd figured they were pretty ancient. He yanked at the dress, once again reminding her of Ecstasy Inc.'s naked policy. "No." It was tough to get the word out when her throat was clogged with so many unspoken yeses.

Blythe glided her fingers over his upper arm and felt his muscles bunch as he reached behind her to attack her bra clasp. She smiled. The Hands Off bra was living up to its name. Made of steel tensile fabric with a locking device guaranteed to frustrate even the most excited male, it was a novelty item she'd purchased to make sure no sexual relationship would rear its hot head while she was on this job.

He growled deep in his throat as he gripped the bra

clasp. The material fell away from her. Blythe hoped she'd saved her receipt so she could return the flawed item.

Why wasn't she horrified at what was happening? But her entire being was into the moment, and it was all Darach's fault. He had to be messing with her mind, because she would never jeopardize her career for this.

This . . . body. This beautiful body. She explored the smooth planes of his chest, paused to touch his nipples with the tips of her fingers, marveled that her light touch could make him groan.

"Tell me who makes your clothing so that I may turn their evil bodies to dust," he said.

Her job. She paused in her tactile exploration long enough to fasten her shawl with fumbling fingers so that it took over where her dress gaped open.

Undeterred, Darach slid his hand beneath her dress and was now working on her panties, the ones guaranteed to increase their clinging power in direct relation to any increase in the wearer's body heat. She must be heating up to supernova level, because her skin felt as if it had absorbed her panties. She'd have to sit in a tub of ice to remove the darned things.

But for right now, she was glad that he was occupied trying to peel off her panties. It gave her more time to assure herself that Darach did indeed feel like a man.

Sliding her palms beneath his pectorals, she paused with her fingers over the same spot he often covered, and gloried in the heat of his skin and the hard beating of his heart. *The beating of his heart?* Vampires didn't have hearts. Or at least that's what she thought legends said.

She'd think about his heart later. All she cared about now was that his pounding heart signaled sexual excitement. Even though she intended to stop him . . . soon . . . she wanted him to be totally involved.

Sliding her fingers over his stomach, she paused only long enough to admit the incredible truth. She was deep in lust with a *vampire*. She was kneeling on the ground with her hands all over him while she tried to remember why she had to keep essential pieces of clothing on.

She remembered. Her *job*. Hmm. She was in danger of losing her panties. She'd guess they were on Ecstasy Inc.'s list of clothing essentials.

Even though she couldn't feel him, he *must* be messing with her mind. That was the only thing that made sense. "Get out of my mind, Darach."

" 'Tis not your mind I'm busy with, woman. This accursed piece of cloth dares to defy me." With a hiss of triumph, he eliminated her panties.

She felt pieces of them slide to her knees. He clasped the pieces and flung them away. Horrified, she watched them ignite into a small, intense blaze. *Ashes.* Her panties were just a tiny pile of ashes.

Darach needed to work on his anger management. "Why did you even bother trying to take off my clothes the normal way? If you could incinerate my panties, I bet you could will all my clothes off my body." Blythe didn't much care about his answer because she was at the most fascinating point in her feels-like-a-man exploration. She skimmed the length of his erection with the tip of her index finger. It was a long, hard journey.

"I wished to show ye how Varin would have done it." His voice was rough with barely contained impatience, heated by barely contained need. " 'Twould have been faster my way, but Varin was a savage with a savage's ways."

"I like Varin's method. It allows more time to build anticipation." *And to think about what a huge mistake I'm making.*

She flung back her head and closed her eyes. *The job. Always the damned job.* The thought of it was like a gnat. No matter how many times she brushed it aside, it was right back in her face.

"There are many ways to enjoy each other's bodies." Darach's lips touched her stomach, the soft underside of her breast. "Ways that ye would never imagine."

Wait. He couldn't be touching her stomach, because she'd fastened her shawl across it. Opening her eyes, she glanced down. Yep, her shawl was still in place. She gazed at Darach. He'd leaned back against the rock and was looking at her out of those incredible blue eyes that held over five hundred years of sexual knowledge. But she'd *felt* him touch her. She was way out of her league.

"Ye worry about your job overmuch. Until ye're

ready to join with me, there are other ways I might pleasure ye. Let me show ye."

Blythe knew that if she scanned his emotions now, she'd find only sexual hunger. She swallowed hard. "Hah! I knew you were in my mind." She scuttled backwards before all her limbs melted at the thought of how he would "pleasure" her. Scrambling to her feet, she backed against a tree, a woody substitute for her rubbery backbone.

Darach's soft laughter mocked her. "I need not touch your mind to know what ye think. This Ecstasy Incorporated ye work for is a cage with bars made of all the things they say ye must and must not do. I dinna trust people who do not believe in the joy of all that is sensual. Close your eyes, Blythe."

His voice was a sexual compulsion. She fought it. Sort of. Her wiser self argued that no woman should *ever* shut her eyes when Darach was around. Her impulsive self said, *Oh, what the hell, go for it. He can't do much damage while your clothes are mostly on and you're attached to a tree trunk.* Her impulsive self was a fool.

"I believe in the joy of sex, just not as a road to longlasting happiness." She'd learned this from hard experience.

"There is no happiness that lasts overlong. There are only moments of intense pleasure that make all that comes between bearable." He paused as though distracted by the thought, then returned to the hunt.

"Ye're safe with me. I willna move from this spot. Close your eyes."

Blythe knew she should resist, but she didn't *want* to resist. She was curious. That was it, she was *curious*. She wanted to know how he could affect her from ten yards away. And she didn't for a minute think he'd leap naked from the ground as soon as her eyes were closed and pounce on her. He wasn't the pouncing kind. Darach was a slide-and-glide kind of guy, and it wouldn't be his feet doing the sliding and gliding.

"Close your eyes. We will speak while we explore what might be. If ye dinna like what I do, ye may open your eyes when ye wish."

Blythe surrendered. She closed her eyes even as she picked over excuses meant to appease her outraged conscience. The best one? It was his voice. It compelled her to obey. It was all *his* fault, a convenient variation on the old theme: The devil made me do it.

"Did ye enjoy sex with the man who caused ye to be banished to Casperwyoming?"

While Blythe considered how she was going to volley his conversational opener, Darach demonstrated what *might be* by closing his lips around her nipple and nipping gently.

She sucked in her breath and tried to fight past the heat of his mouth on her nipple, the slide of his tongue across the sensitive flesh, and the way his lips tightened, pulled gently. The sensation was a ribbon of desire that wrapped her in breathless anticipation with a note that said: Open me. Right now. The opening part was already in progress. She moved her knees apart to accommodate the heavy melting sensation in her lower belly, the feeling of everything inside her spreading, moist with her need to be filled.

Blythe never considered opening her eyes to see if he'd moved. She knew he hadn't, and if she opened her eyes, he would stop exploring what might be. But he'd asked her a question. What was it . . . ? Oh. "We formed a close relationship, and the sex flowed naturally from that. Yes, I enjoyed it, but it wasn't a violent passion, just a warm and comfortable loving." *Keep touching me.*

"The violent passion should *always* come first. I dinna believe in warm and comfortable loving." Darach leaned back against the stone, felt every sharp angle pressing into his back, and smiled at her expression—a mixture of uncertainty and sensual awakening.

He lowered his lids, gathering his desire for her into something so powerful, so intense that she would know what he felt, *feel* what he desired. "There is no greater pleasure than what a man and woman can give each other, and there is no such thing as warm passion. Passion is always heat and flame."

Slowly, deliberately, he skimmed the tip of his finger the length of his erection. He moved the image into her mind, and knew her mind's eye followed his finger's path until it reached the head of his arousal where an anticipatory drop of moisture had formed. "This is what merely the thought of your bared body has done to me."

She slid the tip of her tongue across her bottom lip, and her lip's wet sheen loosed a shuddering, explosive need in him to bury himself in her, to *feed.* Ruthlessly he shoved his physical hunger aside and allowed all that was sexual to take its place.

"How did you *do* that? I didn't open my eyes, but I saw you. I can't think. I have to think." Arching her head back, she lifted her arms and dragged shaking fingers through her hair. But she didn't open her eyes.

The lift of her bare breasts beneath her shawl as she raised her arms made him growl low in his throat. He needed to cup the smooth warmth of her flesh in his hands, to slide his tongue across her nipple and savor the texture of it, experience the almost painful pleasure *she* felt as he touched the sensitive nub.

"Dinna think. *Feel.*" For five hundred years his sensual power had grown, and he called on it now. He would slip into her mind and join with her. She would know not only her own sexual release, but experience all that he saw, felt, imagined. "Know what I know. See what I see. Feel what I feel."

"I don't . . ." Her words died.

"See yourself, Blythe, naked and open to me, so that I might touch ye with my mouth, taste all that excites me." He watched through slitted eyes as she spread her legs farther apart, slid her fingers up the length of her inner thigh, then paused. "Know all through your mind.

Ye need nothing else. Your mind holds power over all sexual pleasure."

"Show me."

Nodding his satisfaction, Darach allowed his own lids to drift shut as he gave himself to the fantasy.

Summoning his power, he drew all that she was to him, became one with her. In his mind, he touched her bare inner thigh with his mouth, his tongue. She gasped and tangled her fingers in his hair.

His senses, so much more acute than when he was human, drove him now. The taste of her skin, the scent of her need, awakened his hungers, for her body and for her blood.

"I am with ye, Blythe. My power is part of ye now. Imagine all ye would do with my body, and know what I experience."

The scene unfolded in his mind. He laid her naked on the ground, then knelt between her thighs. And while night shadows drew intimate patterns across her body, he lifted her hips and covered all her wondrous heat and slick readiness with his mouth. Slid his tongue over the most sensitive flesh of her woman's body and exulted in her ragged moan.

"What would ye do with me, Blythe?" His mind's voice was unsteady, proof of his own need.

"I . . ." She paused as if unable to gather her thoughts, as if she still didn't realize that her mind's pictures would touch him.

And then her first tentative thoughts touched his and

became real in his mind. Even as he slipped his tongue into her and felt her body clench and shudder around him, felt her pleasure at his tongue's invasion, her thoughts rippled around him.

"I want to put my mouth on you. Everywhere." Her mental voice sounded uncertain, fearful of putting what she desired into thought. *"I want to do all the sexual things to your body that I could ever imagine, and I want to lose control."*

"Lose control, woman of Ecstasy. I feed on your desire." He slid his tongue further into her, then out again, mimicking the rhythm of sex while he clasped the firm flesh of her buttocks in his hands to pull her closer, if closer were possible.

Suddenly a door seemed to open in her mind, as though all the possibilities for pleasure became real to her for the first time.

Blythe moved out of his grasp, knelt in front of him, then pushed him back on his heels. She clasped his erection and tightened her grip as she leaned into him. *"You're mine tonight, vampire. Every glorious naked inch of you."* She cupped his sacs in her palms, then slid her tongue across them, leaving a fiery trail of desire. He could feel himself spiraling out of control, fought to maintain the mind connection, fought his need to *feed*.

Then, with a sense of shock, he realized he'd gone beyond any need except his *sexual* hunger for this woman. Never before had he been able to completely dismiss the other hunger.

Her hands and lips touched him everywhere: his throat, his chest, his nipples, his inner thighs. Her fingers kneaded his buttocks, digging her nails into his flesh, and he murmured his enjoyment of the pleasure-pain.

And when her lips closed around the head of his cock and slid smoothly, hotly over him, the feel of her tongue flicking over his flesh, her teeth gently nipping maddeningly sensitive skin, compelled him to finish what he'd wanted to make last long.

He was beyond coherent thought. He raised her face to meet his lips then melded his mouth to hers. His harsh groans swallowed her soft moans. His body shook with sexual need doubled. He felt her mouth on his lips and felt her body's reaction to his mouth, his hands.

With a muffled expletive, his control shattered. He pulled her beneath him and noted with pleasure that she spread her legs for him. He lifted her hips, and drove into her. Blythe screamed her demands that he pound harder, faster. She raised her hips to meet his thrusts with a savagery that drew his lips back in a primitive snarl of triumph.

And when human flesh could contain no more sensations, his orgasm took him, took her. He felt her spasm, felt the tight clench of her muscles around his cock, and felt the waves of unspeakable pleasure spreading through her body. His own release joined hers, and held him prisoner while he fought to capture the moment, the *feeling*. But like the ocean's waves battering his ship, the explosion of his senses drove him before it, and he was helpless in a way he had never known before.

Slowly, reality filtered into his thoughts, easing his pounding heart. Once again he felt the rock pressing into his back, and from long habit, he rested his palm over his chest and gloried in this proof of his humanness. As his breathing slowed, he opened his eyes and met her glazed stare.

"What happened?"

She still stood against the tree, her dress and shawl were still in place, and he still sat across the clearing from her. As he watched, she pushed back her thick fall of hair. He followed the motion, wanting to reach out and slide his fingers through the strands.

"No, don't answer that." She reached behind her to touch the tree's rough bark as though that was her only way to affirm reality. "You reached into my mind, made everything real, but it only happened in my *mind*. I felt my own body's reactions at the same time I was feeling yours. How . . . ?" Her voice trailed off as she skimmed her clothing with fingers that shook. "*Everything* happened in my mind."

"Ye need not know how, only that I can." He slipped his shirt on, fastened his plaid, then stood. When he raised his gaze, she was fumbling with her shawl as she tried to wrap it more tightly around herself. Would she feel guilt now, or worse yet, fear? Mayhap he had been a wee bit too eager. "Ye drew pleasure only from your mind, so ye need feel no guilt about your job." He strode across the clearing, took the shawl from her grasp, and did what she could not.

As she stood facing him, a smile touched her lips. "Could've fooled me. All that pleasure felt pretty global." She took a deep breath, then shrugged. "I cheated. There's nothing I can do to change what happened." She finally met his gaze directly. "I don't think I'd change anything even if I could. I've never had that kind of sexual experience, and I can't imagine anything being that good again. Ever."

Her gaze narrowed. "But that doesn't mean it will happen again. I think Ecstasy is right about not mixing business with pleasure. Sex muddies the water, makes it harder to concentrate." Suspicion touched her gaze. "Maybe that's what you planned."

He shook his head and smiled. She was so intense, so focused on things that really did not matter. In five hundred years he had learned that not many things mattered beyond the pleasure life could give. "I didna plan tonight. If I had, ye would be warm beside me in my bed."

"Right." She frowned, and he knew her thoughts wandered elsewhere. "You called out to Freyja when you climaxed. Who is Freyja?"

It was his turn to frown. He never blurted out things he shouldn't, even in the throes of sexual excitement.

"Freyja is the Northmen's goddess of love and war. 'Twould seem they have much in common."

"I notice that whenever you speak of the Northmen you speak in the present tense." Her gaze was intent on him, and he saw the exact moment when realization widened her eyes.

He stilled. Waiting.

"Do you still guide your ship in from the sea on stormy nights? Do you shout your battle cry . . . Varin?"

He smiled at her. A smile his enemies could tell her was not to be believed. "Only when I have drunk too much and wish to frighten women and bairns."

Chapter Five

A Viking. Blythe walked toward the castle with a silent Darach beside her. She couldn't conceive of the violence he'd experienced or where he stored all the disturbing memories. And what happened when his mental storage facility reached capacity? Did it just explode from the pressure, sending Darach into a downward spiral toward insanity?

She cast him a sideways glance. No, she didn't think insanity would claim him. He was too much in control. It was his control that kept her from reaching his emotions. "So tell me about your life as Black Varin. How did you become Darach MacKenzie?"

He didn't look at her. "We raided this coast and decided 'twould make a better home than our own. We took the name of a clan most would not find strange, then found this place to build our castle. It was a remote area and few could find it. We didna call attention to ourselves for a hundred years. By that time none were alive who remembered who we truly were, neither the real MacKenzies nor the people we had raided."

"What do you do with all the bad memories, Darach? There have to be a lot more than I thought at first. What about your family?" The logical progression widened her eyes. "What about a wife?" Maybe she should have thought of a wife before she gave herself over to all that mind sex back on the path. "Did you ever have a wife?" Automatically she touched the Ecstasy charm at her throat.

"Aye." He walked faster.

Uh-oh. One-word answer. Walking faster. She'd hit a nerve again. "Any children?"

"No."

"What happened?" He was walking so fast now that she had to trot to keep up.

He stopped so suddenly that she trotted a few steps ahead before realizing he wasn't beside her.

She turned to face him and was hit with a wave of anger that almost flattened her.

"Thor's hammer, woman, do ye never leave a man be?" He towered over her, fists clenched and eyes narrowed to blue slits of fury. "Ye're like the healer who pokes and prods at a man's body, asking where it hurts until he aches in a hundred places instead of just one."

"But after all the poking, he heals you. Isn't that what's important?" Blythe swallowed hard to dislodge her fear. She couldn't stop now. All of his anger was protecting a deeper emotion. Years of experience had taught her that.

"Sometimes there is nothing to heal." He clasped her chin and tilted her face up to meet his glare. "Do ye ever think that ye have no right to invade a man's emotions if he doesna wish it? And mayhap ye should try to heal yourself."

She blinked. "Me? What do I have to do with this? I'm perfectly happy." Blythe pushed aside any temptation to define "perfectly happy."

Did she have the right to interfere with his life? Of course she did. In her time, people had to accept help if professionals thought it necessary. No one had the right to reject help. Who would *want* to? *A very old and very stubborn vampire.*

He shook his head, and some of the anger left his eyes. "Ye're not happy. Ye work for a company named Ecstasy that doesna understand its meaning. What does the word mean to ye?"

Too late she recognized Darach's featherlight touch in her mind. She'd already allowed an image of his naked body to form. Now she couldn't even lie.

"Aye." His smile was all self-satisfied male. "Ye're a sensual woman who works for those who dinna wish ye to have sexual desires." He began to walk again.

"Only during working hours." She saw his skepticism. "Okay, so employees are expected to be circumspect outside the job, too. Ecstasy Incorporated is an old, respected company. For years it had to fight the perception that it was just an upgrade from some of the ancient massage parlors that had too intimate hands-on policies. Ecstasy has a reputation to uphold."

He only nodded. "Ye also have unhappy memories."

She was on safer ground here. "Sure. Everybody does. But I don't hide them away. I admit that I have them, then work to heal myself." Blythe glanced away. "Besides, I don't have the kinds of memories you have."

"It doesna matter; memories never go away. They are always there waiting. Ye hide from them by thinking of nothing but your job." He shrugged. "Since I canna change what is done, I choose to push the bad memories aside and replace them with pleasurable experiences." His hot gaze told her exactly what pleasurable experiences he was referring to.

Thank heavens they'd reached the castle. The conversation wasn't going quite the way she'd hoped. As they climbed the darkened stairway, lit only by a few pitiful sconces, she decided to try for one more question. And it definitely would *not* have the word ecstasy in it.

"Who's Jorund, and where did he go?"

Darach stopped in front of her door. The flame from a nearby sconce cast his face in shifting shadows that seemed a little too scary for her taste. Blythe took a deep breath and reminded herself that he was her subject. That she'd never succeed in reaching his emotions if she was afraid of him. And if she didn't succeed, it was back to Casper, Wyoming, the happiness capital of the world.

He leaned forward, blocking out the flame's light and backing her against the door. "I am one of the oldest of my kind, and as such have powers that others do not."

His breath heated her neck as well as her imagination. What kinds of powers? Blythe's imagination happily created a few possible scenarios, all sensual.

"Ian feared Jorund. Feared him with a mortal fear that even madness could not end. Jorund was not one of us, but sometimes sailed on raids when we needed more men."

"Jorund was a regular guy? Didn't turn into a vampire?"

He watched a line of concentration form between her eyes. "Aye. One day they fought, and Jorund almost killed Ian. This was when Ian was still young and hadna changed yet. He would have died like any human." Darach paused, trying to recall things that had happened so very long ago, they were barely memories anymore. "Jorund was a bully, ye ken, and enjoyed destroying those weaker than he. We allowed him to sail with us because of his fierceness in battle. But ever after that fight, he waited to find Ian alone so he could finish what he had started."

"What happened to him?" Her eyes widened as understanding started to form.

"I killed him one night as he crouched behind a wall waiting for Ian."

"But I saw him tonight, felt him brush by me. Who was that? Was it someone dressed as Jorund?"

Darach knew if he entered her mind now, he would find her thoughts racing in all directions, trying to make sense of his words. "It was Jorund."

He looked down at Blythe and waited until she met his gaze. "This is my power. I know a person's greatest fear and can make it real." If he could control the weather, he would order a crash of thunder to make his admission more powerful, but it was not one of his powers. In another hundred years, when his powers had grown, he might be able to call up a credible storm, but not yet. Thunder would probably prove useless anyway. Nothing he had said or done so far had affected Blythe's determination to make him happy. He found he admired her doggedness at the same time as it drove him crazy.

"That's impossible. Jorund was alive, *real*. No one could do that." She sounded as though she was trying to convince herself. "What happened to him? He just disappeared with Ian."

"He was Ian's fear, and when Ian died, he did also."

"No, I don't believe you." Every rigid line of her body spoke of her denial.

"Ye say 'tis impossible, yet ye've spoken with Sparkle and felt Ganymede's power. *Ye've* traveled through time. Do ye think the innkeeper we spoke with would believe that possible? Because ye've not seen something before doesna make it impossible."

He watched those wondrous brown eyes and saw the dawning fear there. It was what he wanted, wasn't it? If she feared him, she would cease her prattle about making him happy. Exhaling sharply, he admitted that he did not want her fearful. But he did need to know one thing.

"What do ye fear, Blythe?" He slipped into her mind. Humans seemed always to think of their fear before answering.

"Nothing. Okay, so you're creeping me out a little. And yes, I'm a bit anxious about my job. But that's it." She glared at him as if daring him to disagree. "And get out of my mind."

He retreated from her mind while trying to hide his smile. Blythe of the brave front did fear something. It was not something he would have expected.

She drew in a deep breath, then reached behind herself to push open her door. "I've had about all the weirdness I can stand for one day. I think I'll turn in."

Darach peered past her into the dimly lit room. He frowned. "I think ye need prepare yourself for a wee bit more 'weirdness.' "

"What?" Turning, she stepped into the room, then stopped. "I can't handle this. You're my witness that this was the feather that broke the ockidor's back. Therefore, I am not responsible for any slaughter or mayhem that follows." She scanned the room. "Who is the slimy, evil . . . ?"

"Moi. And I'm totally devastated." Sparkle rose from beside the fireplace and stretched. She did not look overly upset. *"Mede, our beloved cosmic fraidy cat, ordered me to mess with your room, Darach. See, he couldn't do it in person because he's busy sucking up to the goodness-and-light folks. You do understand the sucking-up concept, don't you?"* She padded over to Darach and peered up at him from sly cat eyes. *"No, I guess you don't. I'd say you never sucked up to anyone in your life. I really admire that in a man."*

Darach had no idea what sucking up meant, but he understood exactly what Sparkle Stardust admired in a man. "Ye need move your mind from your admiration of men back to what ye've done here."

He followed Blythe as she walked further into the room, her eyes wide and disbelieving. "You did this, Sparkle? Why?"

As one, they all peered up at the huge hole in the ceiling, the hole through which Darach's bed had fallen to land beside Blythe's.

Sparkle leaped onto Darach's bed and settled herself comfortably in its center. *"This is all your fault, Darach."*

Darach watched the storm building in Blythe's eyes and knew he should throttle the wee beastie resting on his bed, but against all reason, he felt like laughing. He tried to smother his amusement. "I'm sure ye're verra good at blaming others for your mischief."

"No, really." Sparkle opened her eyes wide, trying to look innocent.

Darach knew no one who was foolish enough to believe those eyes. He glanced at Blythe. Now, this was a woman whose eyes might tempt him to believe in many things if he were not careful.

"Nothing, and I'm saying *nothing,* could excuse *this.*" Blythe flung her arms wide to encompass the gaping hole in the ceiling and his bed resting beside hers. "I really hope all nine of your lives are insured, because you're about to become a squished kitty."

"Yummy, I love a delicious display of temper." Sparkle turned an approving gaze toward Blythe. *"But Darach shouldn't have protected his door so well. I couldn't get through whatever he did to keep me out, so I had to look for an alternate entrance. Luckily for me, he didn't protect your door, and he didn't protect his floor."*

"The bed." Blythe's glare made even Darach uneasy. "Explain the *bed.*"

"Oh, that." Sparkle's tone was a dismissive shrug. *"That was pure chance. I had no idea where everything was in Darach's room. I just made my hole and was completely shocked when the bed fell through. Aren't we lucky it didn't fall on top of your bed?"* She widened her eyes some more to demonstrate her shock.

Darach looked into Sparkle's eyes and knew she had never done anything by chance in all the wicked years of her life. But he chose not to complain. He was starting to see possibilities in this bed situation.

Blythe turned desperate eyes toward him. "Put your bed back, Darach. It can't stay here."

He arranged his face in fittingly sorrowful lines. "I canna do that. 'Tis not within my power." A lie, but it was for a good cause. "And even if I could return the bed to my room, the hole would remain. Ye wouldna wish me to fall through it in the night and land on ye." He smiled at her. "Or mayhap ye would."

Blythe narrowed her gaze at him. "Enjoying yourself, aren't you? Okay, if you won't move your bed, then I'll move mine. There must be a lot of empty bedrooms in this place."

"That's just plain stupid, sister." Sparkle rose and moved to the edge of Darach's bed. *"Think about having this man . . . or whatever, spread hot and naked on his big beautiful bed waiting for you to play with his body. I could tell you some things to do that—"*

"Get out!" Blythe's body thrummed with outrage. She was being attacked on two fronts. She had to get rid of Sparkle so she could concentrate on Darach and his bed.

". . . would drive him crazy." Sparkle continued as though Blythe had never spoken. *"When his body is gleaming with sweat, and his legs are spread wide, and he's trembling with want, and his big, gorgeous cock is stretched so tight you can see the veins, if you put*

your mouth at the base and wiggle your tongue around it'll—"

"Now!" Blythe hated that Sparkle could reduce her to shouting, but she had to get rid of the little witch before she gave in to the temptation of Sparkle's vivid description. There would be no tongue-wiggling in this room.

With a mental huff of disgust, Sparkle leaped from the bed and padded to the open door. Blythe followed her to make sure Sparkle really left, so she caught every mumbled hiss and growl.

Maybe she should try to soothe Sparkle before she left. If she didn't, heaven only knew what the cat would cook up next. "Look, I'm sorry I lost my temper. It's just that this is sort of a working vacation, and Textron is my supervisor. If he finds out that Darach is sharing my room, he'll go ballistic, and my job is important to me."

Sparkle cast a dismissive glance over her shoulder. *"Forget Textron. I hooked him up with Sandy, the underwear woman. Even as we speak, good old Textron is modeling Sandy's transparent briefs in the privacy of her room."*

Talk about double standards. That no-good, sneaking . . . "Transparent briefs? On Textron?" She didn't know whether to laugh or gag.

The glitter in Sparkle's eyes officially signaled that her snit was over. *"No kidding. I peeked. What a waste of transparent briefs. Do you remember those little Vi-*

enna sausages in cans they used to . . . ? No, I guess you wouldn't." She padded out of the room. *"Have to track down my ghosts. They're no-shows again tonight."*

Relieved, Blythe shut the door. Her relief was short-lived. She still had to get rid of Darach. Sighing, she returned to where he stood studying the beds.

"Ye may ease your conscience. We willna be sleeping at the same time. While ye're in your bed, I will be . . . doing things." He offered her his incredible smile that said, *Humor me because I'm gorgeous.*

"Right. Doing things." To be honest, he probably didn't know his smile said that. "No."

His smile faded, to be replaced with his I'm-trying-to-be-reasonable expression. "I can easily protect both of us if ye're in the same room with me."

"I won't need protecting at all if you're not with me." She smiled at him. "Still no. And if you refuse to move, I'll just get Ganymede to find me another room."

"Aye, ye might do that." He looked thoughtful. "But there are no other rooms with beds, so yours will have to be moved. 'Tis not an easy thing to move a bed when the stairs are narrow and winding." He glanced at her from beneath lowered lids. "And ye'll have to share your new room with the beasties already living there."

"Beasties?" This did not sound good.

"Aye. Mice, insects, and other creatures that make their homes in rooms long unused." He stared up at the hole in the ceiling.

"Other creatures?" Her imagination supplied vivid pictures of many-legged hairy monsters crawling across her in the night. She shuddered.

"Aye." The corners of his expressive mouth tipped up.

"Oh." She swallowed hard.

"Mayhap ye would be best served by remaining in this room with me. Ye willna have to go far to make me happy." He didn't try to hide the laughter in his voice.

"Right." *Only as far as your bed*. She understood Mr. Sexy Vampire perfectly.

"Ye may not understand me as well as ye think." The laughter was gone from his voice.

Too late she recognized his touch in her mind. "Okay, we need to get a few things straight if this is going to work." When exactly had she caved? "From this moment on, I want you out of my mind unless I invite you in." And that would be never.

He nodded. "And in return ye'll not mention making me happy again."

She thought about that. If he was in the same room with her, she could do a lot of things to make him happy that didn't require words. And he hadn't demanded that she stop trying to touch his emotions. "I can live with that." But could she live with the ever-present temptation of Darach's overpowering sensuality? She'd have to try.

Darach watched her expressions change. She would

be upset if she knew how easily he could read her thoughts without entering her mind. "Ye need have no worry that I'll spend every waking moment trying to seduce ye. I must keep watch for others like Ian who might return."

Now that she'd accepted his presence, Blythe busied herself lighting several candles she had placed near the fire. He frowned. They had a strange but not unpleasant scent.

"Why don't you sit down and relax before you go out again." She paused to stare intently at him as she touched the small talisman at her throat. "You *are* going out again, aren't you? I mean, the night is your thing. You're not going to sit around watching me sleep, are you?"

"Ye may rest easy. I willna stay the night." He sat down on a stool near the fire. It would not do to become too comfortable while his thoughts drifted to imagining Blythe waiting in *his* bed. "I need to check the castle grounds to make certain all is safe." The scent from the candles relaxed him, and the temptation to stay grew.

"Will there be others like Ian?" She paused in the process of taking the top from a small jar she held.

Darach shrugged. "There should be no more." He drew in a deep breath. Her candles were wondrous. Their scent made him feel . . . content. "But I've sensed a strangeness since I arrived that has nothing to do with Ganymede. I thought the feeling would leave after I destroyed Ian, but it remains. I dinna know what it means." He had not intended to tell her so much, but the words had simply spilled out.

He watched her scoop something from the jar, then rub her hands together. She moved behind him. "Don't think of it now. While you're in this room, let the worries go." He felt her push his plaid from his shoulders and move his hair aside. Darach felt too relaxed, too satisfied to ask her what she was doing.

Then she put her hands on the back of his neck and gently massaged his flesh. Any remaining tension flowed away beneath the soothing heat of her fingers. How many hundreds of years had it been since he'd felt this relaxed, this uncaring of what might happen?

"Tell me about your wife, Darach." Her voice was low, calming, and she used a tone that almost mesmerized him. "And once you've told me, let it go."

Strangely, he did want to tell her. Darach had told no one about his marriage. He'd pushed it from his thoughts five hundred years ago and convinced himself it didn't matter. But his sudden surge of emotion at the thought of telling Blythe about Aesa indicated that the memory had waited patiently, ignored but not forgotten.

Even as he realized what Blythe was doing, Darach could find no reason to stop the telling. It was what he *wanted*. Was this her power? She did not drag memories from a man, but simply made the remembering something he desired. He would think about this later, because the need to speak of Aesa seemed almost a compulsion.

"Most of the men in my clan marry others like ourselves. But I fell in love with Aesa. She was human, but she knew what I was and didna seem to mind." It had been so many years ago; he could no longer remember her face. Darach had lied when he'd told Aesa that her face would remain in his heart forever.

"So you married her. How old was she?" Blythe pushed her fingers through his hair, gently touching his scalp.

Warmth spread from his head to every part of his body, radiating a feeling of well-being. "Ye must understand that I needed to marry young. Once I changed, I would be unable to father a child, and both of us wanted many bairns." He lost himself in the memory. "I was sixteen and Aesa was eighteen."

"You were only a child." Blythe seemed uneasy with his age.

"Ye think of how things are in your time. I was a man at sixteen with a man's responsibilities." He closed his eyes, and Blythe slid the tips of her fingers across his closed lids. The memories flooded back. "We were happy until Aesa grew large with our first child. She became quieter, but still seemed content. I went away for but a short time to secure provisions that would last us through the winter. I didna worry overmuch because her time was still months away, and both of our families would watch over her."

He shrugged, but still kept his eyes closed. “When I returned, she had fled. She had tricked my best friend, Thrain, into helping her get away. Aesa told him that she wished to visit a friend, and that I knew of her intention and would bring her home when I returned. Thrain blamed himself. ’Twas not his fault, but I was overwrought and said words I should not have said. We parted with anger between us. He left with a raiding party that night, and I never saw him again. I searched for Aesa for years, but never found her.”

“Why did she leave you?” Blythe slid her palms down his arms and wrapped her fingers around his clenched fists.

Within the silence of the room, the memories swirled like a whirlwind, carrying with them emotional debris that still had the power to wound. How? He had thought no feelings remained from that time.

“Many years later, long after I had changed and made my home here, Aesa’s brother sent word that she had died. Before her death, she contacted her family and admitted that being with child had changed her feelings. She believed that fleeing me would protect her child from what I was.” Darach drew in a deep breath before telling the hardest part. “She told them that her flight caused her to lose the child.” He exhaled. The rest of the story was easy. “Aesa married another man, who never knew of her marriage to me. She had three children and lived happily until death neared. Guilt drove her to reveal the truth to her brother." He opened his eyes. "I never married again."

Blythe withdrew her hands as he unclenched his fists, then she moved to stand in front of him. Looking into her eyes, he didn't see the pity he would have hated, only a deep understanding.

"Did you hate her for what she did?"

A moment's dark emotion lived in Blythe's eyes, something that made Darach wonder if she was speaking to him or someone in her own past. He shook away the foolish thought. Of course she spoke to him. "I didna hate her, because for many years I knew not what had happened to her. I imagined all kinds of fearful things. When I learned the truth, so many years had passed that the hurt was dulled." He paused. "I felt only regret. For her. For me. For Thrain. And more than all else, I felt regret for the child." He gazed past Blythe into the fire. "I fathered no others."

He felt it then, the soothing touch that was not an invasion of his mind, but more like the warmth of liquid fire flowing over the frigid memories of those long-ago sorrows. Darach knew he could now remember Aesa, his unborn child, and Thrain, but without fear of pain. It was like a battle scar. A warrior could look at the scar and remember the battle, but no longer feel the wound.

"Ye're a powerful woman." For the first time, Darach considered the idea that she might also be a dangerous woman. Foes such as Ganymede and Ian attacked him in a straightforward way. He understood that kind of fighting. But Blythe attacked his vulnerable center, his memories. She could find his weaknesses and exploit them if she chose. "But ye promised that ye wouldna speak of making me happy."

His comment broke whatever spell she wove, because she smiled at him. "Did I say the word 'happy'? I don't remember that word passing my lips. Hey, I keep my promises."

"Hmmph." What else did a man say to such a woman? He straightened his plaid and rose to leave. He felt no hunger tonight, but he would do well to search the area to make sure no danger lurked. "I will protect this room. None will be able to enter it." He reached the door in three strides. "Ye willna be able to leave until I return at dawn." Darach opened the door.

"Whoa, big man. What if I have to—"

"Ye may use the dreaded chamber pot." He smiled at her horrified expression, then turned to leave.

"Wait. I need to ask you one more thing."

"So that ye may plunder another of my memories?" He didn't turn to face her.

She sighed. "Look, I'm only trying to help you."

"And save your job with Ecstasy." Something about that thought angered him.

"Yeah, I guess that too." Her voice indicated that she had moved closer. "But this question is just something I want to know. After you found out why Aesa left you, did that change your feelings about who you were?"

"No." He watched the dying flame in the sconce guarding the top of the stone steps. Ganymede would do well to keep flames burning in all the sconces. The darkness drew evil to itself, and many kinds of evil prowled the night. He knew. "I have known over five hundred years of pleasure with only a few times of sadness. I prefer that to moldering in my grave."

He could almost feel her shudder. "Right. The moldering part doesn't sound like much fun to me either. But why overdose on the sexual part? I mean, you could collect antiques, write history books, lecture on warfare . . ." He turned to see her throw her arms wide to indicate the many things he could do besides dwelling on the sensual.

Darach smiled at her. "Ye still dinna understand. Sex is the greatest pleasure. 'Tis pure. At the moment of orgasm I know no past, no future, only the incredible sensations the body gives. It takes away all sadness, all pain, and replaces them with true ecstasy. I will get no closer to Valhalla on this earth. What else could bring me such pleasure, Blythe?"

For once, she had no answer. As he left, closing the door behind him, he smiled at the thought that he had had the last word in tonight's battle. He doubted this would happen often.

Chapter Six

"Progress report?" Ganymede stood with hands clasped behind his back, viewing the sunset from the castle's battlements.

"Oh, stop playing the conquering laird with me." Sparkle sat on the jagged wall and glanced at the ground far below. She wondered what incredible sex act her ghosts had been performing when they lost it and took a header straight down. She'd have to ask them.

"I drove the vampire from his room." She smiled. Was she creative, or what?

"Great! How—"

"But there's no progress on the ghost front. When I finally tracked them down last night, they were in the dungeon doing the bondage thing. They got caught up in the moment and forgot about the job. They promised to do better tonight." She cast him a hungry glance. "If you'd change into your blond and gorgeous form, I could chain you naked to the dungeon wall and—"

"Forget the sex, we may have a serious problem." His gaze was fixed on the narrow stone footbridge that connected the castle's island to the mainland. "I guess we could defend the footbridge without much trouble."

"Defend?" She twitched her ears forward. "Explain *defend*."

Ganymede shifted his gaze to the hills, which were already bathed in early evening shadows beyond the footbridge. "One of the women I hired today said when she passed through the village everyone was in an uproar. Last night four locals were murdered. Throats torn out, blood drained. Ugly stuff. Anyway, since the villagers need someone to blame, and we're the new kids on the block, they've decided it must be someone staying here."

"The vampire?" Sparkle had her doubts. Slaughtering four humans like that would take a kind of insane feeding frenzy. Darach seemed too much in control for that.

Ganymede shook his head. "He's too smart to feed this close to his home."

Sparkle leaped from the wall to stand beside Ganymede. "No big deal. So we have maybe twenty primitives storming the castle with axes and sticks. What harm can they do?" She had more important things to think about. Like all these women Mede had been hiring.

"It's not that simple. The woman said they're sending for volunteers to join them." He glanced down at Sparkle.

Sparkle cast him an impatient glance. "So take care of it."

"That's the point. I can't 'take care of it.' No destroying of human life. Line five, paragraph three, page ten of my goodness-and-light contract. How about *you* take care of it?" He looked hopeful.

"Uh-uh. No can do. I handle sexual chaos. I don't do the mass destruction thing." She rubbed her head against his leg. "Why not just send all your guests home? Then you could change form and we could have hot sex."

"I'd have to return their money." He seemed distracted. "If I block the footbridge, the villagers will probably give up and go home. What do you think?"

Sparkle sighed her disgust. "Whatever. Now about all these women you've been hiring . . ."

"I needed help, but I didn't want to hire anyone from the village. I don't want a bunch of locals asking questions. And these women just happened by, looking for work. What was I supposed to do?" He tried to look righteous.

"They all have big boobs and hot eyes. Where'd you get them from, Sluts-R-Us? Like no one old and ugly applied?" *Okay, hold on to the temper.*

He offered her a sly glance. "Jealous?"

"Nope." *Yes.* Time to get back to something *really*

important. “You still haven’t explained why I have to be a white cat.” Just thinking about white made her mad. She’d looked at her stomach this morning. It looked . . . round. Butts and boobs should be round. Stomachs should *never* be round.

He smiled at her. “You’re cute when you’re steamed. I like cats. Cats have attitude. I admire that.”

“Good. Problem solved. *You* can be the cat.”

“Been there, done that. Besides, I have to take a human form so that I can interact with my guests. And white is *safe*. This is 1785. The worst of the witch hunts are over, but black can still be an iffy color.”

She widened her eyes. “Oh.” She cast a glance over her shoulder. “I guess white is okay. I can always accessorize.”

He rubbed his hands together as he turned from the battlements. “See? I thought of everything. Let’s go get something to eat.”

“With *my* belly? I think not.” She stalked ahead of him. “This whole thing sucks. I get to be a white fur ball, and you get to be a human. And not even a sexy human. You should’ve had me pick up a blue ox along with the ghosts.”

“Why?” He narrowed his gaze at her.

Her temper improved in direct proportion to his growing anger. “You look like Paul Bunyan, so I figured you’d need the ox.”

“Really funny. See me laugh.” The air around her vibrated with his bad temper.

"Oh, and you forgot to ask where I put the vampire. He's staying with Blythe, so you don't have to worry about hooking her up with anyone." She padded more quickly toward the stairs to avoid fallout from exploding reformed cosmic troublemakers.

"What the . . . ! Get back here and explain yourself, Starbust. You low-down, conniving—"

Sparkle didn't hear the rest of his outburst as she leaped down the stairs. She allowed herself a contented purr. She'd really pissed him off if he was stooping to making fun of her name. Making him mad made her happy.

Blythe hesitated outside her door as she waited for one of Ganymede's new servants to pass on her way up the stairs. The woman would be coming down again quickly when she found she couldn't get in to clean Darach's room. And she wouldn't be stopping at Blythe's door either. Blythe had told Ganymede that she'd take care of her own room. As she watched the woman disappear, Blythe allowed herself a moment to consider Ganymede's hiring process. Every one of the servants looked like she could qualify for the Ms. Galactic Hot-Body title. And there wasn't a servile attitude among them.

Blythe forgot about the servants as she turned back to the door. Okay, this was *her* room, so she'd just open *her* door and go in. When Darach had returned at dawn from whatever he did in the dark, and she would definitely not go *there*, she'd almost knocked him down as she rushed from the room to answer nature's call. No, not call. By dawn it had been a primal screech.

When she finally returned, she told him to forget about protecting the whole room. If he wanted to protect his bed, that was fine, but she had to be able to get in and out of her room. He'd agreed. *Too easily*.

Blythe had stayed away all day while he slept. She'd stayed away because . . . because she had lots of things to do. She'd checked on Ganymede a few times, but she'd learned squat. Then she'd had to fend off questions from Clara-the-vampire-obsessed.

And finally, Textron had trapped her for hours while he tried to weasel every bit of information about her progress with Darach out of her. She had the right animal. He was a skinny five feet ten inches of human weaseliness. Was weaseliness a word? Who cared. It fit him. She'd hugged her secret knowledge about his underwear-modeling career to her chest. When he became too obnoxious to bear, and he would, she'd spring that on him.

Okay, so now she'd just open her door and go into her room. Right. With a sigh, she sat down and propped her back against the closed door. Admit it, she was afraid to go into that room, and she hadn't a clue why.

While she was busy beating herself over the head with her cowardice, Sparkle slunk up the stairs and plunked her ample white bottom next to Blythe.

"So what's up?" Sparkle watched a small mouse scurry across the floor and crinkled her nose. *"I don't know how cats do the mouse thing. Yeck."*

Blythe shrugged. "Nothing's up. I'm just . . . resting before I go inside." Weak. Really weak. "What brings you up here?"

Sparkle shifted her gaze from the mouse. *"Mede's going to be totally ticked in a few minutes, so I thought I'd get myself out of sight."* Her eyes glittered with malicious glee.

"What did you do?" Blythe almost felt sorry for Ganymede. She knew what it felt like to be on the receiving end of Sparkle's manipulation.

"You know how I feel about sex. I mean, forget about the Big Bang theory of how the universe was formed. Sex expands the universe, and that's the truth." She widened her orange eyes to indicate her complete truthfulness.

Blythe couldn't help it, she laughed. "Let's hear it. What did you do to Ganymede?" At least the little she-demon took Blythe's mind off what was waiting behind the closed door.

Sparkle cast a cautious glance toward the stairs. *"Tim and Ed have found sexual bliss with each other. Did you know that?"* She didn't wait for a reply. *"Since they're so happy, I just planted the tiny thought that they could share their joy by inviting Mede to join them in a threesome."* She narrowed her cat eyes to evil slits. *"Then I planted the same thought in Textron's and*

Sandy's minds. Oh, and I suggested that they not take no for an answer, because no matter what Mede says, he really does want to get naked with them."

Blythe could only stare. What did you say to that? Now she had something new to worry about. How would she know if her thoughts were really her own? Fine, so that would be easy. If the thoughts involved depraved and kinky sex with Darach, they were Sparkle's. Blythe frowned. Or maybe not.

"How will Ganymede know that it was your idea?" How will *I* know?

"He'll know. He always knows. And you're probably wondering why I did it." Sparkle batted a small insect out of her way. *"Mede has repressed all his evil feelings, and believe me, he had the evil-feelings market cornered. He's forgotten the joy of being bad. So I figure if I make him mad enough, he'll lose it and do something really wicked."* Her gaze turned militant. *"I want the old Mede back, and I always get what I want."*

A scary thought. Blythe opened her mouth to comment.

"Enough of me. What about you? Why're you afraid to go into your room?" Avid interest glittered in Sparkle's eyes, and behind it, calculation.

Uh-oh. "I'm not afraid."

"Never lie to a liar." Humor had replaced the calculation in Sparkle's gaze. *"Darach's a sexual powerhouse. That scares you. Right?"*

"I don't—"

"Hey, there's nothing to be ashamed of. A few delicious shivers can be a turn-on. Enjoy him. Just think about what he could do to a woman's body." Her voice lowered to a hypnotic purr. *"All that sensual knowledge, all that muscular gleaming body at your disposal. Think about lying beneath him while he rubs that big hard cock between your breasts, then watching him slide down your body until he can put his hot mouth on—"*

"Okay, I've rested long enough." Blythe scrambled to her feet. "All rested up." She fumbled at the door.

Sparkle cocked her head to study Blythe. *"You know what your problem is, sister? You worry too much. You worry about your job, you worry about the weirdness of being attracted to a vampire, you worry about every damn thing except what's most important."*

"And that would be?" Blythe was getting just a little annoyed.

"You should be worrying about the dried-up old prune you'll be in about twenty years who can only look back on what might have been." Her glare effectively stopped Blythe's rebuttal. *"Oh, I know you won't be old physically, but emotionally you'll be a dust ball under the bed of life."*

"I won't—"

"You will." Sparkle stood, then stretched. *"You have a chance few women ever get. You could have sex with a sensual animal of immense power. No puny human male in your time could compete with what Dar-*

ach can give you. Take him, use him, and hold on to the memories."

"So it's all about sex?" There was something troublesome in that thought, something missing. Something beyond the obvious thought that she couldn't have sex with Darach without losing her shot at redemption with Ecstasy Inc.

Sparkle blinked at her. *"What else would you want with him?"*

Blythe sighed as she pushed open the door. "Sure. What more could I want?" As she closed the door behind her, she decided that Sparkle had served a purpose. Blythe was so anxious to get away from the cat that she hadn't thought twice about entering her room.

She glanced across the room at the narrow window. Almost dark. She shifted her gaze to the hearth, where dying embers lit the room. Focusing her attention on the fireplace, she crossed the room, knelt down, then added some wood until the fire blazed brightly. Humming softly, she rose, lit the candles with the lighter Ganymede had given her, then wandered over to where her nightgown still lay across the chair where she'd flung it this morning. She'd been so frantic to escape the room before Darach went to bed that she'd left her things scattered everywhere.

Darach. Blythe closed her eyes. Okay, time for a gut check. She'd have to look at that bed eventually. So what was the worst-case scenario? He could be in his vampire form, really . . . yuck. He could look, well, dead. Bottom line, she couldn't stand here with her eyes closed until he got up, so she'd just open them and look. Drawing in a deep, fortifying breath, she opened her eyes.

It was way worse than anything she'd imagined. *This* was why she'd been afraid to enter the room. Subconsciously, she must have known what awaited her.

Naked. Darach sprawled across his obscenely sensual bed without even a token strip of cloth across his hips.

He slowly lifted his lids to stare at her from those brilliant blue eyes. He smiled, a warm, sleepy smile that invited, tempted. "Ye need stare more quietly, lass. Your ogling woke me."

Blythe forced herself to breathe more slowly. Hyperventilating wouldn't solve anything. "Cover yourself."

Darach looked up at her through a fringe of thick dark lashes. "Make me." He stretched. Raising his arms above his head, he arched his back, a powerful animal with smooth skin flowing over taut muscles. A predator preparing for the night's hunt.

Blythe tried to ignore the powerful-animal part and concentrate on controlling her thoughts. "You know I can't get near your bed." She'd already experienced the walking-into-a-wall sensation when trying to get past Darach's protective shield.

He lifted the corners of his sensual mouth in a smile that taunted. "The protection is gone. Ye may come to me." He gripped his bottom lip between strong white teeth, and she knew he was trying to keep from laughing at her.

She didn't care, because when he released his lip, the full wet sheen of it riveted her attention. What would he do if she moved to his bed, leaned over that incredible bare body, and slid her tongue across that tempting lip?

Whoa. She was losing the battle, and she didn't for a moment doubt this *was* a battle. *Think of something else besides his lip.* Since she was already focused on his mouth, she simply shifted her attention to his teeth. Strong white teeth. She couldn't see any fangs. What happened when he was about to feed? His mouth must change to accommodate long, pointed canines. *What did he look like?* On the yuck scale, he'd probably be a ten.

There, she felt more in control. "Do you always sleep naked?"

"Aye. But usually I pull covers over my body." He pushed himself to a sitting position and leaned his back against the headboard. Absently he put his hand over his heart. "But I didna wish ye to spend overmuch time imagining the covers away when ye returned." He offered her the full force of his smile.

The pure power of that smile rocked her. She countered with defensive thoughts. *Think fangs. Long, ugly fangs. Fangs dripping with blood.* Gross. Okay, she was in control again. "Why, Darach? What's your purpose?"

He lifted an expressive brow. "I would seduce ye. 'Tis no secret." He demonstrated his seduction technique by sliding his hand over his flat, muscled stomach, then cupping himself. His sex was hardening.

Do not look at his sexual organs. Easier said than done. "Am I wrong here? I could've sworn that you promised not to try to seduce me if I let you stay in this room."

"*Let* me stay?" He shook his head, a clear admonition to tell the truth. "I think ye had no choice. And I promised only that I would not spend every waking hour trying to seduce ye." He glanced meaningfully at the pale light of the dying day visible through the arrow slit. "I have many waking moments left."

Blythe refused to let him put her on the defensive. "And you think exposing your body is the only road to seduction?"

"Aye." He looked puzzled, as though she should know that without having to ask. His puzzled look faded, to be replaced by a wicked grin. "Mayhap I could seduce ye with my mind, but I promised ye I wouldna." He shrugged, calling her attention to the total size and breadth of him.

She had to get something straight right away. "So you think a woman would only come to your bed because she desired your body?"

He nodded, his tangle of midnight-dark hair trailing a tantalizing pattern across those amazing shoulders. "What other reason would she have?" He seemed completely serious. "There have been a few who coveted my wealth, but most of the women I bed dinna know about that." He offered her a curious glance. "Would wealth tempt ye, lass?"

She could only shake her head. The thought that this beautiful man believed his only value lay in his ability to give sexual pleasure blew her away. *Saddened her.* "Hasn't a woman ever come to you because she . . . cared for you?"

He raked his fingers through his hair and glared his impatience with her line of questioning. "Your endless blather would shrivel a man's cock until he couldna find it."

Blythe dared a quick peek. Nope, no danger of lost cocks in this room. "Don't you ever want to get to know a woman, become friends with her before the sex part?"

Blythe decided she should have a giant red H branded on her forehead. H for hypocrite. Because, Lord-of-the-universe-forgive-her, she hadn't thought too much about anything except his body since she first saw him. Almost every second thought involved wrapping herself around his bare, muscled body like a greedy sex-glutton eager to suck him dry. Not literally, of course. She didn't think there was a woman alive who could dry up Darach MacKenzie's sexual well, but the attempt would definitely be a life-altering experience.

"Why would I wish to know a woman before I shared

her bed?" Evidently he had decided he'd used up his allotted number of waking moments earmarked for seduction, because he swung his legs to the floor, stood, then strode naked over to the hearth, where his shirt and plaid hung from a hook beside the fire. "If I were to know a woman, I might wish to stay with her. That would be foolish. She would grow old and die, and I would live on to mourn her. I am done with mourning wives and bairns in my life."

"You're getting to know me, and I won't die. So what's the big deal?" Uh-oh. Open mouth, insert foot. "I mean, there's nothing wrong with friendship. It doesn't have to be undying love between two people."

He paused with his back to her, frozen in the act of reaching for his clothes.

And Blythe knew that if she lived to be as old as Darach this memory would remain clear and vivid in her mind always. His body, from broad shoulders down to rounded buttocks and muscular thighs, was an unbroken flow of smooth skin over hard muscle cast in golden highlights from the fire's glow. His sacs hung heavy between his parted thighs, and Blythe's gaze slid the length of his back and settled on their promise. He was every man desired by woman. Savage, beautiful, sensual. And she wanted him with every gasping cell in her body.

The moment passed, and he turned with his clothing in his hand. He met her gaze, and she knew he recognized her hunger. His smile mocked her.

" 'Tis about the body and the joy it can give. Nothing more." He walked back to his bed, sat, then began dressing.

Blythe was speechless. How could she deny what he'd said when he'd caught her looking at him like he was a chocolate cream?

"What do ye enjoy doing when ye're not making people happy?" He didn't look at her as he continued to dress.

"What?" She blinked at him.

"What foods do ye favor?" He still didn't glance at her.

"Foods? Why do you want to know that?" He was bent over, putting on his footwear, and his long hair hid his expression.

"Ye think a man should know a woman before joining with her." He sat up and met her gaze. "So if it will make ye more at ease in my bed, I will hear about your life." Once again, he put his hand over his heart.

She narrowed her gaze on his hand and wondered about the unconscious gesture. Why did he keep doing it? Absently she touched the Ecstasy charm at her neck, and the cool metal refocused her attention on something she'd completely forgotten about since entering her room. The job. She was supposed to make him happy, and *not* in bed.

"Tell me about your heart." Maybe she could surprise him into opening up to her the way he had about his wife. "I'll feel that I know you better if I understand why you do things." She scanned for emotions and found none, had come to expect none. The only time she'd been able to connect with his feelings was when he'd told her about Aesa and his unborn child. Other than that, she'd never gotten past his protective wall.

Darach studied her intense expression and knew he had lost her to Ecstasy. He could simply walk from the room into the night without answering her, but mayhap telling her about his heart would make her feel more at ease with him. He could think of no reason why he should want her to feel more at ease with him other than his desire to bed her, but somehow that did not feel like the whole truth.

"When I became vampire I lost many human characteristics. I found that even though I enjoyed my new powers, I missed many of the things that made me human."

For the first time, he questioned why he should miss anything human. *Because your humanness gave you a sense of belonging. How many centuries has it been since you felt that you belonged to anyone or anything?* Pushing aside that disturbing thought, he continued with his explanation. "Over hundreds of years my power grew until I at last was able to regain the most treasured thing I had lost."

"Your heart." Her voice was a soft murmur.

Darach nodded. "Ye dinna know how much ye value a thing until it seems lost to ye." He turned his head from her to hide his embarrassment over what he would tell her next. "I still canna believe that my heart beats again, and I draw joy from feeling its pounding beneath my hand."

"How long have you had your heart back?" She sat down at his feet and curled her long legs beneath her. "And what do you want to get back next?"

Darach almost forgot her question as she gazed up at him from those clear brown eyes. He allowed his gaze to slide over her long golden hair, but kept his fingers from following the same path. He would finish his tale, then leave this room before he broke his promise not to spend every waking moment trying to seduce her.

"I have had my heart for almost a hundred years now. My power has continued to grow, and I will soon be able to reclaim another part of the human I once was." He felt a tug of anticipation just thinking about it.

"What will you reclaim next, Darach?"

In her need to know, she touched his bare leg with her fingers. He drew in a deep breath at the contact and tried to control his hunger for her body as well as the other, darker need that called to him.

"I wish to see my reflection"—he held her gaze—"as vampire."

He watched her throat move as she swallowed hard, and he clenched his fists, denying the overwhelming temptation of her smooth neck. "I have seen my likeness painted while I am as you see me now, but never in my vampire form."

"Why not?" The question seemed dragged from her.

Darach knew his smile exposed all that was predatory in him. He wanted her never to mistake what he really was, even though her knowing had no part in his plans for seduction. Why would he want to remind her of his true nature? He had survived for five hundred years because he always did what made sense, but this confession made no sense. "I have wiped clean the memories of most who have seen me. All others"—*Look at me, Blythe. See me. Know me*—"are dead."

"Dead?" The word spoke of breathless disbelief. "What are you, a Highland Medusa?" Her face paled even as she clutched the talisman at her throat with shaking fingers.

He must calm her before he left. He should not have told her so much. "I dinna have snakes for hair, and I have turned none to stone, as far as I know. I dinna kill those I feed from, but I have killed those who attacked me."

Darach smiled at her. It would be wise to distract her from thoughts of death. "If ye could choose, what would ye have me reclaim next?"

Her gaze steadied as she thought about his question. "Trying to touch your emotions is driving me crazy, MacKenzie." A slow smile told him she had decided. "I'd like you to cry for me."

"Cry?" She could not seriously wish this for him. "A vampire has no tears, and I didna cry even when I was human. 'Tis not manly. Why would ye wish me to do such a thing?" 'Twas a horrifying thought.

"I'm not talking about wild sobs and a flood of tears. I'd be happy just to have a few token drops. Something that would symbolize human emotion." She looked at him uncertainly.

Darach shook his head, then stood. "Tears are not something I would ever wish for." He strode to the door, then paused to look back to where she still sat on the floor. "Ye must remember your job with Ecstasy. Ye're supposed to make me happy. I dinna think Textron would wish ye to make me sad."

Her gaze grew mutinous, and the pout of those wondrous lips almost brought him to his knees.

"Hey, how about a few tears of joy? What's wrong with that? Geesh, you have no imagination, MacKenzie."

Darach left the room and closed the door quietly behind him. Only then did he grin. It seemed he had spent more time smiling since Blythe arrived than he had in the past five hundred years.

He watched a servant woman pass him on her way down from his room and felt the smooth slide of his fangs. Luckily, she did not look back at him.

As he blended into the moonless night, the nagging thought returned. What did he look like? As he hunted tonight, would his victim wish to cry "yuck" as he gazed into Darach's eyes? Since he would erase the man's memory after feeding, Darach would never know.

His resolution hardened. He would use his power to see his reflection. He would *never* wish for tears.

Chapter Seven

Anyone lucky enough to get a peaceful night's sleep hadn't been running around in Blythe's dreams. She lay with her eyes closed, listening to the dawn sounds of Darach undressing, then sitting down on his bed.

She didn't want him to know she was awake, so she tried to control her urge to yawn. No way could she face a naked vampire after rocking and rolling all last night to the tunes of her top ten nightmares.

Every single fright feature had been there. When grotesque creatures with foot-long fangs weren't chasing her, she was trying to do the deed with Darach while Textron hung over her shoulder reading her contract out loud, and Darach asked about her blood type.

Those weren't the worst, though. Her brother made a cameo appearance. She hadn't dreamed about Mandor for months, so she'd thought that her conscience had decided to give her a break. Fat chance. Once again, he haunted her dreams. Never saying anything, just watching her with accusing eyes. He had a right to all the accusing looks he wanted, because if their situations had been reversed, she would have sat on his bed yammering at him for all eternity.

Repeat after me, I am a happy person. Impatiently she shoved aside any dissenting voices.

Okay, so they were just dreams. Probably caused by that weird onionlike veggie that Caitlin-the-cook, also affectionately known as Caitlin-the-conjurer-of-crappy-food, had served last night.

Blythe needed to put the dreams aside and open her eyes to the real world. But what did you do when the real world was just as freaky as your dreams?

A loud pounding on the door accompanied by Darach's quiet curse ended her mental yo-yoing. She opened her eyes.

Darach had just finished pulling his tunic-length shirt back over his head. He glanced at Blythe. "Are ye naked under those covers?"

"Of course not." *Yes.* She had no idea why she'd decided to sleep nude last night. She *never* slept nude. It was as though a small evil voice had whispered that it would be fun to sleep naked. Where had that idea come from? Small evil voice. Small. Evil. Hmm. *Sparkle.* She was going to have a serious woman-to-interfering-cat talk with the little busybody.

Darach offered her one of his wicked vampire grins,

then cast a pointed glance at her nightgown, still lying across her travel case.

"I have two nightgowns." Now that he was back, she'd have to wait until he was asleep before getting out of bed. Another problem: She didn't know if she wanted to see what he looked like when he slept.

"Aye." His grin widened as he strode to the door, where the pounding continued unabated.

He was ticking her off. "Read my lips, vampire. I . . . am . . . not . . . naked."

Darach chose to ignore her as he stood concentrating in front of the closed door.

"Who is it?" For the first time, she wondered who would be banging on her door at dawn.

"Ganymede and his small minion." Darach didn't sound worried as he swung open the door.

"Sorry to wake you, little lady." Ganymede strode past Darach into the center of the room. "But I had to talk to the vampire before he was dead to the world." His perfunctory glance in Blythe's direction said he didn't give a damn what time it was.

Darach exhaled sharply as he returned to his bed and lay down with his hands clasped behind his head. "Say what needs saying, then leave. I grow tired."

"Sure, sure." Ganymede glanced at the chair and must have decided it wouldn't come close to holding his bulk, because he plunked himself on the end of Blythe's bed.

Blythe couldn't contain a startled squeak as the bed

groaned under the added weight. She clutched the covers under her chin and widened her eyes. Even if the bed collapsed with Ganymede on top of her, she would *not* let go of those covers.

"We've got a problem, blood-sucker." Ganymede seemed unconcerned as Sparkle also leaped onto Blythe's bed and settled herself comfortably on the pillow.

"My name is Darach." It sounded as if he was speaking through clenched teeth. "And I have no problem. Say what ye must, then leave."

Ganymede nodded. "I wouldn't be here making friendly if this wasn't serious."

Blythe gazed into Ganymede's amber eyes and shivered. It was as if those eyes belonged to someone or something completely separate from the big, bluff, uncomplicated man he appeared to be. She scanned his emotions. Anger. Worry. Frustration. And underlying everything, a deep well of unhappiness. Why?

"Does Darach know you slept naked last night?" Sparkle's question was all innocent curiosity. *"Did you enjoy the feel of freedom, of having nothing between you and your yummy vampire except these covers? Did you want to fling them off and slide your naked skin over his buff body? Did you?"*

Good grief. How did you turn Sparkle off? Blythe moved her head so that she could meet the cat's sly gaze. She glared at Sparkle. No way would she let the cat draw her into a discussion about the joys of getting naked while two men were in her room.

Ganymede shifted on the bed, making it dip and creak. "I got word through one of my servants that someone killed four of the locals the other night. Throats torn out." He fixed Darach with a hard stare. "Blood drained. So I sent someone to spy on the village last night. Thought it'd be wise to know what was going on. Word came back that three more were killed last night." Leaning back, he crossed his arms over his massive chest. "All that blood draining sounded like a bunch of vampires having a fun night out. Whatta ya think?" He turned to wink at Blythe.

Blythe stared at him in horror and then shifted her gaze to Darach. She opened her mouth, but nothing came out. How did you respond to something that gruesome?

"Do ye believe I did this?" Darach replied to Ganymede, but his stare scorched Blythe.

Did she think he'd killed those people? What did she really know about his capabilities other than what he'd told her? No. She'd spent her whole adult life reading people's emotions. She would've sensed this kind of savagery in him. *But you can't read his emotions, so what the hell do you know about the real Darach MacKenzie?*

Darach returned his attention to Ganymede, but not before Blythe saw the flash of disappointment in his eyes. Blythe had no doubt he'd purposely let her see what he felt. It worked, because now guilt ate at her.

Ganymede waved a dismissive hand in the air. "Nah.

Too messy. Too stupid. I don't like you, blood-sucker, but you're old and you're powerful. You wouldn't have lasted this long if you went around slaughtering people practically outside your door. But it doesn't matter what I think—all this killing has caused us a problem."

Sparkle daintily licked one paw and studied Blythe. *"Letting Darach see your doubt was pretty stupid, sister. No man wants his woman to think he's some kind of animal."* She paused in her licking. *"Although I think there's something kind of fine about a hot-blooded male animal. Know what I mean?"*

Arrgh! Blythe bit her lip in her determination not to rise to Sparkle's goading.

"What do ye want from me, Ganymede?" Darach's lids drooped, and he visibly struggled to stay awake.

Blythe shifted her gaze to the arrow-slit, where a beam of sunlight shone through. Uh-oh. Sunlight. "Umm, would someone cover the window?" *Please don't tell me to do it.*

"No problem." Ganymede heaved himself from her bed and walked over to hang Darach's plaid from a hook above the slit, effectively blocking the light.

He didn't return to Blythe's bed, but instead paced back and forth in front of the hearth. "We're dealing with a bunch of superstitious villagers here, and"—Ganymede stopped to face Darach—"they're gathering their forces to storm the castle and kill all of us." He finished in an embarrassed rush of words.

"Ye and the cat have the power to stop them, so why

do ye need me?" Darach was losing his battle with sleep.

Ganymede slumped back onto Blythe's bed like a deflated balloon. "I can't harm a human." The admission seemed to have been dragged from the depths of his despair. "I can hurt a vampire or a sassy cat"—he offered Sparkle a pointed glare; Sparkle wasn't impressed—"but I can't touch a human. What can I say, it's a weakness." He shook his head sadly. "And the kitty here is cute but pretty useless in a tough spot."

Said useless kitty pinned her ears flat and growled. Ganymede looked uneasy.

Blythe clutched her covers more tightly. "When will they attack?" This had *not* been part of her travel itinerary. "Why don't you just send us all home?" Even as she suggested going home, Blythe realized she really didn't want to leave Scotland now. *Didn't want to leave Darach alone and unprotected.* What a crock. Darach was the most powerful male she'd ever known. He didn't need her. Somehow that thought made her a little sad. Go figure.

"Returning right now would be problematic." Ganymede offered Blythe his I'll-sell-you-some-beachfront-property-on-Pluto grin. "To get the lower time-travel rate, I had to lock us in to specific dates. No going home early. Sorry." He smiled some more.

"He's lying." Sparkle was still whipping her tail back and forth in a full-blown fury. *"He's just too cheap to give you your money back. Useless cat, my ass. Jerk."*

"Ye want me to protect ye." Darach's comment was nothing more than a sleepy mumble.

"Got it." Ganymede sounded relieved. "I figure you've had lots of practice with the maiming and killing stuff." He rubbed his hands together in satisfaction as he headed for the door. "We probably won't even need you. We're going to pile stuff at the end of the footbridge so no one can come across. That should stop them in their tracks. But if it doesn't, we'll send for you." Humming happily, Ganymede strode out of the room and closed the door behind him.

Sparkle leaped from the pillow and padded to the door just in time for it to almost hit her in the face. *"Frickin' fine. He went off without me. When I get my claws on him, there'll be pieces of cosmic troublemaker raining down for weeks. Someone open the damned door before I get really pissed and knock it down."*

Uh-oh. Sparkle sounded serious. Blythe leaped from her bed, still clutching the cover in front of her. She reached the door and flung it open.

"Thanks." Sparkle padded into the hall. *"Oh, and if the vampire falls asleep without putting up his protection, make sure you take advantage of his buff body. Get your thrills where you can."* She disappeared down the stairs.

Blythe stood staring into the dark. Everything had happened so fast that she'd forgotten to order Sparkle not to give her any more sexy ideas. She frowned. Okay, so maybe a sexy idea now and then wasn't awful, but she didn't like the way Sparkle had blindsided her. She closed the door.

"A good warrior always protects his rear, lass." Darach's sleepy mumble spun her around. "Ye've left yours unprotected, and 'tis a fine one, worthy of protection. A wee peek at it would raise the dead."

Blythe widened her eyes at the realization that she'd done a great job of covering her front but had forgotten about her behind. Could butt cheeks blush? She'd swear that heat was building there even as she gazed at Darach in horror.

"Come to me, Blythe." His lids drifted shut.

After the way she'd shown her doubt of him, she should at least prove that she wasn't afraid to walk over to his bed. "Is your protection up yet?" She didn't want to go splat against it.

"I willna protect my bed today, because ye must be able to reach me." He cracked his lids open a sliver to look at her. "If a mob attacks the castle, wake me." His lids slid shut again, and a slight smile touched his lips. "And if ye truly believe that I kill so easily, ye may feel free to cut off my head or take my heart." He frowned. "Though 'twould be a waste of a fine heart."

She stared, horrified, at him. "What a terrible thing to say. I wouldn't be here now if I believed . . ." Her rant died as she realized he was asleep. She moved closer to study him. Relieved, she noted that he looked as anyone would look when they were asleep. Okay, so maybe not just anyone. He looked a lot better than anyone else she'd ever seen sleeping. Reverse the roles in the ancient tale of *Sleeping Beauty* and she'd kiss him awake any day of the week.

Blythe smiled. Good thing he'd fallen asleep with his shirt on or she might've been tempted to morph into a Sparkle Stardust and perform unspeakable acts of lust on his helpless body. Sighing, she slipped a cover over him. Too bad.

Dressing quickly, she prepared to leave the room and go down for something to eat. She had actually opened the door and stepped into the hall when the realization hit her. She was leaving Darach unprotected. While he was so deeply asleep, anyone could hurt him. Sure, Ganymede wanted him healthy in case he needed Darach to help with the villagers, but what about other enemies? Darach had told only her that he would be unprotected. He was showing more trust in her than she'd shown in him today. She couldn't leave him alone.

With a sense of inevitability, she pulled her door almost closed so no one would get an eyeful, then called to one of the servant women who was starting down the stairs. "I don't feel too well this morning. Could you bring me up something to eat?"

The woman swayed over to Blythe, then smiled at her. "Of course. What would you like?"

Ganymede had sure managed to find the sexiest-of-the-sexiest servants. This woman was gorgeous. And she didn't sound as if she was from Scotland. What would bring a woman like this to such a remote area? She looked as though she belonged in London or Paris. Blythe shrugged the question away. It wasn't any of her business.

"Whatever's being served." She thought about that. "Wait, let's clarify a little. Whatever's being served that's recognizable as human food. And definitely lots of tea."

The woman nodded, then glanced toward the stairs. "Have you met the gentleman above you? I've knocked at his door, but he never answers." She bit her lip and gazed at Blythe out of huge green eyes. "Do you think he might be ill?"

Not so you'd notice. "Ganymede said that he's very reclusive." *And very asleep.* "I don't think he wants to be bothered with people." *Except when he's hungry.*

"Oh." The woman still hovered at the door. "There are rumors that vampires dwell here. Do you know anything of such creatures in this castle?"

The woman didn't look scared, only curious. Strange reaction. Blythe knew that if she'd been told beforehand that she'd be sharing living quarters with a vampire, she would've done some warp-speed travel changes.

"No one's told me anything." *I found it out all by myself.* "Thanks for taking my order . . ." Okay, supply a name for me.

The woman simply smiled and walked away. Blythe frowned. Maybe she hadn't given a big enough hint. As she went back into her room and closed the door behind her, she wondered what she could do to fill the whole day.

Wandering over to Darach's bed, she stared down at him. In sleep, his expression was as inscrutable as it always was. No, that wasn't true. She'd reached his emotions when he'd told her about his wife and unborn child. But there had to be more. Why did he feel the need to guard his feelings so carefully?

Absently she scanned his emotions again. Nope, even in sleep his feelings were closed to her. To be fair, he'd probably spent his whole life protecting himself, so the habit was ingrained. Maybe with someone he trusted . . .

Turning away from his bed, she walked to her travel pack, then stopped as she stared down at it. That's what was *really* bugging her. He didn't trust her enough to let her touch his emotions. And after her maybe-I-do-and-maybe-I-don't performance today, he'd probably never trust her. *He trusted you enough to leave his bed unprotected.* That was her one ray of hope. He'd trusted her with his life for these hours of daylight. And that was a pretty big leap of faith.

Now, how could she amuse herself while she waited for him to wake up? Bending down, she opened her pack.

Yawning, Blythe stretched and unwound herself from her seat on her bed. It had been a perfect day to stay inside reading, all warm and toasty, by the fire's light. That one promising ray of sunshine at dawn had been all there was. Wind had brought clouds and rain. Night would fall in a few hours, and she'd be free of her self-imposed guard duty.

She got up and put her reader back in her pack. It contained all the volumes in the Intergalactic Library, and she'd kept herself busy learning more than she ever wanted to know about vampires. But she was starting to feel hungry, so . . .

Faint shouts erased all thoughts of food. It sounded like a lot of people, and they must be yelling for her to hear them up here. She was hurrying to peer out the arrow slit when Ganymede flung open the door and rushed in. Blythe opened her mouth to make a caustic comment about latched doors being meant to keep people out, but shut it when she saw his expression.

"Wake the vampire. We need him." He turned to rush out again.

Blythe grabbed his sleeve and hung on. "Wait. What's happening?"

"Castle Ganymede is under attack. Can't stop to explain. Look out the window." Then he was gone.

Blythe stood for a moment staring after him, then rushed to the arrow slit. Ganymede had felt so sure that his plan to block the footbridge would stop the mob. The castle stood on an island, for heaven's sake. The bridge was the only way onto it unless the attackers had boats.

She stared down at the teeming mob of angry Highlanders. Right. The bridge was the only way onto the island except at low tide. The mob was ignoring the blocked footbridge in favor of wading through knee-high water to reach the castle, and it looked as if they were dragging some sort of battering ram with them. Great. Just great.

Blythe turned from the window. She had to wake Darach.

Hurrying to the side of his bed, she drew in a deep breath. "Wake up, Darach." Nothing. She turned the volume up a few decibels. "Hey, MacKenzie, time to rise and shine." Nothing. Okay, she'd give her hog-calling voice a try. "Yo, laird of the keep, get up and save the castle!" Nothing. Wow, talk about dead to the world.

She'd have to touch him. Tentatively she shook his shoulder. No response. She couldn't mess around anymore. The shouts were getting louder, and she could hear a resounding boom as the battering ram had a go at the castle's gate. Clasping both his shoulders in her hands, she shook him for all she was worth.

A few minutes later she was winded and no closer to waking him. Frantically she looked around. Her gaze settled on the pitcher of water beside her bed. She grabbed the pitcher and balanced it over Darach's head. This had to work, because she was out of ideas. She emptied the pitcher onto Darach's upturned face. He remained blissfully asleep.

With a defeated groan, she sank onto the bed beside him. "Next time you tell me to wake you, MacKenzie, make sure you leave a percussion bomb to do the job."

Blythe raked her fingers through her hair. Think. There must be something that would wake him. What was the one thing that could wake her out of a deep sleep? Choco-creamian cakes. If the situation weren't so desperate, she would've smiled. When she was a kid, the smell of Mom's freshly hydrated and puffheated choco-creamian cakes was an instant wake-up call.

So what about Darach? He had enhanced senses, but he sure hadn't responded to sound or touch. Taste or smell? He didn't eat . . . She widened her eyes. But he did drink. It was a long shot, but she had to try something. Her only protection was her Freeze-frame, but it wouldn't be much help against a mob that size. She needed Darach awake.

Blythe swallowed hard as she stared at him. Time to dig down to what she really believed. Yes, she'd been alone with Darach, but not in this kind of situation. She couldn't fool herself. What she was about to do would put her in harm's way.

Did she trust him enough? Did she have any hard and fast proof that she *should* trust him? Was it worth taking the chance? No. Sort of. She listened to the growing sounds of chaos outside. Yes.

She went to her travel pack, pulled out her Freeze-frame, then returned to lie down beside him. Even though she thought she trusted him, she wasn't going to be stupid about this. Pushing the top of her dress aside, she pulled his head toward her until his mouth rested next to the pulse point at the base of her neck. If this didn't wake him, nothing would, because her heart was pounding loud enough to attract any vampires within a hundred-mile radius.

"Wake up, Darach. Please wake up." She smoothed his damp hair away from his eyes, then gently dried his face with the end of his cover.

Blythe wasn't surprised at her instant awareness, the clenching low in her belly. Even in sleep, his sexual pull drew her to him. But her sudden fierce need to protect him did shock her. Lying quietly beside her, he was completely vulnerable, or at least Blythe assumed he was vulnerable. Having read about what people believed vampires could do, she supposed she might be wrong. But right now, with his mouth soft on her neck, she'd try to protect him against an army of stake-wielding vampire hunters.

She closed her eyes, trying to make sense of her feelings. No man had ever made her feel protective, so why Darach? He would laugh out loud if he knew she wanted to protect him. He had survived for five hundred years without her help, so he could probably stumble along for another five hundred alone.

Alone. Was that it? Did his aloneness call to her protective instincts? Super. The castle was under attack by a bunch of ax-waving Highlanders, and she was thinking soft, mushy thoughts.

He moved against her neck, and she forgot all about protecting him. What if her wake-up call carried him away? How would she protect herself? Would the Freeze-frame be effective against a vampire? It would immobilize a human for up to an hour or more, but what if it was fatal to a vampire? Would she risk it?

Blythe almost stopped breathing as she felt the warm slide of his tongue against her neck. Her pulse must be pounding out of control by now, an irresistible temptation for a vampire.

He was awake, so why didn't she leap from the bed? She couldn't—she just couldn't. And it had nothing to do with some mysterious vampire power. His mouth moving against her skin, the warmth of his breath soft on her neck, and his low, sleepy murmur paralyzed the part of her brain in charge of life-preserving actions.

"Tell me what ye wish, woman from another time." He had shoved his cover aside and now buried his face in the hollow of her neck. At the same time, he rolled partly over her and slid his bare thigh across her leg.

Bite me would definitely not be one of her requests. She closed her eyes to better savor the erotic sensation of his thigh riding higher and higher until he pressed hard between her spread legs at exactly the right spot. Said spot grew moist and puffed itself up in anticipation. Even through her dress her body responded to his heat and friction. Her body seemed to liquefy, and she absently wondered if all of her erotic fantasies were oozing out of her in a scalding river.

Blythe was so caught up in scalding rivers and erotic fantasies that at first she didn't notice his small nibbles along the side of her neck. It was all part of the sensual package he was delivering. She moaned her enjoyment of the nibbling sensation.

Sluggishly she was trying to remember why she should close her legs when he moved his thigh and replaced it with the hard length of his erection. Pressing down, he rubbed a slow, sensual rhythm against her favorite spot, making her ignore how his mouth had stilled, how the small nibbles had now narrowed down to two sharp points of sensation on her neck.

"There is only so much temptation ye can expect me to withstand. I dinna want to wait longer. I wish to taste ye and join with ye in a way no other ever will." His voice was still a sleepy murmur.

Something about the tasting part should have thrown up a red flag, and combined with the increasing pressure on her neck, that red flag should have been waving wildly. But the complete sensual experience was flowing over her, washing away warning signals.

A raucous shout from the courtyard shattered her strange sexual euphoria. "Come ye, lads. Break down the cursed gate. Then I will carve out the hearts of all the demons who dwell here."

Carve out hearts? Demons? What the . . . ?

"Be still, lass, and dinna look at me." Darach's voice had lost all sleepiness.

The pressure on her neck disappeared even as Blythe

closed her eyes tightly. The pressure she'd felt hadn't come from an ordinary set of human teeth. Those had been sharp canines pressing into her neck. And no, she didn't want to see his big bad teeth close up and personal. She couldn't take either a yikes or yuck experience at the moment.

"What were ye thinking to put yourself in such danger?" He wasn't talking about the carving-out-hearts guy in the courtyard.

She held her breath as he moved off her. Still keeping her eyes tightly shut, she sat up. "You said to wake you if the villagers attacked. Well, they attacked, and I tried to wake you. You didn't warn me that nothing short of an exploding planet would wake you." She shrugged. "I tried the only thing left I could think of."

"Ye could have destroyed us both." She felt the bed shift as he stood.

Her eyes popped open as she turned to glare at him. "So now it's *my* fault? Just like a man." Luckily, he looked like himself again.

His smile was slow, sexy, and made her feel all warm and wet again. She narrowed her gaze. Oh, no, she wasn't going to let him charm her out of her anger.

"If I were like a man, we wouldna need this talk." He glanced at the Freeze-frame resting beside her. "What is that?"

She glanced at the weapon. Fat lot of good it had done her. Once Darach started working his magic, she had forgotten all about it. "It's a Freeze-frame. It can paralyze a human for up to an hour."

"You thought to use this on me?" His expression gave no hint of his feelings.

She could lie. She could tell him it was to protect herself against the howling mob below. But she wouldn't. She firmed her resolve. "Yes. If I had to."

"But ye didna. Why?" His eyes gleamed with a secret knowledge that made her uneasy.

Blythe frowned as she thought about his question. "I don't know. Everything just sort of faded away once you touched me. I couldn't think of anything except . . . sex." Maybe she was carrying this honesty thing a little too far.

His smile was knowing. "Aye. A weapon willna help ye if ye dinna recognize the danger until it is too late."

His smile faded. "Never try to wake me like that again." His gaze was level, serious. "When I'm not fully awake, the blood lust and need to join with ye become one, and I canna fight the temptation." Suddenly he smiled again and relaxed. "If ye wish to join with me, ye must make sure I am awake."

She was so mad that all of her clever retorts tangled in her throat. All that came out was an angry hiss.

"Aye, I understand. Ye wish to thank me for my advice." His smile turned teasing.

Teasing? He was teasing her? Blythe had no time to think about this new facet of his personality because the screams and pounding from below had grown louder.

"You have to help Ganymede." She glanced at the narrow slit. Pale light still shone through it. "But it's still light outside. What can you do?"

"Do the clouds hang heavy?" He had put on his plaid and footwear.

"It's been raining all day, and I haven't seen a break in the clouds." She watched as he strode from her room, then heard him moving around in his room above her. She breathed a sigh of relief when he returned a few minutes later with a large black garment slung across his arm.

Silently she watched him wrap the cloak around himself, then pull the oversized hood over his head. There was nothing human remaining to be seen. His hands were tucked into the cloak, and she could see nothing of his face.

She controlled a shudder. "You look like the Ghost of Christmas Future."

"What?" He was already striding toward the door.

"Can you go out in the light? Won't you incinerate when you hit the daylight?" She huffed to keep up with him as he climbed the steps to the battlements.

"I willna go up in a puff of smoke, but I willna be comfortable." He paused on the steps. "If the sun breaks through the clouds, it will be verra painful." He continued climbing. "But I have no choice if I wish to save others from dying."

As Blythe struggled up the stairs behind him, she was surprised to realize that most of her worry was for him, not the horde of anonymous "others."

"How will you stop them?" She almost slammed into him as he stopped and looked back at her.

She could see nothing past the enveloping hood, only the blue glitter of his eyes. Eyes that changed even as she watched. They seemed to elongate, grow more intense, and Blythe couldn't mistake the eyes of a predator. She was glad she couldn't see the rest of his face.

"I will find the weakest among them. One with a fear that will also frighten the others."

Blythe didn't need to see his face to know that his smile would be feral.

"Then I will make his fear real."

Chapter Eight

"We have a situation here. Where the he . . . Where in heaven's name is the blood-sucker?" Ganymede peered down from the battlements at the mob below. "There must be almost a hundred wackos down there."

Sparkle leaped onto the wall, sat, then gazed up at the cloud-filled sky. "Could have something to do with daylight and instant death. That's just my opinion, though."

"What?" He winced as the battering ram slammed into the gate again and he could hear the distinct sound of splintering wood.

Sparkle cast him a thoughtful glance. "How about opening a big hole and they can all fall in? Technically, you wouldn't be hurting them. They'd be hurting themselves by falling in." Her expression said that she thought her suggestion sounded perfectly logical.

Ganymede yanked at his bushy beard. This was the

last time he'd do the beard thing. It itched like crazy. "Can't do it. The Big Boss doesn't piddle around with semantics. I make the hole. They fall in. I'm directly responsible for hurting them."

"That really sucks." Sparkle sounded sincerely sympathetic.

His mood lightened for a moment. Sparkle hadn't offered much sympathy lately. "Okay, back to brainstorming. How about you? The Big Boss hasn't slapped you with any cease-and-desist orders."

"I don't have the power to put a hurting on them." She perked up. "Hey, what if I make them in lust with each other? They might forget all about carving out our hearts." She shrugged. "Not that *we're* in any danger. You could just change into a cat form and we could get our butts out of here."

Ganymede shook his head. "If I abandoned my customers, I'd have to pay megabucks to their estates. People sue over every little thing nowadays. I'd be headed for bankruptcy court." He paused for thought. "The lust thing could work, but I doubt it. Highlanders love fighting too much. They'd carve out our hearts and *then* make love."

Sparkle's expression said she couldn't imagine anyone with that kind of mentality. "By the way, where *are* your customers? Seems to me that they have a vested interest in the outcome of this. Why aren't they out here cheering you on?"

"They're all in their rooms getting it on. They have

confidence that I can handle this." If the vampire didn't show soon, he'd have to go down and drag him out by his pointed teeth. Ganymede didn't relish the thought. "That's why I took this form. It instills confidence. I look like a good guy. You know, the red-cape syndrome."

Sparkle's snort expressed her opinion succinctly. "Sure. Mede, you can change forms all you want, but no one who looks into those yellow eyes will ever mistake you for the good guy. They're the only things you don't have the power to change. Windows to the soul and all that crap."

Once again, Ganymede felt a twinge of hurt. Sparkle was the only one who could make him feel that way.

Her gaze softened. "But you know what, big guy? I love those eyes." She glanced away. "Always have."

Something tenuous moved between them for a moment, then was gone.

"Hey, there's the blood-sucker." He frowned. "I think."

Sparkle studied the hooded figure that had walked onto the battlements a short distance away. She barely noticed Blythe trailing behind him. "Oh, wow. He looks just like the grim reaper, minus the scythe. What a turn-on." She narrowed her gaze as Darach flung his arms in front of his face and backed toward the stairs. "Uh-oh. Make it dark, Mede."

"Huh?" Ganymede allowed his attention to wander to the Highlander with the biggest mouth, the one threatening to carve out hearts. Just once he'd like to catch a pissant like that when the Big Boss wasn't watching.

"Make it dark, Mede. The vampire can't take the light." Sparkle was sounding more and more frantic.

Ganymede tried to think logically. If he helped the blood-sucker, then he was really helping to keep his customers alive. That was good. And messing with the elements wasn't wrong so long as it didn't hurt any humans. Made sense to him. He smiled. It had been a while since he'd exercised his power.

"Do it *now*, Mede." Sparkle reached out a claw to snag his shirt.

"Sure thing." He winked at Sparkle. "It's show time, babe."

He lifted his arms to the sky. Okay, so he was hamming it up a little. Concentrating, he called in the night and all that was dark. The wind became a gale, the clouds grew black, and darkness rolled in. It was as though dusk had fast-forwarded.

The mob at the gate seemed too focused on their attack to notice or care about the growing dimness. Ganymede smiled. *I've set the stage for you, blood-sucker. Now do your thing.*

"What happened? How did it get so dark?" Blythe brushed her hair away from her face as the wind whipped it in every direction.

Darach allowed himself a brief smile, a smile he

knew she could not see. "Ganymede thinks to make things more comfortable for me so that I can save him from embarrassment." And though Darach would not wish to admit it, he was thankful for the help. It had been many years since he had ventured out on even the darkest of days. He had forgotten the pain.

Darach leaped onto the top of the battlements, ignoring Blythe's gasp.

"Be careful." Her voice was filled with worry. For him.

Had anyone worried about him in five hundred years? He did not think so. He tried to resist a rush of warm feelings for her.

She wanted him safe so that he could save her. Given a chance, she would have used her weapon on him. And she only wished him to be happy so that she would not have to return to Casperwyoming. There, he had hardened his heart against her. *Ye lie to yourself.*

"Why do you have to stand on the wall to do whatever you're going to do?" Her words were swept away on the wind.

"Be still. I must find a worthy fear, and I canna concentrate with ye blathering." He would not tell her that he stood on the wall so she could not see his face.

"Sheesh, what a grouch. And I don't blather."

He smiled at her outraged mumbling behind him, the slide of his lips over his fangs reminding him of what he now was and why she must not see his face while he did this.

Darach stood perfectly still, sliding in and out of the many minds below him. He was hardly aware when the first man saw him and pointed. He cared nothing for the superstitious fears of demons and harbingers of death that flooded their minds. He looked for a deeper terror, one strong enough to become a true physical presence.

The fearful murmurs rose to him, swirled around him. Where was the one fear he searched for?

A man's shout drew Darach's attention to him. "Dinna stop now," the man cried. "We are almost past the gate. The one who stands on the wall above ye might well be the same one who killed your friends and relatives. When I carve out his heart and hold it high for all to see, ye'll know that he was only a man."

Darach smiled as he gazed down upon the blusterer. The innkeeper. The man who felt that women should stay at home. Mayhap the innkeeper would soon wish that he, too, had remained at home, because Darach had found the fear for which he searched.

Closing his eyes, he called five hundred years of power to him, centered it in his mind's eye, and made the man's fear flesh and blood. And as the unspeakable power that only he could wield coursed through him, Darach placed his hand over his heart. *His heart*. Always the bridge between what he now was and what he had once been. *What Blythe still was*. He forced thoughts of Blythe aside as the full force of his power shuddered through him.

He opened his eyes at the mob's shouts of alarm and Blythe's gasp behind him.

The wind had fallen strangely quiet, and within the unnatural dusk, mist moved in from the sea, twining around men, trees, and rocks like ghostly fingers. The shouts of the mob echoed strangely, then even those died.

"There's something coming through the mist. What is it?" Blythe's hushed whisper sounded expectant rather than frightened.

"The innkeeper's greatest fear." When she saw what was about to happen, would she, too, fear him? He must have already frightened her with his loss of control when she'd woken him. He did not want her fear, and he would not look beyond that realization.

Silently he listened as battle cries drifted over the loch, distant at first but growing louder as whatever was approaching through the mist drew ever nearer. Then he heard the first sound of a vessel, the quiet swish of a bow cutting through the water, the muted splash of oars. He could hear others behind the first.

The people below seemed frozen with terror, as well they might. The innkeeper's fear had not been a harmless one.

Suddenly the mist parted, and Darach saw what had sailed into the loch from the sea.

"Viking longships." Blythe's voice held more awe than fear, and he prayed it would remain so.

The quiet broke with a vengeance. Shouting their

dismay at the disaster descending on them, the Highlanders splashed through the water in a frantic attempt to reach the mainland. Once on shore, they scattered in all directions, desperately fleeing from the Northmen now pouring from their boats. Because of the mist, Darach knew that the Highlanders could not see that there were only three boats, but from the bloodcurdling shouts of the warriors, he doubted it mattered overmuch.

"Black Varin! 'Tis Black Varin come to slay us!" The innkeeper's terror-filled wail rose above the general chaos.

"Black Varin?" Blythe was now leaning over the wall in an attempt to see all that was happening.

Darach did not look down at her. "Methinks the innkeeper's imagination has doomed him." He riveted his attention on the figure who was splashing ashore to pursue the innkeeper.

"Who *is* that?" Her voice was breathless, disbelieving.

Darach exhaled deeply. " 'Tis supposed to be me, but legends grow beyond all reason as time passes." He shook his head. "Black Varin would scare even me."

"No kidding." Her two words held sincere agreement.

Darach narrowed his gaze on the creature dragged from the innkeeper's soul. And creature it truly was.

"He must be almost eight feet tall." Strange, but she still did not seem afraid. "And would you look at all that wild black hair and that bushy black beard."

Darach watched as the innkeeper desperately tried to flee from the ax-wielding giant. The innkeeper was overweight and not used to running. Darach could almost hear the man's labored breathing as he stumbled away from the castle. The massive Viking gained on him with each long stride. They soon disappeared into the darkness.

"What will happen to all those people?" For the first time, Blythe sounded worried as she watched the other Northmen, shouting bloodthirsty oaths in their own tongue, pursue their prey until all were out of sight. "Will the Vikings kill them?"

" 'Twill depend on what happens to the innkeeper."

"I don't understand." She still peered into the darkness.

"Ye dinna need to understand. Trust me to do what must be done."

"You're pretty arrogant, aren't you, vampire?" She still didn't look at him.

"All vampires are arrogant. 'Tis part of our vampire oath." He was teasing her, and it amazed him that it gave him pleasure.

"Oh, please." Blythe shifted her gaze back to him. "Did you see Black Varin? The eye patch, the scars, the broken nose, the missing front teeth? And what was he chanting with each swing of his ax?"

"Kill, kill, kill."

She shook her head. "You sure have improved with age, Viking."

Darach remained staring across at the mainland as his features returned to their human form. When the change was complete, he flung back the hood, leaped from the wall, and guided Blythe back to their room.

Before going into the room, Blythe ordered some food to be brought up to her. No way did she want to eat with the others. Ganymede would be asking questions about Darach, Sparkle would be offering helpful hints for a fulfilling sex life, Clara would be sharpening her wooden stake, and Sandy would be all excited about her newest underwear revelation, probably invisible briefs with built-in pheromones.

Textron? He'd be bugging her about her progress making Darach happy. How did you bring happiness to someone who had just visited disaster on so many? How did he live with the responsibility, *the guilt?* Okay, so she was laying some of her own baggage on him. *Happy. You . . . are . . . happy.*

"Did what ye saw today make ye fear me, Blythe?" Darach sat cross-legged beside her on the floor in front of the hearth as she ate. He gazed into the fire, his dark hair a shining curtain around his face, his eyes gleaming in the firelight.

She studied her last bite of burnt whatever before answering. "No. I was in awe of your power, but not afraid." She looked up at him and smiled. "Now, the you that climbed out of that boat? He was a different story. If you hadn't been next to me, I would've been running and screaming like everyone else."

What did that say about her feelings for Darach? Blythe pushed aside a tangle of emotions to reach what she truly believed. "I guess what I'm trying to say is that I trust you to keep me safe from danger."

"But who will keep ye safe from *me*?" His thoughts seemed turned inward, his question for himself alone.

Blythe shrugged and tried to smile. His question made her uneasy. "A hero will appear." She'd meant her answer to be flip and funny. It fell flat. She hadn't believed in heroes for a long time.

Darach didn't seem to think it was funny either. He turned to study her. "Why did ye fear the Northman so much? Was it only his fierceness, or mayhap his ugliness?"

Blythe thought about that. "Anyone who runs around yelling 'kill, kill' is one scary dude. And I guess it's natural to fear what you don't know or understand. Okay, so the ugly part had a little to do with it."

Something about her answer bothered him. She could sense it even through the slashing grin he offered her. "Ye dinna know or understand *me*."

"Hah, and whose fault is that?" She thought about the fear factor. If he were going to scare her witless, it should've happened today when he woke up. But even that didn't upset her too much. Was it the "all's well that end's well" philosophy? She didn't know.

His glance shifted to the arrow slit. Night had truly fallen. "Ye tried to touch my emotions today."

She sighed. "Yeah, it's part of my job. Remember?

But even out on that wall, I felt nothing from you. I might know and understand you a little more if you'd let me in."

His gaze returned to her, and his smile held secrets she couldn't even guess at. "I did not guard my feelings out on the wall."

Blythe frowned. "Then why couldn't I feel any of your emotions?"

He rose in one lithe motion and stretched. "Because I felt none. When I use my power, I do so because I must. I dinna allow myself to feel."

"To avoid guilt?"

"What do ye know of guilt, Blythe?" His gaze sharpened.

"Nothing." Fine, so she was a hypocrite. She wanted him to expose all his deepest emotions, but she had no intention of reciprocating.

His glance said he didn't believe her. Taking his sword from where he had propped it in the corner, he strode toward the door.

"Wait. What about Black Varin? What will happen to him? Are we safe from him?" She still wasn't clear on the scope of Darach's powers.

"Black Varin lives. He will murder and pillage just as the innkeeper feared he would." He reached for the latch. "I must destroy him and his men."

Blythe's heart pounded out her sudden fear for him. "Take me along. I can help." Had those stupid words come from her mouth? "I have the Freeze-frame. It will even the odds a little." Dumber and dumber.

Darach's smile said he thought her offer was pretty stupid, too. "Ye doubt that I can do this alone?" He shook his head. "Ye dinna know me if ye think that."

Blythe narrowed her gaze on him. Well, hell. It was okay for her to think her offer was dumb, but it really ticked her off that he thought her help had no value. She knew her logic was flawed, but she didn't care.

"You see, that's the problem, Varin-the-real. I can never *know* you if you won't let me into your life. And I have to know you so that I can do my job. I think I'll just tag along on your search-and-destroy mission to get rid of Varin-the-fake." She held her hand up as he opened his mouth to blast her. "Hey, just ignore me. I won't say a thing." Well, hardly a thing.

"Ye canna come. 'Twill be too dangerous." He glowered at her.

"You're beautiful when you're angry." That should stoke his fire. "And how can it be dangerous when you just said you could take care of the situation with one hand tied behind your back?"

"I didna say that." He bit on his bottom lip as he thought about his next words. "A warrior canna be beautiful. 'Tis unmanly."

Blythe grinned at him. *The more things change, the more they remain the same.*

Now that he'd expressed his opinion on the concept of male beauty, Darach dismissed her. "Ye must stay here." He yanked open the door.

"Make me." Maybe throwing a direct challenge at him wasn't too smart. She knew darn well that he *could* make her. So she rushed into speech before he could consider all his options. "I'll follow you. I can't make you ha . . . Oops. Forgot I couldn't mention the H word. I can't do my job if I'm never with you. Besides, I'm safer with you than I would be staying here. What if Varin-the-fake comes back here while you're gone? Sure, you can protect this room, but I'd be pretty traumatized if he murdered everyone in the castle."

Darach frowned. "What does 'traumatized' mean? And Ganymede would take care of his own." He didn't sound too certain, though.

Blythe went in for the kill. "If I were traumatized, I'd be so upset that I couldn't function normally. I'd become seriously depressed. I might even turn off my emotions to protect myself." *Like you*. "And I wouldn't count on Ganymede for anything. The only thing he's looking out for is his own skin." Maybe she wasn't being fair to Ganymede, but she'd say whatever was necessary to convince Darach.

She watched Darach's eyes and knew the exact moment he made his decision. "Ye may come. Mayhap ye need to see all that I am. But I dinna wish to answer questions."

"Hey, mum's the word." Sort of. She passed up her shawl in favor of the warmer cloak. No one could convince her that this was spring. Then she grabbed her Freeze-frame before she could think any deep thoughts about the consequences of dumb decisions.

Once outside, she clasped her cloak more closely around herself. It was so . . . dark. The clouds had cleared away, but even the moon's light didn't do much to push back the darkness. Would she ever get used to not seeing artificial lights from buildings and sky vehicles? *You don't have to get used to the dark. You're only here for two weeks.* Something about that thought disturbed her, so she pushed it aside.

"Do you have superhuman strength?" Inane questions were a great way to push back the darkness.

"Aye." He was peering at the ground as though he could really see something there.

"How about superhuman speed?"

"No. If I did, I would surely use it now to escape your endless blather." He sounded like he was speaking through clenched teeth.

"You know, I'm really starting to hate that word 'blather.' " She followed along behind as he walked away from the castle. His gaze was still fixed on the ground. "What're you doing?"

"I'm following the footprints of Black Varin and the innkeeper. The rain has made the earth soft, so I can see them clearly." He moved more quickly around rocks and through small stands of trees.

When he stopped speaking, the silence closed in on Blythe. A silence so complete that it made her uneasy. Life was never silent in her time. She knew she shouldn't, but she had to break the silence.

"Okay, since I can't see squat, I'll add superhuman eyesight to your list of powers."

"Ye may also add superhuman patience."

She chose to ignore his sarcasm. "I know you have enhanced senses. Can you fly or shape-shift?"

He kept walking as he stared at the ground, seeing things she couldn't hope to see. "Would ye wish to mate with me as we fly above the earth?" He sounded interested in the concept.

She didn't intend to answer his question, so she countered with her own question. "Why do you have to turn everything into something sexual?"

"Because it fashes ye so, and because the thought of being inside ye excites me."

Give him points for honesty. She wished she had a snappy comeback, but words eluded her.

"I canna fly now, but 'tis a power I will gain in mayhap a hundred years. The older I grow, the more I will be able to do. And I . . . change when I take my vampire form."

This was getting more and more interesting. "So, do you change into a bat?"

Darach offered her a horrified glance. "Why would I wish to be a bat?"

He had a point there. "You're right. If I could change shapes, I'd probably want to be a giant woolly pandercat."

"Pandercat?" He shook his head and returned his attention to the ground.

"I'll explain later. How about becoming invisible? Can you do that?" She was almost breathless with excitement over all the info he was giving her. Fine, so she was breathless because he was walking too fast and she was out of shape.

Without warning, he stopped completely and turned to face her. "I canna become invisible. I dinna *need* to become invisible."

He was baiting her, waiting for her to ask the expected question. She absolutely would *not* ask . . . she asked, "Why not?"

His smile was a slow slide of wicked anticipation. "Why would I wish to be invisible when I can do this?"

She had no time even to question what "this" was before she knew. Suddenly he was gone from in front of her. And at the same time she felt him flow *into* her.

It was a slow heat, filling her, touching her in an erotic glide, merging yet remaining separate. She could feel the pounding of his heart in counterpoint to hers, the immediate sensitivity of her nipples responding to his male presence, his male hunger. And the pressure of his erection touching her from the inside, an intimate stroking low in her belly, caressing secret places no man's body could ever reach. Deep inside who she was.

She spread her legs in an attempt to ease the building pressure, compelled by the instinct to take him inside her even though he was already there.

"Good Lord!" She flung off her cloak in response to the spreading heat.

"Ye called, mistress?" His voice, his laughter, thrummed through her.

"Can this make me pregnant?" She felt her orgasm building, her senses wrapping around his arousal, clenching it tightly within her.

"Aye. 'Twill fill ye with all the possibilities for sensual enjoyment. Ye will give birth to a craving for all the joys the body can give." His voice was thick with desire. *"And ye will never again be satisfied completely with what your time can offer."* His need burned into her body, his greed for all that was sexual wringing a cry from her.

Then he began to move, the rhythm of his thrusts quickening, driving her closer and closer to something so huge that it spread across her whole life's horizon. She braced herself against his thrusts as he drove deeper and deeper. There was no limit to how deep, how hard he could plunge. All she knew was that she had to reach . . .

Her climax rushed to meet her, and she embraced it, screaming her joy and squeezing every last moment from that mindless pinnacle where only physical sensation dwelled. And as she held her breath to experience the last few glorious tremors, she heard Darach's groan of completion. Then she felt his presence leave her.

Just like a man. He got what he wanted, then left. Somewhere along the way she'd closed her eyes. She opened them to find herself lying on the ground with

Darach beside her. She didn't remember falling.

Blythe took some small comfort in seeing his shocked expression. This must not have been business as usual for him either. Someone had to break the silence, so it might as well be she. "You were right. Being invisible has its limitations." She had to ask. "How did you do that?" Hmm. Hadn't she asked that question before?

He didn't meet her gaze as he rose and helped her to her feet. "Ye learn many things in five hundred years."

What happened when he reached one thousand? No woman would survive sex with him, but at least those future lovers would have known—

"Ecstasy." He touched the small charm at her throat.

"What?" Was he in her mind again? She checked. Nope. Mind empty.

"What we felt was true ecstasy, not this Ecstasy Incorporated ye work for." He returned his gaze to the ground and continued walking.

Okay, she got the picture. He didn't want to discuss what had just happened. Fine with her. It was his loss. Now he'd never hear that she hadn't known the meaning of mind-blowing sex until him. She followed him on legs that still felt shaky.

But that was all it had been. She wouldn't even consider that it had been something more. *Stop thinking. Say something.*

"What about things that can harm you?" *Can the trembling and throbbing still going on inside me do damage?* She tried to remember the list she'd made after her research. "Holy water?"

"No."

"Crosses?"

"No."

"Fire?" *How about the way I'm still burning for you, vampire? Is that terminal?*

"I would burn just as ye would burn."

"Daylight?" She *knew* sunlight was a danger.

"I wouldna burst into flame, but light causes terrible suffering. The pain would drive me mad, and if I stayed in the sunlight overlong, the pain would kill me."

Blythe nodded. It had taken courage for him to walk out into the daylight this afternoon. She clamped down on her budding admiration. She had to keep thinking of him as only a sexual animal, one she had to make happy.

He quickened his pace like a predator who senses his prey close by. Blythe smiled as she struggled to keep up. It was incongrous to think of an eight-foot-tall Viking, with an ax, as prey.

She did have one last question. "What do you fear, Darach?"

He offered her a long, hooded stare.

"I fear *ye*, woman from another time."

Chapter Nine

"Me?" Blythe stared at him with wide eyes as she clutched her cloak tightly around her body to ward off the night's chill. "Why would you be afraid of me?"

Because of how ye tempt me. Mayhap Blythe would do better to use her cloak as protection against *him*, for when his mouth touched her warm, bare flesh, it threatened to unleash the beast in him. Only centuries of practice controlling his hunger stood between Blythe and death. And yet, each time he had reached orgasm with her, the explosion of his senses had taken him beyond his desire to feed. In five hundred years, only Blythe had been able to do that.

"Well, why do I make you afraid?" Her tone said that if her hands were free, she would place them on her hips.

Darach smiled into the darkness. He sensed that he was close to the end of his hunt, but before continuing along the path, he would give her an answer.

"Ye look at the world through different eyes. And sometimes when ye speak with me, your ideas make me think differently, act differently." He shrugged and glanced at her. "I have done things in a certain way for five hundred years. Ye disturb my life."

Darach could see the white flash of her smile, and was reminded of the feel of his mouth on hers, the slide of his tongue across her teeth, the warm, wet tangle of her tongue with his. Odin's fire, a score of Valkyries could beckon to him and he would still think of this woman from Ecstasy.

"Disturb your life? You mean that I take you out of your comfort zone?" She brushed her hair away from her eyes, and he followed the motion hungrily.

Darach nodded. Absently he decided that he would feed tonight, sparingly, just to make sure his hunger was at its lowest when he was around Blythe. He would find someone completely undesirable, someone with huge warts and a love of garlic.

"Interesting." She followed him as he moved warily down the path. "Just for your information, you take me out of my comfort zone, too. Big time."

"Shh." He held his finger to his lips. What he sought was near. Strangely, he felt no danger. But he would not take any chances with Blythe's safety. "Ye must stay here while I go ahead. I will come for ye when 'tis safe."

"Fine." She stopped walking.

He narrowed his gaze on her. "Ye agreed verra

quickly. 'Tis not in your nature to be left behind."

She smiled at him, but Darach was not certain he believed that smile. "I'm not stupid. I don't want to have a front-row seat to the Ugly Viking versus Stupid Innkeeper grudge match. So long as you don't lock me in a room without a bathroom, I'm okay being left behind."

Darach nodded and left her standing in the moonlight. He would not look back and be affected by her forlorn expression. He strode quickly away.

He slowed as he entered a small clearing ringed by large boulders. Taller than a man, the stones could easily hide a waiting enemy. He did not worry overmuch, because even if the Northman caught him unawares, Darach would have little trouble defeating him. But years as a predator had taught him to prepare for the unexpected.

Only the dead awaited him this night. Darach relaxed as he sensed no living thing in the clearing. Instinctively, he knew the innkeeper no longer lived.

Within seconds he found the man's body. He was sprawled between two giant boulders, his face frozen forever in a twisted mask of unspeakable terror. Darach raked his fingers through his hair and fought back the guilt. It was always so. You would think after five hundred years he would no longer react like the human he had once been. He had done what he must. One man had died so that many could live.

"Is he dead?" Blythe's quiet voice was right behind him.

"Aye." Darach would not berate her for following him. He had expected nothing less. He only regretted that she should see this. "He bears no marks. His fear killed him."

"A heart attack?" She did not sound frightened as she peered around Darach.

This was not a woman who would run screaming into the night. He admired that in her, but also feared that her courage might eventually prove her undoing. Darach frowned at the thought.

"Ye may call it what ye wish." Darach glanced down at the massive footprints of the Northman. They ended only a hand's span from the innkeeper's body.

"And Black Varin?" She moved to his side, then slipped off her cloak.

"Black Varin was the innkeeper's fear. He and his Northmen ceased to exist when the innkeeper died." It was done. He would guide Blythe home, then return the body to the kirk. Afterwards, he would feed, then begin the hunt for those who had killed the villagers. If they were vampires, he must destroy them.

Darach usually felt no emotion when he knew he must hunt. It was merely a thing he had to do. But he felt a strange weariness of spirit tonight that tempted him to stay with Blythe, if only for her companionship. *Ye never needed companionship before. Why do ye need it now?* Darach had no answer.

As Blythe bent down to lay her cloak over the dead man, Darach stopped her. "Ye need not do this. I will return to take him home."

She didn't argue as she put her cloak back on. They walked silently to the castle, and Darach wondered if she wished she had chosen another place, another time, to visit. He would not blame her.

Once inside her room, Blythe watched Darach leave. Would he come back after taking care of the innkeeper, or would he stay away until dawn? She wasn't sure which she wanted.

She needed some time alone to regroup. Too much had happened, and she had to make peace with her warring emotions. She couldn't make anyone happy if she didn't know how she felt about anything. Calm was a prerequisite for any of Ecstasy's Happiness staff.

But she'd avoided her job too long. Time was running out, and she had only reached his emotions once. Textron wouldn't count that once as any kind of success. And if she failed, she'd be failing her family as well as herself. Blythe frowned. Somehow that argument didn't pack the emotional punch it once had.

But it would be better if he came home tonight. After the day he'd had, he might be more open to her. She pushed aside a whisper of guilt. He'd be better off for her help.

Blythe pulled her nightgown over her head—no more experimenting with naked nights—and propped herself up in bed to wait. Picking up the research notes she'd made on vampires, she crossed off *holy water,* crossed off *fire,* crossed—

The demanding meow outside her door caught Blythe by surprise. Sparkle. For a moment, she considered ignoring it. Probably not a good idea. Sighing, she got out of bed, then pulled open the door.

"Hey, sister, do I have some hot stuff for you." Sparkle stared up at Blythe with bright, excited eyes. *"You want some dirt on your boss? Come with me."* She started to turn away.

"I can't." What kind of trouble was Sparkle trying to get her into now, because Sparkle Stardust was *always* about trouble. "I'm not dressed, and I'm waiting for—"

"Forget dressed. Everyone's in bed. No one will see you." Sparkle's tone said that she'd be fine with Blythe running through the castle naked. *"This is too great to miss. Did you bring anything to record sound?"*

"Well, yeah." Blythe touched the Ecstasy charm at her neck. "But—"

Sparkle's gaze grew sly. *"Here's how I see it. You want to get it on with the vampire, but you won't because of your boss. I don't know how he'd find out if you didn't tell him, but I guess you're all hung up on the honesty thing. Honesty's just plain dumb, but that's only my opinion. Anyway, your boss can make or break your career, but while he's telling you that sex on the job is bad, he's doing it with the underwear lady."* She tried to mold her little cat face into a sympathetic expression, but the wicked glitter in her eyes negated the effort.

"Now, if you had a recording that proved old horny Textron was also playing around on the job, it seems to me he couldn't say much about what you were doing."

"Blackmail?" Somehow it didn't sound so awful when Sparkle described it. Or maybe Blythe's moral fabric was unraveling as fast as her resistance to a certain sexy vampire. Because, heaven help her, she *wanted* to make love with Darach, not in her mind or while he shared her body, but in the time-honored *normal* way. She frowned. If the word "normal" could ever be attached to Darach.

"Sure. If it works, do it. That's just me, of course." Sparkle seemed pretty sure of Blythe's response, because she started down the winding stone steps without a backward glance.

Blythe watched her disappear around a curve in the stairwell. Sparkle didn't know that it wasn't all about Textron. It was about her family, her brother, and what had happened to them because she put pleasure before business.

Sparkle padded back up the steps to stare at Blythe. *"Look, sister, I know there's more to your story than what you've told me, but there're special times in your life that you can't let slip by, because they'll never come again. Live in the moment. Don't think about the past or the future. Drain every last drop from now, savor it, and remember it. You can beat yourself up over the 'big bad' you did tomorrow."* She gazed at Blythe with her cat eyes that gave nothing away. *"Go for it."*

Blythe thought about that. Yes, she'd always feel the guilt, but making love with Darach wouldn't kill her family again. In fact, Mandor would probably laugh and tell her to live her life to the fullest for all of them. So if she stripped off the hair shirt of guilt for her family, that left her job. And if no one but Textron would ever know, and he was afraid to tell on her . . .

"Are you coming?" Sparkle's short well of patience sounded empty.

For a mini-moment, Blythe balanced goodness, honesty, and fair play against making love with Darach. Okay, soul-searching over. She followed Sparkle down the steps.

Once outside Sandy's room, Blythe looked to make sure no one was around, then put her ear to the door. "Drat. I can't make out what they're saying."

"Give me your recorder." Sparkle's eyes gleamed wickedly in the darkened hallway.

Blythe pressed the E on her Ecstasy charm to start the recording, then lifted the chain from around her neck. She put it on the floor in front of Sparkle.

Sparkle carefully batted the charm under the door until only the chain remained in sight. *"There. The recorder is inside and can pick up every grunt and moan."* She stared up at Blythe, joy gleaming in her eyes.

Blythe studied the cat. "You really get off on this kind of thing, don't you?" She kept her voice to a whisper, although she suspected Sandy and Textron wouldn't notice anything even if the whole MacKenzie clan marched down the hall playing their . . . She bit her lip trying to remember the ancient Scots' instrument of choice. Got it. Playing their bagpipes.

Sparkle stared at her as though she'd said something really stupid. *"Sure. Who wouldn't?"*

Half an hour later, Sparkle had wandered away and Blythe had resorted to sitting on the floor. Blythe leaned her head back against the wall and tried to decide if she'd recorded enough. Probably. She stood, then leaned down to—

"Ye tempt me in any position, woman, but this . . ." Two large male hands cupped her behind. "This is beyond the power of even an immortal to resist." The hands glided over her nightgown—smoothing, heating, and obviously appreciating.

Blythe straightened with a startled squeak. *Darach.* "Don't sneak up behind me like that." She retained enough sense to keep her voice to an angry whisper. She turned to face him.

"Why would ye be here in your nightclothes?" His gaze was a mixture of amusement and suspicion.

Lie. She needed a big believable lie. "I was on my way down to see if I could get something to eat when I dropped my charm." She searched her mind to make sure he wasn't in there taking notes. Nope. She could keep on lying.

"In your nightclothes?" He bent down, pulled her charm from underneath Sandy's door, and handed it to her.

"Yes, well . . ." She bit her lip. "I was really hungry, and I figured that no one would be up at this time of night." Quickly she put the chain around her neck and pressed the C to stop the recording.

"Hmm." His gaze said he wasn't sure if he believed her, but that he would give her the benefit of the doubt. "Go back to your room, and I will bring food to ye."

Blythe didn't need to be told twice. She almost ran up the stairs. If she were quick, she could take a little listen to Textron before Darach returned. She pressed the Y for play.

"Oooh, I love your sexual package, Texy-poo. It's so . . . compact."

Compact? Blythe did some mental eye-rolling. She didn't know how much of this she could listen to without gagging.

"I can't believe you're naming a new product after me. I love you for that, Sandy." Unidentifiable sounds of passion. "The Textron Testicle Cup. It gives me shivers just thinking about it. Come here, baby." Moan, grunt, shriek, growl.

Okay, heard enough. Blythe turned the recorder off. She smiled. Textron Testicle Cup? Probably the size of an egg cup. She sighed as she plunked herself on her bed. That was mean. She couldn't blame Textron for what he looked like, but she sure could blame him for being a jerk.

Blythe didn't have long to think about what she'd done or what she planned to do before Darach returned from the kitchen with some bread, honey, and ale. He set everything on the table beside her bed and silently watched her eat.

"You know, that tasted pretty good." She smiled at him, then glanced away. "Did you take care—"

He returned her smile as he put his finger over her lips. "Dinna speak of it now. Think only of your senses and the pleasure they can bring you. The soft texture of the bread, the smooth sweetness of the honey, the quenching of your thirst. Feel the fire warming your skin and imagine the softness of your bed."

"I understand what you're doing, but it doesn't work for me." She met his gaze directly. "I need to know what's happening."

Darach studied her with hooded eyes. "Ye canna change what has happened, Blythe, and the future is always uncertain. Ye can only control what happens now, and I choose to feed my senses rather than dwell on sadness."

Blythe sighed. Darach and Sparkle had the same message. Maybe she'd try the living-in-the-moment thing. "Will you stay the night or go out again?"

For someone who seemed intent on avoiding worry, he was looking troubled. " 'Tis not long till dawn so I willna go out again this night, but tomorrow night I must find what is killing so many."

That didn't sound good. "Do you think the killers are vampires?"

He glanced at her from those amazing blue eyes. "Aye."

"Oh." Judging from the number killed, there had to be a lot of insane vampires out there. "Can you call in some help? You can't destroy all of them yourself."

His smile returned. "Ye have little faith in my power. I need no help destroying them. And I must, or else people will eventually find enough courage to attack the castle again." He reached over and ran one finger the length of her clenched jaw. "This is my duty for the time I am here. I canna shirk it, ye ken."

She stuck out her bottom lip. Just because she understood his duty, that didn't mean she had to like it. And why did she care anyway? She didn't know the answer to that.

Blythe had planned to try to sneak up on his emotions tonight so that in some small way she could earn the big bucks Ecstasy Inc. was paying her. Okay, so Ecstasy wasn't paying her big bucks and all this sneaking around trying to catch Darach unawares was growing old. She'd just ask, he'd say no, and they could get on with the rest of the night.

"Look, vampire-of-steel, I've got mental bruises from bouncing off your emotional wall, so I'm going to flat-out ask you this time. Will you open up your emotions and let me take a look so I can make you ha . . . cheerful, chirpy, and content?"

Blythe was purposely staring into the fire so she didn't have to meet his long-suffering gaze.

"Aye."

"Hey, no is okay with me. I understand . . ." She widened her eyes as she turned to look at him. "*Yes?* Did you say yes?"

His gaze met hers. "Ye may touch my emotions this night." His mouth softened and his eyes grew hungry, letting her know that he hoped she would touch other things as well.

"Why now?" Blythe knew she shouldn't question good fortune, but she had to know.

A crease formed between those incredible eyes. "Ye drive me mad with your questions, challenge me with your beliefs, care that I am safe, and . . . ye make me laugh." A slow flush rose to his face.

Embarrassed? Her big bad vampire was embarrassed? Something cold and hard inside her was melting into soft and mushy. And it had nothing to do with sex. That Darach, with all his power, chose to show her his vulnerability moved her in a way she wasn't ready to examine.

"Anything else?" She knew a big silly smile was pasted to her face.

Blythe could almost feel him drawing in a deep breath, and recognized that what he was about to say was difficult for him.

"I . . . trust that ye wish the best for me, and I find that I wish to share my feelings." He frowned. " 'Tis a need I have never felt before, and I dinna understand why I feel it now with ye." He offered her a sudden bad-boy grin that completed the melting-and-mushy process. "Mayhap 'tis old age creeping up on me."

Blythe bit her lip to keep her own emotions from spilling all over him. *I trust.* Words she'd never expected to hear from him. Words she would treasure always, made all the more precious because she sensed they were not words he had said often during his five hundred years.

Blythe drew in a deep breath of her own. Okay, time for calm. Time to move into professional mode. Through force of habit, she pressed the E on her charm. She probably wouldn't need to prove anything to Textron once she told him what she knew about him, but her Ecstasy work habits were too firmly ingrained for her to ignore them. She'd probably end up erasing everything.

Blythe slipped off the bed and hurried to the container that held all her work equipment. She did a mental inventory as she knelt down and pulled out the things she'd need. Mood candles, relaxation mat . . . "You'll have to take off all your clothes for this." Manipulator gloves, restorative balm . . . "Oh, and we'll do this in front of the fireplace. Heat strengthens the effect." She rose with everything in her arms, then turned around. As though in slow motion, her things slid from her grasp to the floor.

"Ye said I must remove my clothing." His crooked smile was the practiced tool of the tempter. "Did I do something wrong?"

"No." Was that trembling croak really her own voice? "No." Okay, that was better. Stronger, more assertive. "Everything is just fine."

Fine? Try magnificent, overpowering, stupendous. With the flames leaping and snapping behind him, he was the incarnation of all that was carnal and wicked. Temptation in human form, a beautiful naked demon come to rip her professional persona from her and replace it with a drooling greedy sex fiend.

She would *not* let this happen. *Wide, powerful shoulders, arms thick with muscle.* He was her client, and she would remain calm and professional at all times. *Sculpted pecs and flat, ribbed stomach*. She'd done this hundreds of times before, and she'd always handled her job with cool precision. *Slim hips, powerful thighs roped with muscle, and long, strong-looking legs.* This was about her career, and she could never forget that she had to keep her mind on business if she expected to help him. *Long, narrow feet* . . . Feet? She thought his feet were sexy? She was one sick puppy.

Now if she could only close her jaw and remember how to speak, they could get this show on the road. *And his whole yummy body was covered with smooth golden skin, probably warm from the fire's glow.*

"Did I ever tell you that you don't look like a vampire?" Time. She needed time to gain control.

He seemed puzzled. "What should I look like?"

Blythe shrugged her shoulders. "Pale, anemic. Oh, and you should feel sort of cold and clammy. You know, kind of a fresh-from-the-grave effect." She was babbling.

Darach frowned. "Some vampires might appear pale because they dinna walk in the sunlight, but my skin has always been as it is. Would ye wish me pale and . . . clammy?" He didn't seem overly concerned about not measuring up to vampire standards.

"Nope. You're great the way you are." Shakily she walked over and spread the mat in front of the fire. "Just lie down on your stomach, and I'll—"

"Ye didna look at one part of my body."

He stood right behind her, making her nervous. She couldn't seem to spread the mat smoothly. It kept bunching up in different spots each time she tried to lay it down.

"I didn't look at your face. Do you want me to look at your face?" She turned her head and glared at him. "Yep, it's your face. Can we continue now?" Rotten, lousy mat. She clenched her teeth as she wrestled with it.

"Ye know what part I speak of." His low, husky voice was suggestive of red velvet and black satin found in dens of sin and sensual pursuits. The male scent of him was redolent of hot, moist places with a hint of spice meant to entrap, enslave.

Blythe was breathing hard as she stared at the accursed mat. She didn't look up when he took the mat from her and laid it smoothly in front of the fire on the first try.

"Ye must look at me, Blythe, else ye willna be able to concentrate while ye make me . . . happy." His voice was the devil's temptation minus the apple.

He was kidding, right? He really thought that looking at him would help her concentrate? Unfortunately, she understood what he meant. If she couldn't look at him and separate sex from her job, then this whole thing was doomed to failure.

Okay, she could do this. She turned and looked at his "sexual package." She already knew that it wasn't *compact*. And at least one part of him was already happy, so she didn't have to exert any energy there.

"Breathe, lass. I dinna wish ye to faint."

"I don't have to be reminded to breathe." Inhale, exhale, inhale, exhale. There, she'd remembered how to do it. "And I never faint." That much, at least, was true. She had no patience with newbies in the business who passed out after scanning the emotions of a client with serious mental problems.

Darach scooped up the items she'd dropped, put them down beside the mat, and then stretched out on his stomach. He rested his head on his forearm. "Ye must tell me what ye wish me to do."

I wish you to stop looking so absolutely amazing. He was one smooth, flowing line of yumminess from his strong back over his rounded buttocks to the backs of his thighs and legs.

"I'm setting seven candles around you. Scientists have created chemicals that when burned emit scents that can directly affect . . . Well, I won't go into anything technical, but they each will have a specific effect on you." She spaced the candles so that they wouldn't interfere with what she did, then lit each of them.

" 'Tis amazing," he said in awe of the seven different-colored flames of the candles.

For the first time since landing in the past, she felt pride in what her time could offer. "Now I'll activate the mat. You'll feel a slight tingling. Relax into it and let it make you feel good."

Thank heaven, now that she was getting involved in her work, she was falling back into a professional attitude. "I'm going to smooth some cream on you. It'll feel cool and soothing. Enjoy it." Blythe quickly squeezed the cream onto his back, then rubbed it in with slow, firm strokes.

Her slow, firm strokes were completely professional until she reached his buns. At that point, her firm strokes took on more of a clasp-and-squeeze quality. Fascinated, she watched him clench his cheeks. "Do you know that you have a dimple in each cheek when you clench your buttocks?"

"Ye have a liking for dimples?" His voice was already

soft from the relaxing effects of the candles and the mat.

"They have a definite aesthetic quality when found on certain body parts." She was feeling pretty mellow herself.

She blinked to clear her mental processes. No mellowing on the job. "The cream is to prepare you for the manipulator gloves. The gloves work in conjunction with my power to calm and reshape your emotions."

"Why do ye bother telling me this?" His voice was now only a husky murmur.

"I just think you'll have less anxiety if you understand what I'm doing." Okay, now came the hard part. "I'm going to scan your emotions, Darach. I want you to open them to me. Once I see what we have, I'll start the healing process."

As she spoke, she slipped the gloves on. Calling them gloves was probably misleading. They were nothing more than thin strands of conductive fiber interspersed at regular intervals with tiny nodules that acted on the body's nervous system to complement what she was doing mentally.

She paused as a thought occurred. "Since you're not really human, could this whole thing hurt you?"

"It willna kill me."

Blythe didn't miss the humor in his voice. She firmed her lips. He wasn't taking any of this seriously. Well, he would. She smiled. He most certainly would.

"I'm connecting to you now." She leaned forward on

her knees and placed her gloved hands on his back. "Open your feelings to me, Darach."

Closing her eyes, Blythe began her scan of his emotions. At first she felt nothing, and she sympathized with how hard it must be for him to open a door that had been closed for so long. But she'd take care of his rusty hinges before the night was done.

Then suddenly they were there, five hundred years of emotions hitting her with enough force to tumble her mind end over end—wave after wave of elation, grief, passion, rage, remorse, and every other imaginable feeling.

And as the intensity of his emotions drove her back on her heels, she threw up her hands in a futile effort to ward off some of them.

Dizzy and disoriented, she still realized that two emotions were missing. Two emotions that said much about Darach MacKenzie. She found no despair. She found no love.

Her immediate reaction? How could anyone exist without love for five hundred years and not know despair? *He's a vampire. Maybe vampires can't love.* The thought bothered her.

"When ye wish for something, ye may not like what ye get." His tone said he knew exactly what she was feeling.

"I'm fine." Right. Fine. Ecstasy Inc. would probably have to add an addendum to their advertising: *Rates for vampires may be higher due to increased risk of uncontrolled hysteria by our Happiness staff.*

She could handle this. Leaning forward again, Blythe began a slow massage of shoulders, back, buttocks, thighs, and legs. The healing process was a partnership between twenty-fourth-century science and her natural power. With each stroke of her fingers she sent her power flowing through him, coating all his negative emotions, feeling them shrivel and lose their power to affect him, and filling the empty spaces they left behind with comfort and a sense of well-being.

Finally she was finished. While she was working, she had blocked out all other sensations, all other thoughts. As she leaned back and stripped the gloves from her fingers, the world came rushing back.

She remembered the feel of his supple flesh beneath her fingers, admired the gleaming ripple of muscle as he flexed his shoulders, and drew in her breath with alarm as he slowly turned over.

"I'm finished. You can dress now." She needed to stand up and put some space between them. *Feet, move.* Her feet didn't think moving was such a big deal.

He reached up and cupped her chin in his big hand. "Look at me, Blythe."

She couldn't avoid it without seeming childish, so she glanced down at his face. His eyes looked lazily content, his mouth soft and relaxed.

"Ye've helped me know more peace than I've felt since I was a bairn. Ye have a wondrous power." He rubbed the callused pad of his thumb across her bottom lip. "I would repay your gift."

"No, no, that's okay. I mean, this is my job. But if you really feel strongly about the paying thing, I'll have Textron send you a bill." *Mindless-babble attack.* Absently she touched her charm to turn off the recorder. She had the evidence she needed, if she decided to use it.

"I insist." He slid his fingers down the curve of her neck and along the top of her bare shoulder exposed by her nightgown.

Blythe had never thought so many goose bumps could squeeze onto such a small section of skin. Kind of like the ancient conjecture about how many angels could stand on the head of a pin. She shook her head to clear it. Why was she thinking of angels when temptation incarnate was breathing down her neck?

"I don't think—"

He shook his head and offered her his resistance-is-futile smile. "Ye need not think for the rest of the night. Each of us has power. I have felt yours. Now it is time for ye to know mine. I will make ye verra happy."

"Hey, I appreciate the thought, but I'm already as happy as I can be. Gee, any more happiness would be dangerous to my . . . happiness." What exactly did *that* mean? How could he reduce her to seriously stupid by just looking at her?

Propping himself up on one elbow, he drew her head down to him. "Never as happy as I can make ye." He touched her earlobe with the tip of his tongue before whispering in her ear. "I will try verra hard not to bite ye."

Uh-oh.

Chapter Ten

Blythe watched, mesmerized, as he stood up, helped her to her feet, and then carefully blew out each of her candles. The small plumes rising from them symbolized an ending to the scientific and enlightened method of achieving happiness and the beginning of Darach MacKenzie's way.

And she had no doubt that after five hundred years, his dark, sensual, and exciting path to happiness would be totally satisfying, if fleeting. Because she still firmly believed that the path to lasting happiness didn't pass through the quicksand of sexual indulgence. But hey, she was just about ready to test the sensual waters and hope she missed the quicksand spot.

He said nothing as he clasped her hand and led her to his bed. She let herself be led, but that didn't mean she'd completely committed herself. There was still inner turmoil to quell, battles of conscience to be won.

When Darach reached his bed, he released her hand, then tossed the covers aside and lay down. She stood staring at him, the temptation to fling herself atop his bared body almost silencing her noisy inner conflict.

"Lie with me, Blythe. I have allowed ye to use your powers to bring me peace, so your obligation to Ecstasy is finished. Now ye may freely come to my bed so that I may show ye that there are joys beyond mere peace." He touched her with his gaze—warm, convincing.

Of course, she'd already experienced a few of his joys beyond peace. "Is that why you let me touch your emotions, Darach? Did you concede the battle so that you could win the war?" Blythe didn't really believe it, but she needed the air completely cleared before she made her decision.

His gaze never wavered. "Ye dinna believe this." He patted the bed beside him. "Sit and tell me what fashes ye."

She eyed the bed, saw no obvious trap, and sat down. "Is the bed magic?"

Amusement crinkled the corners of his eyes. "No. Why would I need a magic bed?"

Why indeed? *He* was the magic, and he needed no bed to help him. "Look, I haven't been completely up front with you. Sure, I didn't want any sexual complications to compromise my work, but that wasn't the whole story." This would be hard, but she felt she owed him some explanation for her attitude. After all, he'd bared his body and his emotions to her.

"I never thought it was." His gaze seemed to reach into her heart and had the same effect as an unexpected visitor when her house was a mess. No way would she let him in.

"One thing you have to know about me is that back home I was always late for everything. I mean, I was *never* on time. It drove my family crazy, especially my brother, Mandor. He was always on time." Blythe paused to gain strength. The telling would get harder now.

" 'Twould be easier if ye would invite me into your mind so ye wouldna have to bear the pain of speaking about it out loud." He didn't suggest that she forget about it, or advise her to save it for another time if it upset her.

"No, I'll be okay." She appreciated that he understood her need to tell her story. "Ecstasy decided to have one of their regional conventions on some backwater planet because it would be cheaper. They insisted that my parents and at least my brother or I attend."

"Backwater planet?" The line between his eyes said he was struggling with the planet-other-than-earth concept.

Blythe sighed. So much to explain, so little time. "My brother wasn't going with us. He had no particular plans; he just didn't feel like going."

She swallowed hard. Would her past ever pack less of an emotional gut punch? "This was during the time that I was exploring sensual solutions with my client. I wanted to spend time with him, so I begged Mandor to take my place. He agreed."

Blythe crossed her arms over her chest and began to rock back and forth. When she was little, this sometimes helped ease the pain of a stomachache. It did squat for a heartache. "They'd just entered the convention hall when an antiquated heating system exploded. They all died."

Gently he slid his fingers over her cheek. "I sorrow for ye. 'Tis never easy to lose those close to us, and guilt doesna reason. Still, ye canna blame yourself for your brother's death." His voice was low and soothing.

But even the almost hypnotic comfort of his voice couldn't put a dent in her self-loathing. "I blame myself for *all* their deaths. I told you that I was always late. If I'd gone with my parents, they wouldn't have even been in the convention hall. They would've been sitting in my hotel room waiting for me while I put on my makeup."

She paused, expecting him to tell her once more that she wasn't really to blame. Instead, he again clasped her hand. "Even after five hundred years, I think of things I might have changed if I had but known what would happen. I shouldna have left Aesa alone while she was with child. I shouldna have spoken in anger to Thrain. Mayhap then the child would have lived, and I would still know Thrain's friendship. Were these things my fault, Blythe?"

Blythe shook her head as she watched him trace comforting circles on the back of her hand with the pad of his thumb. "Up here, I understand the logic of what you're saying." She tapped her forehead. "But not here." She placed her hand over her heart. "That's why I feel that I have to make it up to them somehow. And I can only do that through Ecstasy. The job was everything to them, and they had such high hopes for my future in the company. I have to make it to the top for them, and I can only do that by not making the same sexual mistake again."

Still holding her hand, he turned on his side to study her. "And this makes your family happy, seeing ye suffer for what ye believe ye did? Do they sit around in their afterlife speaking of what a wondrous day it has been because ye cried over them?"

"No. They wouldn't want that." Their clasped hands now rested on her lap. Opening her hand, she glanced at his palm and absently wondered why his lifeline didn't run all the way down his arm. Maybe the line ended at the moment he became vampire. Silly thought.

"Ah, I understand. Your sadness makes *ye* happy." He nodded his satisfaction at his reasoning.

Blythe frowned. What was he getting at? "No, I don't enjoy being sad."

His gaze suddenly speared her. There was no soothing or sympathy there now. "Then why do ye make yourself suffer if it makes neither ye nor your family happy?"

"I told you that I owed—"

"That is the argument of the weak, and ye are not a weak woman." He moved closer as he turned his hand over so that he could once again clasp hers tightly. "Ye must have the strength to accept what canna be changed and instead remember the things about your family that made ye laugh, that made ye family."

She couldn't look away from his eyes and the truths reflected there.

"Celebrate your life as they would wish. Live it not only for yourself, but for them. Dinna live it for this Ecstasy Incorporated, because if its leaders had not been so worried about cost, they would have chosen a safer place. If ye must place blame, place it on them."

Finally, she was able to tear her gaze from his. She thought about his argument.

He squeezed her hand. "Did Ecstasy know that ye werena happy?"

She shook her head. "Not a chance. Oh, they run psychological tests each year, but I've taken enough of them to know how to manipulate the results."

Blythe took a deep, cleansing breath. He was right. She'd been weak, because it was easier to wallow in her misery than to drag herself out of the pit she'd dug.

She smiled. "You would've made a great shrink, Viking."

"Shrink?" There was that line between the eyes again.

Without thinking, she traced the line with her finger. "You're right, and I was wrong." She held up a warning hand. "Now, don't get carried away with that, because I'm usually right."

Darach released her hand and lay on his back again. He reached out to smooth the cream silk of her gown where it stretched tight across her back. The slide of the fabric beneath his fingers, the faint smoky scent of the candles, and the quiet sound of her breathing aroused him. He tried to ignore the darker element of his enhanced senses, the awareness of her blood coursing beneath the soft skin at the hollow of her neck.

"Come to me, Blythe." Darach forced himself not to use any compulsion on her. He wanted her to join with him freely. "Let me give ye joy this night." He smiled at her, knowing how his smile could make women bend to his wishes. "Dinna think tonight. *Feel.*"

She looked at him, a small smile turning up the corners of her lips, and he felt her acceptance in that smile. "Feeling sounds pretty good, but we need to get a few things straight first."

He forced back a groan. Why could nothing be simple with this woman? But surprised, he realized he wanted her badly enough to agree to almost anything. Resigned, he nodded his agreement.

"First, I want this totally natural." Absently she ran the tip of her fingernail around one of his nipples.

His nipple immediately became the center of all that was pleasurable, so painfully sensitive that he felt he would moan if she even breathed on it. "Aye. Natural." What in Loki's flame did that mean?

"I don't want you in my mind, or in my body." She seemed to think about her words as she moved her finger to his lips, gently tracing the shape of his mouth.

Darach never wasted opportunities. He clasped her finger to still it, then slowly slid his tongue across the pad while he held her gaze captive. Then he closed his lips over her fingertip, letting her see the intent in his eyes, the joy he took as he circled it with his tongue, and the promise that his tongue could bring pleasure to many other parts of her body.

As her eyes darkened, he released her finger. "Mayhap ye will explain how I can bring ye pleasure without being in your body."

"You know what I mean." Blythe used the finger he had released to circle his other nipple, and the damp slide of her finger across his flesh almost put an end to her sexual negotiations. "I don't want you totally inside me like last time, only the ordinary male parts." She seemed to consider this. "Of course, in your case they aren't really ordinary." She pursed her lips as she attempted to make herself clear to him. "I want this to be a completely normal experience, just like any man and woman would have."

Darach could tell her that joining with a vampire would never be a "normal experience," but she would soon find that out for herself. He nodded. "I have agreed to your wishes, and now I have one thing I desire of *ye*."

He almost smiled at her cautious nod. She might

trust him in certain matters, but she still did not always know what to expect from him.

"When I ask ye to close your eyes, I would have ye do so until I give ye permission to open them again." It was a stupid request, but he still found that he could not take the chance that she might look on him with horror.

Her gaze sharpened. "You change, and you don't want me to see it."

She was beginning to know him too well. The thought was not a comfortable one. "Sexual excitement causes my blood lust to rise and the change happens whether I will it or not. I can control my desire to feed, but I can do nothing about my vampire form."

Blythe frowned. "But that first time on the way back from the inn—"

"Ye closed your eyes. I can choose what images ye see in your mind, but I canna change the reality. If ye had opened your eyes, ye would have seen me in my vampire form." *Whatever that might be.*

"You don't think I could take the shock?" She was smiling, but he saw the doubt in her eyes.

Her doubt solidified his determination that she not see him. "I dinna know, but soon I will have the power to see my reflection. 'Tis something I have looked forward to for centuries."

"Yeah, I guess not being able to see yourself could cause problems. How do you shave?" She ran her fingers along the side of his face.

He clenched his jaw. If she continued to touch him, she would see his vampire form whether he wished it or not. "With great pain and much blood. 'Tis fortunate that I heal so quickly."

Silence fell between them as he waited for her decision.

Finally, she stood and in one smooth motion slipped her gown over her head, then dropped it to pool at her feet.

Darach smiled. Most women he had known would have waited with downcast eyes and flushed cheeks for him to slip their clothing off, either from real or pretended timidity.

Even though the thought of sliding the silk, warm from her body, down the wondrous length of her legs caught at his imagination . . . and other things, he understood her desire to control what happened between them. His smile widened. The thought of a woman who would not merely allow him to do what he wished with her body, but would demand that she be a full participant in their joining excited him.

She knelt on the bed beside him, then leaned back on her heels to study him. "Teach me, vampire, the pleasure that has kept you from despair for five hundred years."

Blythe knew that he would touch her now, and she hungered for it. This lovemaking wouldn't be like the slow, beautiful opening of a flower bud. Forget it. She hoped Darach wasn't expecting that of her. She was in full bloom and about to fall off her stem. She wanted him that badly. It was almost embarrassing.

Instead of reaching for her, he pushed himself to a sitting position and leaned his back against the headboard. His wicked smile told her he knew exactly what she wanted and was going to make her wait. Blythe didn't *want* to wait. She raised one brow in a cool, silent question, while she mentally rolled around on the floor, kicking and screaming.

"Make me want ye, Blythe." Five hundred years of sensual knowledge shaped what she now read in his expression—eyes dark with carnal promises, full lips that whispered erotic secrets. "Make me want ye without touching me. Invite me in and show me your dwelling, woman from another time."

Blythe could scuttle away now, run from his sexual challenge, but she wouldn't. It was important that he not be the only one to give pleasure tonight. She wanted to drive out the memory of all the women who had come before her, give him as much joy as he gave her.

Like, yeah. She could count on one hand the number of lovers she'd had. But a five-hundred-year advantage didn't mean squat when you were motivated. And she was motivated.

"Watch and learn, vampire." Okay, she'd delivered her big bad boast. "By the way, you never had something like a harem with fifty women versed in a thousand ways to pleasure a man, did you?" She bit her lip at the horror of the thought. She'd be hard pressed to come up with five, but she'd do the best she could with what she had. She cast him a furtive sideways glance.

His sudden laughter startled her. "Fifty women? What would I do with fifty women?"

She was sure he could think of something.

He shook his head, and his hair, shining in the fire's glow, shifted across his shoulders. "Ye fascinate me, Blythe. Ye make it verra hard for me to play the brooding vampire intent on seduction when ye make me laugh in the middle of my enticements."

And with those simple words, he relaxed her. She smiled at him. "Thank you."

Sliding from the bed, she stepped back. Blythe was very good at focusing, and she now turned all her attention to her body. What could she do to make him want her? If she could turn *herself* on, wouldn't that arouse him as well? No other ideas came to mind, so she began to move.

The slow, seductive movements of the Kovan dance lent themselves to what she wanted. At no time in her life would she have dared perform this dance. She would dare it tonight.

Bending forward from the waist, she allowed her hair to hang free, hiding her face while the strands swung gently with the subtle side-to-side motion of her hips. She ran her fingers through the strands while she conjured erotic images of Darach in her mind. And as the familiar heaviness low in her belly began to build, she touched her nipples and rolled them between her fingers until they were hard, sensitive nubs.

Still bent at the waist, she slid her fingers from her knees, up her inner thighs until they met at the already wet, swollen lips guarding the spot she wouldn't touch, that only *he* would touch tonight. But she could certainly tease.

Spreading her legs further apart, she changed the sway of her hips to a more suggestive hip thrust. At the same time, she spread the lips so that he could see, *imagine*.

"Let me see your face." His demand was hot and thick with his need.

"Not until I'm ready, vampire-with-no-patience." She'd wanted her response to come out light and teasing, but it ended up slut-husky. Talk about being into your role.

Slowly she straightened. But before he could see her face, she turned her back to him, bent again at the waist, opened her legs wide, and drew only her fingertips up the backs of her thighs. Then she spread her palms over each cheek and rotated her hips in the age-old invitation to mate.

Her breath came quickly now as sexual images of Darach played in her mind—his hard thighs spread for her, his sex engorged, ready to thrust into her. She felt a desperate need to fill the aching emptiness, *now*.

"Show me your face, Blythe. Dinna make me come

to ye." Was there just a hint of desperation in his guttural threat?

She hoped so. But it was time that he saw her face anyway. That was the whole point of the Kovan dance. Not the sexual movements, but the moment when the lovers saw each other's expressions.

Straightening, she turned and looked at him. Blythe knew that her face was flushed with sexual excitement, her eyes filled with what she wanted from him, her lips parted as she tried to draw in enough breath to keep her pounding heart beating.

But her sexy strategy had backfired. Her breath caught on the flare of hunger in Darach's eyes. Eyes that looked somehow different—larger, slightly slanted, with pupils so enlarged that they turned his eyes black. And his lips . . . She couldn't look away as they parted and he slid his tongue across his lower lip to moisten it.

"Come to my bed, Blythe, before 'tis too late."

Too late for what? But she moved to the bed and once again knelt beside him. He would touch her now, and she'd explode in an orgasm to end all orgasms.

He didn't touch her.

"In all things sexual, anticipation is part of the pleasure." Reaching out, he drew an imaginary circle around her breast. His finger lingered a breath away from her nipple.

Close. So close she swore she could feel a shadow of sensation. Her nipple reacted as though it truly had been touched—became hard, aching, sensitive. So sensitive that she had to bite her lip to keep from begging him to . . .

"Pain and pleasure are sisters. Waiting, imagining how it will be, is pain. But it increases the final pleasure tenfold." He splayed his fingers and drew them over her stomach, so near that it seemed the air between her body and his fingers heated. "Lie beside me, Blythe." His voice was a hypnotic murmur of invitation.

It seemed impossible to look away from his intent gaze, impossible even to blink. Somewhere in the teensy section of her brain that still functioned, she duly noted the continuing changes in his eyes—they were large, elongated, still with that intriguing slant. And the pupils were so black that she felt if she made the effort she could see into his soul. But she didn't think that would be a smart thing to do, so she didn't try.

Still holding his gaze, she lay down next to him. Finally changing his position, he knelt above her. "Spread your legs for me, Blythe."

Without hesitation, she moved her legs apart, then watched as he skimmed his fingers along her inner thighs, never quite touching her flesh, and paused a whisper away from . . . *She couldn't stand this.* She was wet with her readiness, her body open and wanting him to touch her right *there*.

She was desperate. If he wouldn't touch her, then she'd do it herself. But even as the thought was born, it died. Nothing would relieve this need, this *agony*, except his touch.

Blythe glared at him. "Touch me or I'll hurt you. Bad." She spoke through clenched teeth.

His smile was slow, mocking, sensual. " 'Tis a terrible threat, yet it holds a certain . . . attraction." His eyes flared with a hunger that made her shiver. "Tell me what things ye would do with me so I may decide whether the eventual pleasure is worth the risk." His smile faded. "If it gives ye any comfort, I suffer now as much as ye do."

"I don't think so." Her cranky mutter sounded whiny even to herself.

A flash of what could only be described as pain touched his eyes. Maybe she was just imagining it, but his face seemed somehow leaner, his cheekbones sharper, his eyes . . . Something about his eyes . . .

"Close your eyes. Now." His harsh command brooked no disobedience.

Blythe closed her eyes and waited. A thread of fear twined around her heart, her lungs. She breathed hard to rid herself of it, and tried to ignore the rapid pounding of her heart.

"Dinna open your eyes, Blythe. Ye willna see, but your remaining senses will grow sharper, sensations more intense." His breath warmed the sensitive skin at the base of her throat. "I have waited long for this."

"Not really. I mean, it's only been a couple of days. You have to work on the exaggeration thing." She swallowed hard. Oops—maybe she shouldn't call too much attention to her throat right now.

His soft chuckle once again eased her fears. "I dinna exaggerate. I canna remember wanting any woman as much as I want ye, so I have truly waited overlong."

Silence filled the space between them.

"I feel your unease, Blythe. Do ye wish to stop?" His voice was calm and even, giving nothing of himself away.

Instinctively Blythe reached for his emotions. Disappointment. Sadness. And even a touch of the despair she hadn't found before. Searching within herself, Blythe recognized the same emotions at the thought of not having Darach tonight.

"You don't escape that easily, vampire. If you don't finish what you started, your immortal status could be in danger." She reached up and laid her palm flat against his body.

His chest. She could feel the hard pounding of his heart. "This is who you are to me, a man whose heart beats the same as my heart. Okay, so your skill level in certain areas exceeds mine, but not by much. And we don't like the same foods, but that's pretty normal between two people. Oh, and our life expectancies are about the same." She smiled. "So all in all, I'd say we're just a normal couple. In fact—"

He kissed her. No gentle preliminaries, just a hot, hungry plundering of her lips. Since her mouth was already open, ready to enlarge on their compatibility, his tongue found easy access. He had no interest in exploring. As his tongue stroked her, tangled with her tongue, and generally tried to draw her soul from her body with his mouth, she felt . . .

She felt the press of his fangs against her lips.

He froze as soon as he sensed her stillness.

Blythe had known this moment would come, knew that her response was important in a way she didn't even fully understand yet.

Tentatively she slid her tongue the length of each fang, memorized the smooth texture, and recognized the damage each could inflict on a human body. She couldn't repress a small shiver, not so much from fear, but more as a reaction to finally touching what made him essentially vampire in her mind. This was the real deal.

She faced the reality and accepted it as part of Darach. "Make me remember this, vampire." She touched the tip of her tongue to the sharp point of each canine. "So that even if I live to be a thousand, I'll recall the taste and feel of you. Make this a forever experience."

"Ye have great faith in my power to please ye." He touched the side of her face with fingers that shook slightly. "As ye should." The amusement was back in his voice.

He traced a familiar path as he kissed the sensitive skin behind her ear, the side of her neck, then paused at the base of her throat. Her parade of goose bumps dutifully followed behind.

"I can hear the flow of your life beneath your skin, imagine the taste of it on my tongue. 'Tis a seductive call when a woman excites me." He slid his hands over her shoulders, down her arms, then covered her breasts with his large palms. "And ye excite me verra much."

Blythe heard his words, but all she could think about was the feel of his hands on her breasts. And when he replaced his hands with his mouth, circling each nipple with his tongue, then closing his lips over one and teasing it until it was a hard nub of concentrated sensation, she tangled her fingers in his long hair to anchor herself to earth.

As he moved to her other nipple, she felt the slide of his fangs against her skin, the heat of his mouth on her nipple, and erotic sensations she'd never imagined she could feel from a man's mouth on her breasts. Darach was right. Without her sight to distract her, all sensation was focused on his touch.

Blythe was greedy. She wanted to explore his body and learn what gave him pleasure. As Darach shifted his position to kneel between her spread legs, then kissed a path over her stomach, she ran her hands down the smooth plains of his back and gloried in the flow of muscle beneath her fingers.

Darach moved lower still, and she held her breath—imagining, anticipating. And when his lips finally touched her inner thigh, she exhaled sharply. He moved higher, ever higher, and she released her hold on his hair. She needed something stronger to keep her from liftoff. Desperately she grasped the headboard behind her and hung on.

He paused, his mouth a wish away from where she needed him to be, from where he'd better get to really fast or else she'd launch without him.

"If your legends teach that only a woman's neck tempts a vampire, they are foolish." His breath was hot between her thighs, his voice thick with desire. "Life flows hot and tempting here also."

Her femoral artery? As if *that* really mattered in the scheme of incredible sex? She felt the prick of his fangs, and the unexpected erotic jolt made her arch her body, lifting her hips in silent entreaty.

"Ye need have no fear, though, for a greater temptation awaits here." He put his mouth on the spot that was far too ready for him.

Blythe screamed. She hadn't meant to scream. She'd never screamed when a man touched her before. But this was too . . . "Are you doing something to enhance my senses?" Her words were forced out between frantic gasps for breath.

"Your feelings are your own."

He slid his tongue over the spot, and Blythe whimpered her appreciation. This was pitiful. She needed to release her grip on the headboard. She needed to torture his nipples with her lips and tongue. She needed to cup his sacs while doing sexy creative things with her mouth on them. She needed to nibble her way up the long, thick length of his erection, then slide her lips over the head. She needed to swirl her tongue around and around the head before taking him deep into her mouth, then—

He slipped his tongue inside her at the same time he slid his hands beneath her buttocks and lifted her to meet his mouth.

Blythe's deep, ragged groan surprised her. She didn't make those kinds of uncontrolled sounds during sex. A blissful sigh or tasteful "Yes!" were about it on her vocal-reaction scale.

And as he began a sensual in-and-out rhythm with his tongue, Blythe felt the smooth slide of his fang against the spot guaranteed to make her—

Scream, cry, and beg. She did all three. At once. Loudly.

"I want you *now*, vampire. Don't make me say that again."

She felt Darach lean back on his heels while still holding her buttocks firmly. His breathing was a harsh rasp. "I canna wait longer." He sounded apologetic.

He was sorry he couldn't prolong her torture? He was kidding, right?

Then she felt the nudge of his sex between her legs. She held her breath so she wouldn't miss a second of sensation—the slow, sensual slide into her, her own wet readiness, the feel of her body stretching to accommodate the thick head, her body's automatic clenching around the hard length of him, and above all else, the sense of him filling her inch by incredible inch.

Blythe couldn't hold her breath or her need for one more second. Exhaling sharply, she released her white-knuckled grip on the headboard and reached for him.

Darach must have come to the same conclusion, because with a hoarse cry, he thrust into her so deeply, so completely that it wrung an answering cry from her.

Blythe pulled him down to her as he plunged again and again. She rose to meet him, a primal mating that swept everything before its blind, unstoppable surge to fulfillment.

And as her orgasm took her, Blythe only recognized one truth. She had to anchor herself. *Now*. Bits and pieces of random thoughts drifted without meaning through her mind. *So much pleasure. Bite down hard on something so you can stand it.*

No, that was wrong. You bit down on something for pain. This wasn't pain, but something just as intense. And she needed, she needed . . .

The explosive pleasure that was a thousand times more than pleasure ripped a scream from her throat that was echoed by his cry seconds later. As he plunged deep into her for the final time, she sank her teeth into his shoulder and hung on, aware only of his skin's heat and the male taste of him.

When the final shuddering spasm faded, Blythe realized he hadn't moved off of her . . .

"Ye bit me. I think 'tis supposed to be the other way around."

He *couldn't* have moved off of her, because her teeth

were still locked on his shoulder. Regretfully she released him.

"Ye may open your eyes."

Blythe lifted her lids as he moved to her side and propped himself up on one elbow. "Ye would have made a vampire all would envy." His smile was easy and relaxed.

I could get used to waking up to that smile. She blinked. Had she really thought that? Nope, wasn't *her* thought.

She glanced away from the clear mark of her teeth in his shoulder. *He'd* done it all for her. The orgasm she'd had with Darach MacKenzie was the high-water mark for all future orgasms. He'd given her . . . complete joy.

What had she given him? A set of teeth marks. "I want you to know I wasn't totally selfish. I did incredible sexual things to your body in my mind."

"Ye must show me these 'incredible sexual things' verra soon." He pushed a strand of damp hair from her forehead.

She felt boneless, and when she glanced at him, he looked pretty satisfied, too.

"You know, we're sort of alike." Blythe turned on her side to face him. She smoothed her fingers over the teeth marks in his shoulder.

"We are nothing alike." He seemed to think about that. "Except for a love of biting."

"We each have our own demons." Could Darach MacKenzie exorcise them for her?

"Everyone has demons."

"We're each hardheaded." She frowned. That wasn't a great positive for compatibility.

"*Ye're* hardheaded. I am always reasonable." His smile was all smug male superiority.

"We make amazing love together."

"Ye're right. We are much alike."

He laughed. He really laughed. Never in all her life had hearing a man laugh brought tears to her eyes. It did now.

"Ye're crying." He frowned as he wiped a tear from her cheek with the tip of his finger.

"From joy. These are tears of happiness." Frantically she blinked them away. "Tears are a natural expression of emotion."

His lips tipped up. "Ye still wish to see me shed tears."

Blythe shrugged. It sounded silly saying the words. "I guess so. I mean, tears say it all. They're a physical expression of emotion. They don't lie."

Silence stretched between them.

"Darach, I think I'm ready to see you in your vampire form." Blythe hadn't planned to say that. The words just seemed to pop out. But once they were out, she realized they were true. She liked him enough now, felt comfortable enough with him, to not be horrified by any physical changes. They'd just shared the greatest intimacy a man and woman could achieve, so if she wasn't ready now, she'd never be ready.

"No." He didn't hesitate, and his tone said there would be no discussion.

"You've seen *me* when I've just gotten up in the morning. That has to be way more scary." She offered him a blinding smile meant to turn his determination to mush.

"No." He glanced at the arrow slit where pale light was visible. " 'Tis time for me to sleep, and I must protect my resting place." He offered her a smile meant to soften his hint that she get her bottom off his bed.

"Ye're a warm, loving woman, Blythe, and tonight was wondrous, but I willna allow ye to see me in vampire form." He drew in a deep breath. "I dinna want to take any chance that ye might look on me and say 'yuck.' "

"Yuck? You think I'd say yuck?" Outraged, she climbed off his bed. "I can't believe . . ."

He was asleep. That quickly he'd closed his eyes and escaped her nagging in sleep.

Blythe smiled. Not a nice smile. Here was a challenge she could sink her teeth into. Hmm. Maybe she'd sunk her teeth into enough tonight. But she *would* see him in his vampire form. Not out of morbid curiosity, but because she wanted to know and understand every facet of Darach MacKenzie.

Why did she want to know? That was a very scary question.

Chapter Eleven

"You know, Mede, you're one lucky laird that I was here to fix things for you." Sparkle seemed pretty pumped as she leaped onto the table in the great hall. "Can I hook people up, or what?"

"Yeah, with the wrong people." He shouldn't have brought her here. He'd thought she could help him, but he'd forgotten the scary twists her reasoning could take. "This is your revenge, isn't it? You think I used you." Ganymede slumped on the bench with his elbows propped on the table.

"Hey, friends are for using, so what's the big deal?" She paused to scratch a sudden itch behind one ear. "I hope that's not a flea. Look and see if it's a flea. Did you bring flea powder?"

Resignedly Ganymede parted the hair behind her ear. He peered closely. "Yep, it's a flea." He returned his elbows to the table.

Sparkle widened her eyes, then wailed. "Get it off! I hate bugs. Get it off now, now, *now*!" Frantically she shoved her head against Ganymede's hand. "Get it off fast, or I'll change into human form and lay some pain on your stomach that the pink stuff won't fix."

Ganymede's glum expression lightened for a moment. "No, you won't, because it takes too much effort to change." He parted her hair again and watched as the flea leaped from Sparkle onto the floor. Smart flea. "It jumped onto the floor."

With a small cat huff, she sat down and wrapped her tail around herself. "What I put up with for you. And what makes you think I matched up the wrong people?" She blinked her big orange eyes at him.

She didn't get it. "Look, I brought six paying customers here. Three men, three women. Let's do the math. If each man hooks up with one of the women, the Cosmic Time Travel Agency has fulfilled its obligation and no one asks for a refund." Just thinking about the situation he had on his hands steamed him. "Now let's look at how you've screwed everything up."

She glared at him. "I'm all ears."

"Two of the men are in love with each other, and one of the women is getting it on with a vampire. Another of the women can't find a man because *they're all taken*, so she's resorting to talking to the servants. Do you think she'll want a refund? I think yes. The only pairing that worked out the way I wanted is that Textron and the underwear lady."

"Hah!" Sparkle managed to twist her cat face into a scornful expression. "The only reason your underwear lady is doing the deed with Textron is so that she can sell her products to his company. She's offering a discount along with a free Ecstasy logo on all the briefs she sells to Textron. They're going to have you deliver the order on your next time-travel tour. That's so romantic. Not."

"You listened in on their private conversations?"

"Well, yeah." She offered him a so-what glance.

"I'm okay with that. But what about the vampire? If he sucks sweet little Blythe dry, the agency is going to take a big hit." Ganymede always had his eye on profit margins. He didn't need his insurance rates raised because of something stupid like one of his customers getting offed by a vampire.

"I have a feeling something good could come of that relationship." She frowned. "Of course, that's bad, because good things happening are bad for my image. Was that clear?"

Nothing was *ever* clear with Sparkle. "You're dead wrong, babe. It'll never happen."

"Wanna bet?" She had that sly look again.

"Sure." He couldn't lose. "So what do I get when I win?"

"You get me in my human form for a whole month of creative sex." She tipped her head to study him. "Make sure you're in your golden-god form."

"Even though there's no chance you'll win, what did

you have in mind?" Ganymede started to smile. He'd pretty much figured out what she'd say.

"A month of creative sex with you in your golden-god form." Her orange eyes glittered with laughter. "I believe in win-win situations."

His smile faded. "By the way, what happened to my ghosts? Haven't seen them around. I'm not paying them to lie down on the job."

"Guess you won't be paying them, then, because all they've been doing is lying down on the job." Her gaze swept the table. Probably searching for more fleas. "Last night I found them in the vegetable bin. They said all of those different-shaped veggies opened up lots of new erotic possibilities." She lifted her gaze to his and yawned delicately. "You have to admire anyone with that much stamina and drive to excel."

He was getting a headache. Good thing it wasn't a stomachache, because he was just about out of the pink stuff. "We still have to get rid of the vampire."

"Why? He saved our butts the other night, and Blythe would probably take us apart if we tried to hurt him." Sparkle glanced down at her stomach. "Does my stomach look flatter? I've been cutting out dessert."

"Your stomach looks great." Maybe the blood-sucker wasn't such a bad guy after all. Sparkle was right. Darach had been pretty decent about helping to get rid of that mob, even though Ganymede had done most of the tough stuff.

Sparkle stood and prepared to leap from the table,

then stopped. "That flea's down there. Do something about it."

Ganymede rubbed his forehead. The headache was getting worse. "I'll call in some of the servants to find it." If he was lucky, they'd never find the flea, and Sparkle would be trapped on that table until it was time to leave.

"There's something wrong with those women you hired, Mede." She sat down again, evidently ready to outwait the flea.

"Right." He walked over and rang the bell that would summon the servants. "They're all beautiful women. Maybe that's what's *wrong* with them."

For once, she didn't get mad when he hinted that she was jealous. She narrowed her clever cat eyes on the women who hurried into the hall. "No, there's *really* something wrong with them. I sense everything sexual in humans, and there's something dark and twisted in all of them that I can't quite get a handle on. Think I'll do a little investigating."

"Knock yourself out, babe." He needed to lie down in a dark, *quiet* room.

Blythe sat in the chair watching Darach sleep. He'd be awake soon and her day would officially begin. Funny how within such a short time she'd become a nocturnal creature.

She'd slept until early afternoon, then gone down to the great hall only to be waylaid by Textron. He'd tried to squeeze information from her about her progress with Darach, but she'd kept her mouth shut. At any point she could've cut him off by playing the recording that proved she'd succeeded. She hadn't.

Then the jerk had made a few sly innuendoes about her relationship with Darach. She could've stopped that dead by playing the recording of his little session with Sandy. She hadn't.

Why? She wasn't quite sure yet, but something important seemed to be shifting in her life. For some reason, Textron hadn't been worth bothering with today. Which was pretty crazy, because anything pertaining to her job always took precedence.

Right now? The only important thing on her horizon was the man sleeping in this room. She smiled. He thought he'd escaped their argument this morning. Wrong. She was wound up and ready to rumble.

Lazily he rolled onto his back and opened his eyes. He'd kicked off his covers during the day, and she'd spent some quality time mentally dividing his body into sensual zones. Then she'd decided what kinds of erotic stimulation would be most effective in each zone. Hey, she was organized in all things.

"Did ye enjoy your day?" His voice was still warm and husky from sleep.

Not as much as I'll enjoy my night. "It was okay. I had my daily argument with Textron, ate something wild and strange for dinner, and chased Clara, the vampire-slayer-in-training, away from our door twice.

Oh, and as far as I can see, Ganymede isn't hatching any plots against you." Blythe smiled. "I think he's too worried about what Sparkle will do next." Her smile faded. She really didn't want to tell him her next bit of news, but he'd find out anyway. "Three more people from the area were murdered last night."

He closed his eyes for a moment, and when he reopened them she recognized his resolve. "I must destroy the vampires tonight." Sitting up, he absently rubbed his palm across his incredible chest. " 'Twould help if ye'd find out where the killings took place while I bathe and dress."

Blythe didn't *want* to leave the room while he bathed and dressed. She wanted to see and experience it all, maybe even gain some tactile insights. Was this what an obsession felt like? She was beginning to wonder.

She quickly scanned his emotions. Relieved, she found him open to her. Resignation. Regret. No, she supposed this wasn't a good time to argue with him about her desire to see his vampire form. He had enough to worry about.

Hurrying down to the great hall, she caught Ganymede on his way back to his room. "I'm sort of worried about all these killings in the area. How close to us were the three last night?" Did she sound casual enough?

Ganymede pulled at his beard. "Nothing for you to worry about, little lady. You're completely safe here in the castle with me to protect you." He glanced around to make sure none of the other guests were nearby.

"The killings last night were closer to us than the others. Maybe two, three miles east of here. So I wouldn't go wandering outside the castle after dark."

Blythe nodded. She didn't have to pretend fear as she hurried back to tell Darach.

He only nodded when she gave him the news. Silently he strode to the corner to retrieve his sword, then headed for the door. Darach MacKenzie, the inscrutable one. It drove Blythe crazy when he reverted to his emotionless self.

"I want to help, Darach." It never ceased to amaze Blythe what kinds of absurdities came from her mouth when Darach was around.

"Help?" His tone was dismissive. " 'Tis too dangerous. Ye'll stay here where ye'll be safe."

Nothing motivated Blythe more than being told she couldn't do something. *Or knowing that someone she . . . cared about was walking into danger alone.* "I could stay close behind you like I did the other night and watch your back. The Freeze-frame will stop anything, and I know how to use it."

He raked his fingers through his hair. She was beginning to recognize the gesture. It was a nonverbal communication of *You're driving me nuts, lady.*

"Ye willna come, and ye willna argue about it. I dinna know how many vampires there are, and ye would only distract me from what I must do." He seemed to think that the final word had been spoken. *His* word.

Not likely. "I'm coming, and I'm helping. Are you going to walk? You know, you really might want to push the flying thing up on your list of powers. It would do you more good than just being able to see your reflection. Just my opinion, though."

"Aye, I'm walking. I keep several horses in the stable, but I can move more quietly on foot. Besides, the vampires will be close, so I willna need to ride." He reached the door, pulled it open, then turned to smile at her. "Ye will stay here and dream of me tonight, Blythe." He closed the door quietly behind him.

He really didn't know her if he thought she'd sit here all night wringing her hands and playing the helpless lady of the manor. She flung on her cloak, tucked the Freeze-frame into her pocket, and rushed to the arrow slit to see where Darach was headed. Thank heaven the window faced east. She watched him cross the footbridge, then follow a path winding into the darkness. She was lucky the moon was full tonight, because she hadn't brought anything to light her way.

Time for action. Blythe rushed to the door, reached for the latch, and slammed into Darach's protective shield. She couldn't believe him. He'd trapped her in this room.

Okay, calm down. Think. The window wasn't an option. She glanced up at the ceiling. The hole? Darach had shielded the door to this room, but maybe he hadn't bothered with the door to his old room since he wasn't using it anymore. It was worth a try.

It only took her a few minutes to put the chair on top of a small table and the stool on top of the chair. She actually managed to crawl through the hole before her makeshift tower collapsed. Hurrying to his door, she yanked it open. She felt a slight jolt that told her he'd protected the door from anyone trying to enter, but not from her escaping. Of course, she wouldn't be able to get back in, but that didn't matter. Yes! She was free.

Fifteen minutes later, she was riding a gray mare across the footbridge. Okay, so she was feeling a little smug. One thing that Darach MacKenzie *didn't* know about her was that she knew how to ride.

She was about twenty minutes behind him, but if she kept the mare at a trot and followed this path heading east, she should catch up with him. Blythe didn't think beyond the catching-up part.

Ten minutes later, she was almost ready to admit that Darach must have turned off the path somewhere when she heard the sounds. Ugly sounds. Growls, howls, and shrieks that were human and yet not human.

Gut-check time. She could still turn the mare around and race back to the castle. But in the primitive part of her where fight-or-flight reigned, fight won. She wouldn't run away if there was a chance of helping Darach. A less primitive part of her was asking, "And you expect to do what?"

She'd know when she got there. Firming her resolve along with her spine, she dismounted and tied the mare's reins to a tree. She wouldn't take the horse too close to whatever was happening for fear that the panicked animal might bolt and leave her stranded.

She moved closer to the noise, trying to use boulders and trees as cover. She didn't worry about being too loud, because no one would hear her above all the other sounds.

Unexpectedly, she rounded a large boulder to face a nightmare scenario. Blythe froze.

Darach stood with his back to her in the center of a small clearing, his sword unsheathed and ready. Spread in a semicircle around him were six creatures that looked a lot like Ian. Each wielded a short, deadly-looking ax similar to the one Jorund had carried. Slowly they closed in on him, their insane cries echoing eerily in the silence of the night.

Blythe drew in a sharp breath and fumbled in her pocket for her Freeze-frame. She wouldn't look into the glittering blue eyes filled with insane rage. She wouldn't dwell on the long, yellowed fangs exposed as the creatures curled their lips in vicious snarls. She wouldn't stare at their misshapen bodies and clawed fingers. And she definitely wouldn't scan their emotions.

"Go home, Blythe. Now." Darach's voice was calm, with no inflection to tell her if he was angry or afraid.

How had he known she was behind him? "I can't do that, Darach. Do what you have to do, and I'll take care of myself." Yeah, right. At least he was too occupied to reach into her mind and read her uncertainty.

She thought he would argue, but he said nothing more. Blythe watched the creatures draw closer to him. Darach's attention never left them.

Unexpectedly, a strange sensation hit her. It felt . . . as if she'd morphed into a human magnet. It was as though a power within her were drawing some unknown entities closer and closer. She shook her head to try to rid herself of the sensation.

The sensation was so strong that she almost didn't feel Darach in her mind until he spoke. *"I know your greatest fear, Blythe. They come for ye. Run home to your room before they catch ye."*

No! He wouldn't do this to her. Yes, he would if he thought it was the only way to make her leave. Blythe's heartbeat felt as if it were pumping a few thousand beats per minute. She widened her eyes and stared into the darkness beyond the clearing.

She heard the rustling first, as though hundreds of tiny feet were moving through the undergrowth. Then came the distinctive chittering sound. Louder and louder. They were coming for *her*.

She tried to scream, but her voice seemed locked in her throat. She tried to run, but her feet were frozen to the ground. Her breaths came in gasps of pure terror. Her mind seemed incapable of doing anything but repeating over and over, *"They're coming. They're coming."*

Suddenly they burst out of the night. Hundreds of

round pink bittyfluffs racing toward her on their tiny yellow feet, focusing on her with their huge purple eyes. Chittering at her as they came.

Blythe put her hand over her mouth to keep from screaming her terror. She was a small child again, leaning over a crate of bittyfluffs that had just been flown in by space freight. Everyone wanted one for a pet, and she was searching for the exact one she wanted Mom to buy for her. But she'd wandered away from Mom, so that when she lost her balance and fell into the large crate, there was no one to pull her out. Bittyfluffs were small, cuddly, and *suffocating*. Overly friendly, they piled onto her face, and for every one she pushed away with her little hands, two more took its place. She couldn't scream because her mouth and nose were full of pink fur. And she couldn't breathe, *she couldn't breathe!*

Stop panicking. Think logically. You didn't die. Mom came along in time to save you from suffocating. Logic didn't help. She'd had an unreasoning fear of bittyfluffs her whole life.

I'm sorry, Darach. So sorry. Blythe turned and ran, away from the bittyfluffs, away from her lifelong fear.

With her heart pounding, she hiked up her dress and raced toward her horse. She could outrun the bittyfluffs with their short little legs. *Who will help Darach?* Run. She had to keep running. *What if those creatures kill him?* No, she had to get away from the bittyfluffs. *He's alone back there facing six of them*.

Her headlong flight slowed. For the first time, her lifelong fear clashed with an even greater fear. *Darach could die.*

Breathing hard, she stopped and bent over at the waist to prop her hands on her knees. As her pounding heart slowed, she made her decision. Her fear of bittyfluffs was in her mind. What Darach was dealing with back in that clearing was real.

Did she have the courage to go back? For Darach? Turning, she looked back down the path and didn't miss its symbolism. If she retraced her steps now, she'd be choosing to revisit her childhood nightmare. It was time. She started back toward the sounds of battle.

Halfway back, she met the herd of bittyfluffs. They hopped and chittered at her. She kept walking, never looking down, not even daring to think for fear she'd break and run. They followed her as though she were some strange pied piper. When she almost tripped over one, she glanced down into its huge, adoring, purple eyes. *This* was what she'd feared her whole life.

She'd read an ancient quote once to the effect that to overcome fear you should surround yourself with what frightens you, understand it, and then it can't hurt you anymore. Easier said than done. Holding her breath, she leaned down and touched the bittyfluff with fingers that shook. It chittered its excitement. Jerking her hand away, she forced herself to breathe. *There's nothing to be afraid of. Just pet it.* The second time was a little easier. She stroked the bittyfluff, concentrating on the smooth fur beneath her fingers, the big purple eyes that shone with joy that she was touching it. Her tension slowly eased.

Straightening, she drew in a deep, fortifying breath. She'd braved the bittyfluffs. Their fearsome memory would never have the same power over her again, because she'd faced the reality today. They were just fuzzy little animals, not the monsters of her childhood nightmares.

Blythe strode back into the clearing with her Freeze-frame ready. She was in time to see Darach kill one of the vampires. Four down, two to go. She refused to look at the gruesome death scene as she focused on Darach.

He'd probably been right. He didn't need her help. What kind of physical power did it take to kill these insane creatures? She shook her head. That was wrong. They'd once been human, and she needed to give them the dignity of that memory.

Unexpectedly, one of the remaining vampires slipped behind Darach, who was completely involved in his life-and-death struggle with the vampire in front of him. Darach didn't seem to realize that danger was creeping up from behind.

Without thinking, Blythe raised her Freeze-frame and fired. The vampire froze in place, his clawed hand stilled in the act of bringing his ax down on Darach's unprotected head.

At the same time, Darach dispatched his enemy with

one deadly stroke from his sword, then whirled to face the vampire behind him.

Time itself seemed to stop. Darach grew still, sword raised to strike, while she stood with her Freeze-frame in her hand. She and Darach stared at each other, past the frozen figure of the last vampire.

Darach was in his vampire form.

Only the herd of bittyfluffs seemed unaffected by the drama playing out in the clearing. Like a giant amoeba, they moved together in a pink blob, chittering their joy at being alive in this place of death. The irony wasn't lost on Blythe.

As Darach lowered his bloody sword, he drew in a deep breath, and Blythe knew he was preparing to change to human form.

"Don't." Her voice was only a murmur, but he heard her and stood waiting.

Blythe understood that what she did, how she reacted within the next few minutes would determine something very important. Her relationship with Darach? They had a sexual relationship, but was it more than that? Did she *want* it to be more than that?

Yes. And that was the most frightening admission she'd ever made.

Blythe slowly returned her Freeze-frame to her pocket, almost afraid to move too quickly, afraid that she'd lose him. She stepped around the frozen figure of the vampire to stand in front of him. He seemed bigger, larger in ways that went beyond the mere physical. Deliberately she stared at his face.

"You can relax, vampire. I'm not going to say yuck." She smiled up at him and hoped her smile told him in some way the wonder she felt.

"Tell me what ye see." His voice was harsh with the remnants of the violence he'd just experienced, demanding with his need to know what she saw.

And underlying everything, Blythe felt his uncertainty. *That* was what moved her. She knew her eyes glistened with her own emotion as she reached up to slide her fingers along his clenched jaw.

"You're beautiful, vampire, in any form." Blythe put her finger across his lips to stop him from rejecting the unmanly description of him as beautiful. "Shush. This is my time to speak, and I'll use any words I want." She took her finger from his lips and tapped him firmly on his chest. "And you'll be quiet and listen."

His eyes widened, and Blythe almost laughed. She'd bet not many people had ever talked to him that way. But she'd braved a whole herd of bittyfluffs tonight. Next to that, facing him was nothing. She studied his stoic expression. Fine, so it wasn't "nothing."

She exhaled slowly, letting her emotion go. Her description had to be clinical, not colored by her feelings for him. He had to believe she told him the truth, not what she thought he wanted to hear.

"Your face is more angular now. Knife-edged cheekbones. Your eyes are larger, elongated, and a little slanted. Your pupils are so big that your eyes look black." She offered him a small smile. "If the eyes are the windows to the soul, then your windows are wide open and letting in the breeze."

She tilted her head to try to get a better perspective on him. "Your nose looks about the same; maybe the nostrils are a little more flared. Your mouth . . ." She needed exactly the right words here. "Your mouth looks larger, but not in a bad way. The lips are fuller, probably to accommodate your enlarged canines. I can't see your fangs the way I could see them on the others. I guess if you snarled at me they'd be exposed."

"Dinna tempt me, woman who cannot follow directions." His voice was starting to sound more normal.

Blythe offered him her complete smile. "All in all, you're quite a yummy package." She gazed directly into his eyes. "I officially invite you into my mind to check on the truthfulness of what I just told you."

He shook his head. "I trust ye on this."

Blythe had never expected his trust on something so important to him. "You've given me a wonderful gift, vampire." Standing on tiptoe, she kissed him. It didn't matter that death surrounded them, that he still clutched a bloody sword, or that small pink fur balls crowded around them. She kissed *him*, the vampire and the man.

With an inarticulate growl, he dropped his sword and gathered her to him. Lowering his head, he touched her lips gently with his, then deepened the kiss.

This was no searing passion, but a thank-you, and somehow a branding more real than all the heart-pounding excitement of his previous kisses. It confused her just when she'd started to think she understood what Darach MacKenzie was all about.

He released her, then drew his hands over her shoulders and down her arms as though to assure himself she was really there. "I wish ye to turn your back while I finish this. Then we'll go home together."

She didn't question him. Turning her back, she wondered what he was doing. No, she probably didn't want to know.

"We may leave now." He moved to her side.

Blythe looked over her shoulder at the clearing. The vampires were gone, including the one she'd paralyzed with her Freeze-frame. "How did you do that? Where did they go?"

"I returned their bodies to the elements. 'Tis what they would wish." He guided her along the path as her faithful bittyfluffs followed behind.

She stopped to stare at him. "If you can make them disappear like that, then why do you bother fighting them with your sword? Even a gun would make more sense. I'm not good with dates, but I seem to remember that some kind of firearm existed in this time. Wouldn't it be a lot easier and safer to skip the first step?"

Darach paused as they came in sight of the horse. It snorted and stared walleyed at the herd of bittyfluffs. "We must wait a moment to assure Arnora that the pink creatures willna harm her." He looked down at a bittyfluff that had planted its round pink bottom on his foot. "What are they? I took them from your mind, but they're passing strange. I dinna understand how ye could fear such as these."

Blythe sighed. "They're bittyfluffs, and it's a long story." *A story that she wouldn't be around long enough to tell.* The truth of that thought made her really . . . No, she didn't want to think about what it made her feel. "You haven't answered my question about the vampires."

He stared over her shoulder at a past only he could see. "They were all warriors. We believe that only those who die bravely in battle earn what ye would call heaven. The Valkyries choose the bravest of the slain and escort them to Odin's Hall, Valhalla. 'Tis a promise all in my clan have made to each other, that we will allow each to die as a warrior. I would wish such a death for myself."

Blythe nodded and glanced away. When she looked back, Darach wore his human features. He led her toward the horse.

"Methinks we should walk back. The bittyfluffs will follow ye, and they wouldna be able to keep up with Arnora." He offered her a smile. "Ye understand that they willna leave ye. Ganymede will be verra angry when he realizes he must take all the bittyfluffs with him when ye leave."

When ye leave. The words hung between them. Darach's smile faded, and Blythe met his unwavering gaze. Darach looked away first.

"Ye feared the bittyfluffs, yet ye returned. Why?" He still didn't meet her gaze.

"For you." Geez, this was getting too intense. "I guess I prioritized my fears, and decided I was afraid for you more than I was afraid of the bittyfluffs." She shrugged to suggest it was no big deal.

Darach didn't buy it. He stopped and waited for her to meet his gaze. "Ye're a brave lass. I dinna believe there are any in Odin's Hall with more courage. I . . ." He drew in a deep breath. Whatever he'd been about to say would go unsaid.

He strode the few steps to Arnora, untied her reins, and led her back toward the castle. Blythe walked silently beside him.

"There is something I must tell ye. I didna tell ye before because I didna wish to frighten ye."

As if she hadn't been scared witless from the moment she'd ridden away from the castle? Blythe supposed there were degrees of fear. "Spill it."

"Spill what?" He looked puzzled.

"Tell me about whatever it is that's going to scare me." Talk about a language barrier.

He nodded. "There were seven vampires. One ran when I entered the clearing."

Blythe shuddered to think that Darach would have to kill again. "Why did he run? All the others I've seen couldn't wait to attack you. And why don't they try to kill each other?"

"In their madness, they have no ability to reason, only the instincts of a predator. They dinna try to kill each other because they sense their sameness, and traveling in a pack makes them more efficient killers. They attacked me because they have no memory of those they once knew, no understanding of what they do, only a need to kill any they meet."

"And that means?" She didn't think she was going to like this.

"The one who ran was sane enough to seek to escape. I dinna know why he returned before complete madness took him, but he is more dangerous than the others because he can reason." He fixed her with his gaze. "Ye must always stay near me, and never leave the castle until he is destroyed."

Blythe wrapped her arms around herself and shivered. The cold had nothing to do with it. "What's happening, Darach? Why're so many coming here at once?"

Within his gaze she saw the vampire he truly was. "I dinna know, but I intend to find out."

Chapter Twelve

Blythe had returned to help *him*. She had faced her greatest fear because she thought he was in danger. Darach glanced at the woman who walked beside him. The wonder of her sacrifice filled his heart. Through force of habit he laid his hand across his most valued possession to assure himself it still beat.

If not for Blythe, his sorrow would be almost beyond bearing. He had just killed six warriors, men he had known through the centuries. And most likely he would slay another before the night ended.

Darach knew of only one way to deny grief its prize. Stoically he rebuilt the emotional wall that Blythe had breached. If he didn't feel, he could think clearly. He must discover what was driving so many of his clan to madness. Before, there had only been one or two every few years. Even the women who hunted them had not caused this kind of horror.

"You're brooding. I can tell." Blythe hooked her arm around his as they walked toward the castle. "You need to let it out or else it'll eat a hole in you from the inside out."

Darach stared straight ahead at the castle's dark silhouette, stark against the moonlit sky. "I canna 'let it out.' I must discover who has caused this."

He felt her attempt to touch his emotions, and firmed his lips along with his resolve to keep her out. If she could not reach his feelings, she would at least believe he had some. She would be upset to find that he had none, *must* have none until this was over.

Unexpectedly, the unknown vampire's presence touched him..He stopped and stared at the castle.

"What's the matter?" Blythe sounded uncertain.

"The vampire waits outside the castle." He pointed to a part of the wall shadowed from the moon's light. "Stay behind me. I wished to see ye safely inside the castle before we battled, but I must reach him quickly before he kills." He handed her Arnora's reins, then unsheathed his sword.

"Before he kills? Kills whom?" She hurried to keep up with him as he began to run across the footbridge.

Darach saw clearly what Blythe could not. The vampire had a woman trapped against the castle wall. But as he drew closer, Darach sensed something familiar about the vampire. His back was to Darach, but there was something in the set of his shoulders, the long gold hair, the tilt of his head, that stirred memories.

Darach stopped a short distance away from the rogue vampire, dread building in him along with desperate denial. He sensed Blythe close to him, but she was wise enough to remain quiet.

The vampire had to know Darach was behind him, but he didn't turn, only concentrated his attention on the terrified woman cowering against the wall. While Darach watched, the woman stabbed at the vampire with a wooden stake. Darach recognized her now. It was Clara, the woman Blythe said wished to be a Buffy.

"Ouch." The vampire's exclamation was derisive. "I hate to disappoint such a bonny lass, but I must tell ye that stabbing me in the heart willna kill me. I have no heart. And ye should never hunt vampires with a twig. A twig breaks too easily." To demonstrate, he yanked the wooden stake from Clara's shaking hands and broke it in half.

"Your cross is a fine talisman"—he clasped the cross that hung from her neck and examined it—"but it willna make me cover my eyes and run from it." He released the cross. "Ye've only done one thing that has truly fashed me." He wiped a hand over his plaid. "Ye've soaked me with the holy water ye flung on me, and 'tis a cold night to be walking around in wet clothing."

He moved closer to the terrified woman and reached for her. "Ye should never anger a vampire."

Darach had faced many things in his life, but this . . . ? He did not think he could survive this. He might have banished all feeling, but this transcended emotion. This spoke to who he was, who he had once been.

"Thrain." He spoke the name he had once uttered so fondly.

The vampire turned slowly to face him while Clara, speechless with terror, ran for the safety of the castle. "I didna think ye'd remember me, Varin."

His gaze locked with Darach's, and emotion flooded his eyes. " 'Tis Jamie I've been these many centuries, but on this night that will see my death, I choose to be the Northman, Thrain." He unsheathed his sword. "I didna stay to fight with the others because this should be between only the two of us. I wish to see Valhalla before dawn."

"No." Once again, Darach's emotional wall was crumbling. Mayhap Blythe had weakened it so that it would never stand again. "Ye canna ask this of me." Not remember Thrain? How could he think that Darach would forget him? They had played together, fought together. So many memories. They had each received their sword on the same day, and shared the pride of feeling as though they were truly warriors. Until they'd hacked the legs from his mother's table, and she'd chased the no longer brave warriors down the hill. Darach barely remembered Aesa's face, but Thrain's would never fade.

Thrain stepped closer. "I would have slain that woman if ye hadna saved her. I am not so mad as the ones ye killed tonight, but I canna resist the blood lust.

When I learned that this cycle of the moon was your duty, I knew that I wished to die by your hand, so I came. I didna want to wait until I couldna reason. I would control when and how I die."

Darach's complete rejection of what Thrain asked pounded through him with each beat of his heart. Thrain seemed much like Darach remembered him through the mist of so many years. Tall, powerful, with intelligence gleaming in the blue eyes that all of Darach's clan possessed. But as Darach gazed into his friend's eyes, he saw the beginning of madness, the slight clouding that signaled the start of what could only end in death. He also saw the battle Thrain fought to hold back the madness, to go to his death with dignity.

"What happened?" Darach needed time to think. There must be a way to save his friend. There were so many lost years between them, so many things that he wanted to say.

"The women who hunt us have found a way to use the bog myrtle without coming near us. I dinna know how they do it." He fingered the Thor's hammer talisman at his neck, a gesture that brought back memories of so many days spent together in their youth. "I had met with the warriors ye killed tonight to talk of the old days and share a night of friendship. Sometime during that night the women struck. I have no memory of what happened until I woke and found myself bound."

His expression grew bitter. "When they were finished

with us, they left us for the morning sun to find. I was able to free myself, and then I freed the others. We had lost so much blood that all we could think of was the need to survive. The others could not stop once they started feeding. They gorged themselves, and by the time they finished, they were doomed. I tried to stop, but I didna stop soon enough."

Killing fury roiled in Darach; the need to destroy lived and breathed in him. "Tell me what these women fear, Thrain."

Thrain smiled for the first time. "I've heard of your power. May Odin grant ye the chance to use it on them." His smile faded. "They despise men, whether vampire or mortal. They use us sexually, but other than that, they feel we serve no purpose in their world. I know of no fear they all share. They believe that what they do will make them immortal. What then could frighten them?"

Thrain's gaze grew intense. "But they've grown greedy. When one of their number died even though she had joined with a vampire, they decided that each must mate with many vampires in order to assure their immortality. I dinna know how they found us, but I suspect they use their wealth to employ an army of spies.

"But we have spoken enough. It is time." He reached up and removed the Thor's hammer talisman from around his neck. Then he handed it to Darach. "Ye gave me this when we were but lads as proof of your friendship. I give it back to ye tonight. Keep it and know that I always valued and honored that friendship. May we one day meet in Valhalla." He raised his sword.

Darach stood holding the talisman, staring across the chasm of so many lost years and the knowledge of what he *had* to do, at the man who had been his closest friend. But the duty to his clan was clear. He must do what Thrain wished.

Darach lifted his sword. And for the first time in his long life, he knew true despair.

Blythe watched in unblinking horror as the drama unfolded. They weren't really going to fight, were they? The harsh clash of swords answered that question.

Darach wouldn't really kill Thrain, would he? With a motion so swift that her eyes couldn't follow it, Darach brought his sword to Thrain's neck.

Blythe opened her mouth to shout at Darach, but nothing came out. Ultimately, this had to be his decision. This moment was like so many of her nightmares about her family. She would watch them walking into that convention hall, but no matter how hard she tried, she couldn't yell a warning to them.

The moment hung suspended for what seemed to Blythe like a million heartbeats.

"Do it." Thrain's voice grated with his knowledge of imminent death.

With a vicious curse, Darach flung down his sword and backed away from Thrain. "I canna."

Way to go, vampire! Blythe felt as though her voice

and feet were freed at the same moment. Even her brain cells must have been frozen, because suddenly she could think logically again. Time for her to offer an alternative to life-and-death combat.

Dragging Arnora behind her, she rushed between the two men and held up her hands. "Wait. I have an idea."

Darach glared at her. "Go into the castle, Blythe."

"Not until I've told you my idea." She turned to see if Thrain was listening to her.

Thrain was staring mesmerized at the herd of bittyfluffs crowding around her. "What are these creatures?"

"Bittyfluffs." Impatiently she waited until she had both men's attention. "Here's the problem, as I see it. Thrain, you have too much human blood. You need less human blood and more vampire blood. Right?"

Thrain nodded, puzzled. Darach continued to glare at her.

"It seems the solution is simple. Thrain, you need a wound that'll get rid of some of the blood you have now. Not enough to kill you, but enough to weaken you. Then you bite Darach and take some of his vampire blood." Blythe frowned as she thought out the details. "I hope you all have the same blood type. I guess you might have to repeat the process a few times, because you couldn't take that much of Darach's blood all at once. And I'm assuming that once you've gotten back the correct balance of vampire blood to human blood, the negative symptoms will disappear." She offered them a brilliant smile. "It's so simple I'm surprised you guys didn't think of it."

Darach didn't return her smile. "We canna bite each other."

"Why not? You bite everything else." She couldn't believe he was rejecting her plan.

" 'Tis the law of our clan."

"That's a pretty dumb law, if you ask me." Everyone should be allowed to bite in an emergency.

"I didna ask ye. 'Tis the law and we canna break it." Darach was wearing his I-must-be-patient male expression.

"Why not? Who's going to tell? A little bite in the dark. No one will ever know." She was trying really hard to be reasonable here.

" 'Twould not be honorable." Thrain entered the fray.

"Excuse me? Dead is pretty permanent, pal. Maybe you should rethink the death-before-dishonor attitude." She was getting steamed now.

Both men offered her their stubborn-mule expressions.

"Well, hell." There had to be a way around this. "Does the law say anything about giving blood, or does it just forbid biting?"

Darach looked puzzled. "It only forbids the biting. It says nothing about the giving of blood, because without the biting there would be no blood to give."

"That's what you think. I don't know when the first

human-to-human transfusion took place, but I'd bet it came after 1785. You guys are about to become medical pioneers. First, though, I have to get something from Ganymede." *Please let Ganymede have remembered to bring an emergency medical case.*

"Who is this woman, and why does she speak so strangely? And I still dinna understand what manner of creature these bittyfluffs are."

Thrain's confusion would have been funny if the situation weren't so desperate.

Darach gazed intently at Blythe. "Can ye help Thrain, lass?"

"What're you willing to do to save him?"

"Anything." His gaze never wavered.

"As long as it doesn't involve him biting you." She shook her head. "I don't understand that, Darach."

"The clan is only as strong as its laws. Those who break the laws when it suits them weaken the clan." He rubbed the back of his neck. "According to clan law, I should have killed Thrain." He offered her a half smile. "Ye may take some comfort in knowing that I have broken at least one law tonight."

Blythe couldn't help it. She leaned into him and kissed his chest where his shirt gaped open. "Let's hear it for law-breaking. And look, no cuts or bruises. You're getting better, vampire."

He smiled at her, but his eyes looked weary. "Mayhap ye will search my body later for wounds in places other than my chest."

Blythe gazed directly into his eyes. "If you'd killed Thrain, you'd have suffered a mortal wound here." She placed her palm over his heart. "You did the right thing, Darach."

He nodded. "I'll return Arnora to the stable, then take Thrain up to our room and hope we dinna meet Clara. 'Tis unlikely, though. She has probably locked herself in her room." He glanced down at the bittyfluffs. "Ye must come to the room for a few minutes before ye get what ye need from Ganymede. The bittyfluffs will follow ye, and I will keep them in the room until ye return." He forced a smile. "Ye dinna wish to upset Ganymede with a herd of these creatures in *his* castle."

Fifteen minutes later, Blythe returned to her room with the rolling medical case in tow. Luckily, she'd caught Ganymede at the right moment. She'd found him surrounded by his two male guests, Textron, and Sandy. Sparkle sat nearby cleaning her face and trying not to look amused as Ganymede made desperate excuses why he couldn't join any of them in a threesome, foursome, or any other number combined with "some."

They'd stopped talking when they spotted Blythe, but she'd already heard enough. She curled her lip at the thought of Textron and Sandy. But at least Ganymede had been so busy trying to escape them that he just told her where the case was and didn't ask her why she wanted it.

Once back in her room, she faced Darach and

Thrain. She tried to ignore the sea of chittering pink covering every surface. "I sure hope these guys did what they had to outside."

The two men glanced at each other as though that thought hadn't occurred to them.

"We will put them outside the door. They willna leave ye, so we dinna have to worry about them terrorizing the others." Darach herded the bittyfluffs out the door, then slammed it before they could run back in. "I have learned a lesson from this. Someone else's greatest fear can become a plague on the one who called it forth."

Thrain seated himself in the chair while Darach sat on the stool beside him. Darach's gaze was inscrutable while Thrain's was openly hopeful. Blythe knew Darach well enough by now to understand that he wouldn't allow himself to show hope when he feared it might be a false hope. How many disappointments had he suffered in his life to develop this kind of attitude?

"Thrain, I'm not going into any complicated explanations right now, but you need to know that I'm from the future. Luckily for us, medical science has reached the point where procedures that at one time had to be done in a hospital by doctors can now be done routinely by anyone who can read directions." She frowned at his blank expression. Okay, so much for explanations.

"I'm going to read these directions, then I'm going to fasten parts of this small machine to each of you. This is called a Transfusomatic, and it'll locate a vein, check for blood compatibility, and then draw blood from each of you. The blood that's drawn from Darach will be transferred to you, Thrain." She immediately buried her nose in the directions so that she didn't have to face their startled expressions.

A few minutes later, she was ready to start. As she fastened the machine to Thrain, he fixed his gaze on her throat and his lips lifted to expose his sharp canines. Blythe shuddered. "Stop staring at my neck."

He shifted his gaze as Darach growled low in his throat and half rose from his stool.

Blythe had never been a huge fan of protective men, but tonight, in this time and place, she thought one particular super alpha male was pretty special.

"Explain the directions to me, Blythe, and I will take care of Thrain." He stared at his friend. "Ye understand that ye dinna need to be tempted by a woman's closeness when ye are not yourself."

Thrain only nodded.

A short time later, it was finished, and Blythe knew she needed to get away from the room, away from these men, away from the trauma of this night. "I'll dispose of the polluted blood and—"

"No, ye have done enough. Thrain will sleep in my bed, and I will protect it. No one will be able to reach him, and he willna be able to leave the bed." He smiled at Thrain. "Do ye feel any different?"

Thrain glanced at Darach and Blythe, then smiled.

"The blood lust has lessened, and my mind seems clearer."

Blythe watched the tension slowly drain from Darach. He placed a hand on his friend's shoulder as Thrain walked over to Darach's bed and lay down.

"I need some fresh air. I'll be back in a little while." Blythe didn't wait for Darach to reply. She just grabbed her shawl and fled the room. A hundred bittyfluffs chittered with joy as she closed the door behind her. "Hey, guys, let's go look at the moon."

When she reached the battlements, she simply sat down with her back against the wall and stared at the moon. Then she cried. Loudly, messily, interspersed with gasps for air so that she could cry some more. No delicate weeping for her.

Blythe was barely aware when Darach sat down beside her, shooed the bittyfluffs away, then pulled her against his side. He didn't try to stop her tears, which was a good thing, because this crying business was serious stuff. Finally, she felt that she had cried her total lifetime's supply of tears, so she tapered off to a few sniffles. Then she wiped her eyes with her shawl.

"I'm sorry, Blythe. Ye shouldna have seen what ye did tonight. Ye're upset, and 'tis my fault." He pulled her head against his shoulder.

She looked up at him, and in the moonlight her eyes still shimmered with tears. "Upset? I'm not upset. And I'm not crying for me."

Darach frowned as a bittyfluff crawled into her lap.

Enough. He needed to be alone with her so he could discuss this crying. "Dinna move." Rising, he herded the bittyfluffs off the battlements and into the tower, then closed the door on them. Then he returned to sit beside Blythe. "If ye're not upset, then why do ye cry?"

"For you, for Thrain, for those men you had to kill tonight, and for Ian." She made it all sound perfectly reasonable. "None of you can cry. When a man dies, he should always have someone to cry for him. A mother, a father, a . . . Oh, I don't know. Someone who will *miss* him." She waved her hand to indicate the many people who should be weeping over their dead loved ones.

"And someone needs to cry for Thrain. You sure can't. Don't you understand how he honored you? He traveled here because he wanted to be with his best friend when he died. He didn't want to die at the hands of someone cold and impersonal, an executioner. What did you do to deserve that kind of friendship from a man you haven't seen in over five hundred years?" Fresh tears slid down her cheeks.

"Because I canna cry doesna mean I dinna care." Darach was sure of himself in most situations, but he did not know what to do with this woman's tears.

"I know, I know." Blythe wiped at her tears. "And I'm crying for you, too. I've scanned your emotions, but you're hiding them from me again. The things you've had to do tonight . . . I can't imagine that kind of horror. I guess you feel that you won't have the guts to do what you have to do if you're busy letting your emotions hang out. So I'm letting them hang out for you." She hiccupped and offered him a watery smile. "Doesn't make a whole hell of a lot of sense, does it?"

Suddenly his carefully constructed self-control shattered. He'd thought he was so strong, but never since he became vampire had he been tested so. Never had he been forced to destroy as he had tonight. Never had he been faced with the choice of slaying a friend or breaking a clan law. And never . . . had a woman cried for him.

It had been easy to believe himself happy in his sensual world before this.

He had to find a violent expression for all that roared for release in him. Raking his fingers through his tangled hair, he stood, then lifted his face to the moon. "Ye wish to see my feelings, to know how much I care?"

Blythe looked wary. "Well, maybe not right now. I'll take your word for it."

It was too late. Darach needed to rend, tear, destroy. He could easily wreak havoc with his mind, but tonight he must use his hands, feel the destruction on a physical level.

With an inarticulate cry, he ripped away a section of the battlement wall and raised it high above his head, then heaved it to the courtyard below. The explosive sound of the huge section of stone wall hitting the ground had barely faded when he turned his fury on the tower itself. He ripped the door off, sending the herd of terrified bittyfluffs crowded on the other side of it fleeing down the steps.

Through his red haze of fury, he could hear Blythe shouting at him to stop, but he couldn't. Frantically he looked around to see what else he could destroy. Why had he chosen this place to vent his feelings? There was nothing here that satisfied his need. 'Twould have been better if he were in the great hall. He could have thrown tables, torn down walls, brought the whole cursed building down around his head. While he contemplated doing just that, Ganymede thundered up the tower steps.

"What the hel . . . What the heck are you doing? You're destroying my castle and waking the dead with all that blasted noise." Ganymede thought for a moment. "Well, I guess on a night like this the dead are already awake, but you're scaring my guests."

"Leave . . . me . . . be." Darach thought about the satisfaction he'd get from tearing Ganymede apart. 'Twould be a gratifying alternative to bringing the castle down stone by stone. "And 'tis *my* castle, so I can do what I wish with it."

Darach's killing rage had eased enough for him to be aware of Blythe stroking his arm and murmuring to him. "Calm down. You're okay. We'll deal with everything together."

She spoke to him as she would a wild animal she was attempting to soothe. Mayhap she understood better than he did the beast that lived just beneath the surface of the emotionless face he showed the world. A beast he'd not set loose before this.

"Woman trouble, right?" Ganymede slapped Darach on the back and almost propelled him through the gap in the battlement wall. "Hey, I understand where you're coming from, vampire. Sparkle makes me want to annihilate continents, destroy whole solar systems when she gets started." He frowned. "Can't have that kind of fun anymore, though. Anyway, why don't you make up with Blythe here and let the rest of us sleep?" Ganymede tried to look fatherly as he turned to leave. "And what's that herd of bittyfluffs doing in this time? Almost knocked me down as I came up here." Without waiting for a reply, he stomped down the steps.

Darach stood bemused for a moment, trying to get a mental picture of the wee bittyfluffs knocking Ganymede down. He couldn't do it.

He forgot about Ganymede, though, when he realized Blythe had been unusually quiet throughout the whole exchange. Flexing his shoulder muscles to release some of the tension still thrumming through him, Darach looked at her. She still had her hand on his arm, but he couldn't interpret the emotion in her eyes.

"Ye'll tell me now that tearing buildings down is not on Ecstasy's list of ways to earn lifelong happiness." He put his hand over hers, and she didn't pull away. 'Twas a good sign.

Her lips tipped up in the beginning of a smile.

"You're right. And Ecstasy doesn't believe in alternate roads to happiness. The only acceptable road is the company road."

"Mayhap your leaders would add destruction to their list if they had to kill seven people they knew." He couldn't control the bitterness in his voice.

Blythe leaned into him as a cold mist rolled in from the sea, blotting out the moon. The smell of rain was in the air. "If it's any comfort, wild, uncontrolled crying is also not on their list, but it made me feel a whole lot better." She led him over to the shelter of the tower as light rain began to fall, but she didn't step inside the doorway. "Want to know a secret? I think you're right about the folks at Ecstasy. They're too rigid. They don't allow for differences in personalities. As far as they're concerned, if I can't bring you happiness with scented candles and a little body and mind massaging, then forget it. You're doomed to eternal sadness."

"When ye return to your time, will ye still work for them?" *I dinna wish ye to return to your time.* Somehow his admission came as no surprise. But it was a foolish wish. After what she had seen this night, she would feel only relief at leaving.

If he told her of his many homes, of the wealth he had accumulated over the centuries, would she stay? No, he did not think that would influence Blythe.

Why did he want her to stay? *Because ye're not finished knowing her.* Darach suspected he would need an eternity to "know" this woman from another time.

"Stay with Ecstasy?" She shrugged. "I'm not sure. It's the only place I've ever worked, and my family's ties are to the company. But if I stay, it won't be because I feel guilty. That's one thing I'm certain of."

Darach glanced up as the rain fell harder. "Ye should get out of the rain."

"No."

Surprised, he looked at her.

"I don't feel clean, Darach. Oh, I know I'm not covered with blood, but that's the way I feel." She flung off her shawl and lifted her face to the rain. "I want this cold rain to pour over my body and make me feel clean again." Blythe shifted her gaze to him. "And I want your body to cleanse here." She placed her hand over her heart. "The rain can't reach that."

His body instantly reacted to her suggestion. "Ecstasy wouldna approve."

"We've broken your clan rules and ignored Ecstasy's guidelines, so . . ." She shrugged. "Let's live selfishly tonight. This isn't a forever thing, vampire. It's to forget for a short time what happened tonight, and it's to reaffirm life."

She smiled up at him, but her eyes held no laughter. "Is that deep, or what?" Her smile faded. "Make it so hot and hard that you'll drive away all of tonight's ugliness. If you don't, I may never have sweet dreams again."

He reached for her.

Chapter Thirteen

"Dinna remove your clothing." Darach grasped her hand as she reached for the top of her gown.

Blythe frowned. "I think the cleansing concept requires clothing removal."

"Aye, I agree, but ye cheated me out of that pleasure last time. I willna be denied now." He began to undo the top of her gown, frowning at the laces that seemed to stretch on forever. "I believe your gowns were made by bitter hags who hoped to keep all women virgins. I must unlace ye to your waist. Why?"

Her smile teased and taunted. "To drive impatient vampires into a sexual frenzy."

"They do it verra well." Darach was tempted to dissolve the laces, but Blythe would be upset if he ruined another of her gowns. He undid only a few laces and could wait no longer to touch her. Peeling her gown down to just below her breasts, he studied the offending piece of cloth that cupped them. "I dinna know why ye wear this. Your breasts are wondrous, and it shouldna take a man so long to reach them."

"If you don't touch them soon, I'll be forced to cry some more, this time for me." Her voice was heat and desire.

Five hundred years of self-control were useless around this woman. "I wished to take off each piece of your clothing one by one, then touch, taste, and enjoy the sight of your body. This wish lasted"—Darach counted—"only five laces." He closed his eyes. "I canna wait through even one more lace." Concentrating, he indulged his impatience.

When he opened his eyes, Blythe stood naked before him; her eyes were wide with shock and her clothes were scattered around her feet as she stared at his own bared body. He suspected her shock was because he had rid both of them of their clothes so suddenly.

But he knew his own eyes must be wide as well. Blythe's body affected him as no other woman's had in all his many years, not because she was the most beautiful, but because she was the most beautiful to *him*.

From the rain-darkened hair that spread across her smooth shoulders, to her full breasts meant to fill a man's palms, down the tempting flow of her stomach and hips to her long, enticing legs, she was all softly rounded woman. He would never tire of sliding his fingers across her warm, golden skin as if touching the sunlight he could never know.

"Mayhap after I've made love to ye a thousand times, I will learn more patience." Darach knew he had given her false hope, because it would never happen. A thousand times was nothing. A thousand *years* would not extinguish the longing that burned in him for Blythe. And he refused to hide from what he had just admitted.

"I don't want restraint from you, Darach. And don't even think about being patient." She stepped into his embrace, and he closed his arms around her.

"I've had a lifetime of being patient. I endured being stuck in the hellhole of happiness—Casper, Wyoming. My whole adult life has been a song of perseverance. I could never get angry with clients, never hurry along their journey toward the happiness finish line. Do you have any idea how many times I wanted to kick some butts across that damned line so that I could go home?" Blythe blinked up at him as rain sluiced over her bare shoulders. "I've never admitted that to anyone." She frowned. "Even myself."

"Enough." Darach placed a finger over her lips. "Dinna talk. Dinna think." He pulled her close against his body, glorying in the feel of the rain's cold bite against his back and buttocks, and the searing heat wherever his body touched hers.

Leaning away from him, she lifted her eyes to the stormy sky, and her skin gleamed as the rain slid down her face. "I've never felt this free in my whole life."

Holding her steady with his arm around her waist, he leaned down and covered her nipple with his lips, teasing and nipping until she whimpered and pushed away from him. He let her go.

"Whoa. *You* don't do it all this time. Last time I missed out on all that touching and tasting stuff. My turn now, vampire." She flattened her palms across his chest, then rubbed a slow pattern of seduction.

Moving close to him, she slid her tongue over each of his nipples and nipped as he had. At the same time, she ground her abdomen against his sex, trapping his erection between their bodies.

The heated friction tore a groan from him. But before he could react, she trailed her hands down his body even as she slipped to her knees in front of him.

Darach spread his legs, wanting, *needing* her touch on all that was a sexual part of his body. And right now, he could not think of any part that was not. Only the cold rain pouring over his body kept him from going up in flames.

Slowly, wantonly, she kissed a hot path up the inside of each of his thighs while her fingers kneaded his buttocks. And when her nails dug into each cheek, the pain was also sexual. He slid his fingers through her wet hair as his body tightened, aroused almost to the point that he could endure no more. But he did, because he wanted her mouth . . .

She cupped his sacs in her palms, then put her mouth on each, sliding her tongue over skin stretched tight in readiness.

He put his hands on her shoulders to steady himself.

No woman's mouth had ever come close to bringing him to his knees, but Blythe's mouth was silk and heat. And more than just the physical pleasure her touch was giving him was the knowledge that she gave with joy, with caring. For him.

She paused to look up at him. He knew that the wet strands of his hair hung dripping beside his face, every muscle in his chest and shoulders bulged with the rigid control he needed now, and his eyes must be starting to change to those of the hungry creature that wanted Blythe in *every* way. The creature would *not* have her in one important way.

"Your eyes are changing," she said. Her gaze was filled with awe and a desire she did nothing to hide, rather than the fear he would see in any other woman's eyes. "Thank you for trusting me enough to let me see it."

Could a woman's words be a sexual thing? It must be so, because her words touched him as a caress would, gliding across his pounding heart and moving down to where all sensual pleasure was now centered. 'Twas a revelation. For all his years as vampire he had ignored any words that women said during sex, because usually they were only words telling him what they wished him to do. He felt the slide of his fangs and knew he could not control his need much longer. But he would do so until Blythe was ready.

As she stared at him, he felt the moment held something tenuous, a discovery that was still hidden, and a promise that was not yet fulfilled.

Then she lowered her head and touched his erection with her mouth. He threw back his head and allowed the rain to beat down on his upturned face as all physical sensation narrowed to the touch of her lips, her teeth.

She slid her tongue the length of his arousal, then touched the base with the tip of her tongue and moved it in a way that made his whole body shudder. Where had she learned that? Mayhap he did not want to know. But he wondered about nothing more as she nibbled her way around the head of his erection, then paused.

And even though he thought himself prepared, when she slid her lips smoothly over the head and surrounded his flesh with all her heat and passion, he felt that his heart stopped, then began to beat again with a pounding demand strong enough to shatter his body.

Dimly he heard thunder and knew that jagged streaks of lightning lit the sky. Wind whipped about them and the rain became a punishing torrent. And he was part of the storm, driven before it by the torture of her mouth firm around him as she mimicked the motion of sex, sliding down on him, then retreating. Her tongue circled and played with his flesh, and her teeth scraped lightly along its length.

With a savage growl, he tangled his fingers in her hair and pulled her from him. She looked up at him, and as the storm battered them, he saw the same wild need as his.

He was close to losing control, but as had always happened with Blythe, his need to bury himself between her legs overwhelmed any compulsion to feed from her.

Grasping her beneath her arms, he lifted her to her feet. Driven completely by his senses now, Darach backed her against the tower wall.

"Now!" Her one-word command was whipped away by the wind, but he heard it.

As she spread her legs, he cupped her slick buttocks and lifted her to meet his thrust. Shouting his triumph, he buried himself in her, felt her muscles clench around him, and shuddered as the heat of their joining flowed to every part of his tensed body.

With a growl that would have done credit to the fiercest vampire, Blythe clasped his shoulders and wrapped her legs around his waist.

Darach braced her against the wall and plunged into her again and again. Her cries grew more frenzied with each thrust. As she gripped his shoulders, she lifted her body so that she could drive herself down on him, forcing him deeper when deeper wasn't possible.

He felt the power of his release building, and when it slammed into him, every muscle in his body seemed to lock. In that moment of stillness, Blythe found her own climax, clenching around him so tightly that he cried out with almost unbearable pleasure. Spasm after spasm rocked him, and there was no thought, only the desire for it to never end.

When he returned to his body, he was slumped against the wall with Blythe clinging to him limply.

She looked at him but said nothing. Was that good or bad? But words could be left for later, because now that he did not have sexual excitement to warm him, the cold rain pouring over his bare body made him shiver. Blythe must feel the same.

Quickly gathering their clothes, he guided her back to their room. The bittyfluffs had piled into a huge pink mound beside the door and were all sleeping. "Will they feel cold out here?"

"Nope. Bittyfluffs are tough. They come from a cold planet. All that pink fur keeps them warm." She hesitated at the door. "What about Thrain? I need to put my clothes back—"

Darach pushed open the door. "Thrain is asleep and will continue to sleep for the rest of this night and all day tomorrow. His body needs time to find its balance."

Once inside, Blythe dried herself and then scrambled into her bed. He knew that she watched him as he built up the fire for the night; then she patted the bed beside her. "We'll have to share my bed tonight."

He climbed under the covers with her and lay on his back. She rested her head against his shoulder, and he felt strangely content. He had felt many things with women, but contentment was not one of them.

"It's funny, but I always thought I needed lots of foreplay to get me excited enough to feel that I'd had a WOW sexual experience. You've shot down that theory." She snuggled against him, and he put his arm under her shoulder and pulled her closer.

"Foreplay?" Darach frowned. Whenever she used a word he did not understand, it reminded him that she was from another time and would soon return there.

"It's the erotic stimulation that comes before sex. You know, the touching and kissing." She smiled. "We were so crazy out there that we didn't even have a meeting of lips."

He laughed softly. "Ye dinna understand, Blythe. Every moment we spend with each other, no matter what we are doing, is erotic stimulation . . . foreplay."

"You're right. I never thought about it that way." She looked away from him. "Tonight was the greatest lovemaking I've ever shared. Why does it get better each time I'm with you?"

Shared? Did sharing have anything to do with it? Mayhap. They had come together tonight out of a shared pain, a need to forget if only for a few moments. But beyond that, each time he made love to her he wanted her more, because . . . he cared for her. And the caring frightened him more than an attack by a hundred berserkers. It was his turn to look away.

"I think the satisfaction grows because we know more about each other, are more at ease with each other's bodies." That was only part of the truth for him, but it was all he was willing to tell her, because there was no future in his caring.

He could gift her, though, with something she would prize. "I enjoy speaking with ye, and I feel safe telling ye things I have never told another. Ye can make me laugh, and I feel happy when ye're with me. 'Twill sadden me when ye leave." Darach closed his eyes. There. That was as close as he would ever come to telling her that he cared.

Darach felt the butterfly touch of her lips on his cheek and the warm skim of her breath. He felt her smile. "Thank you."

She lay still for a while, but he knew she did not sleep. There was one thing he would ask her before she slept. "While I was enjoying our short but verra exciting foreplay, ye wiggled your tongue against the root of my cock. Where did ye learn such things?" Darach braced himself for her tale of a talented lover who had taught her well. He would listen stoically, but if he ever had the man within his power, he would tear him apart. Darach had never felt jealousy before Blythe. 'Twas truly a violent emotion.

"Sparkle told me about that." Blythe laughed. "I wouldn't listen to the other things she wanted to tell me."

The tension drained from his body. "Ye might wish to make a list of Sparkle's ideas."

"Mmm. Will do." She turned into his arms, and a few minutes later her even breathing told him she slept.

Darach lay the rest of the night watching her. He tried to make sense of what he felt for Blythe, then told himself it did not matter. She would not wish to stay in his time, and he could not blame her for that. And he would not abandon his duty so that he might follow her to her time. The fact that he was even thinking in terms of her time and his time told him he was in serious trouble.

Darach had thought himself happy in his world before Blythe burst into it. But now? He had not recognized the loneliness of his life until he was no longer lonely. He had not understood that sex could be even more intense when it involved his emotions, and his emotions were very much involved with Blythe.

As the gray light of dawn shone through the arrow slit, he still did not know what he was going to do with his feelings for this strong and caring woman from a future time. And in the end, what he felt meant nothing if she did not feel the same way.

Reaching out, he fingered the talisman she still wore. Darach resisted his urge to melt it into an unrecognizable blob of metal; he wanted nothing associated with Ecstasy Incorporated touching her. He wanted to be the only ecstasy in her life. And the power of his wish surprised him.

Darach smiled as Blythe slowly wakened. His smile faded, though, as he remembered his duty, a duty to keep Thrain safe and to find those who were destroying his clan. After what Thrain had told him, he must look with suspicion on any women he did not know.

He must ask Blythe to see what she could find out about the women who worked in the castle. He had expected the women who hunted his clan to turn their attention to him eventually because of his power, but he had not realized that they had become so voracious.

He had grown careless, thinking himself safe from them because he assumed they could not gather a force large enough to attack him here, and arrogant because he had considered a group of women too weak to defeat him. If not for his constant thoughts of Blythe, he might have suspected the servants sooner. When he woke this eve, he would search out their thoughts, but for now he must rely on Blythe.

Darach clenched his fist around the talisman at the thought of his own greatest fear—being bound and helpless—then jerked his hand away as his voice poured from the talisman.

Blythe sat up, her eyes wide and still confused by sleep. "Who turned that on?"

"What is this? How are my words coming from it?" His heart pounded madly, and anger built as he realized that these were the words he had said when he told Blythe she had made him happy.

Fully awake now, she bit her lip as she touched the talisman and the words stopped. "This is a machine that can record sounds. I recorded what you said because I needed to give Textron proof that I'd done my job."

He felt he would explode with anger, and she did not even look guilty. "Who gave ye the right to steal my voice to share with Textron? Did ye also save what I said during our lovemaking to prove how much joy your body brought me?"

Blythe narrowed her gaze on him. "That's really cold, MacKenzie. No, I didn't record our lovemaking. I only recorded what I needed as proof." She sat up, yanked the cover off them, and wrapped it around herself. Then she climbed from her bed. "I can't believe you're so bent out of shape about it."

"Mayhap ye're used to machines such as this, but to me 'tis like a stranger listening to something that should be private." He felt betrayed. Why?

Still clutching the cover to her, Blythe raked her fingers through her hair. "All right. I'm sorry if the recording upset you. What else can I say?"

Calm yourself. It doesna matter. He lied to himself. It mattered because he had let himself care for her and had forgotten that all *she* cared for was Ecstasy Incorporated. But he needed to regain his control; control was what had allowed him to survive for so many centuries when others had not.

Blythe watched the coldness settle into his gaze and shivered. Was this the same warm man she'd laughed with last night?

"I had forgotten that ye're here only for Ecstasy. 'Twas foolish of me to think it anything more. Ye may use my words so that ye dinna have to return to casperwyoming." Each word was a cold chip of ice.

She couldn't believe this was happening, and she didn't know why his anger was bringing her close to tears. "If I didn't have to use the latrine so badly, we'd have it out right now, vampire. Don't you dare leave before I get back, and you'd better not be asleep either."

Blythe didn't bother to dress, just wrapped the cover more tightly around herself and rushed from the room. With the whole herd of bright-eyed bittyfluffs running behind her, she raced to answer Mother Nature's call. She didn't even take the time for her usual curses aimed at the pitiful excuse for a toilet. Blythe didn't know when flush toilets were invented, but if she decided to stay . . . Whoa, where had that come from? She didn't have time now for deep, life-altering thoughts.

As she hurried back to her room with bittyfluffs in tow, she composed brilliant and biting sarcasm to fling at Darach's stubborn head. Okay, so she was being a little stubborn, too. Blythe refused to give him the satisfaction of knowing that she'd already decided to erase the recording, because with what she had on Textron, she wouldn't need to use Darach's words. She just hadn't gotten around to erasing them. He was so arrogant that he'd think she was doing it for him. Of course she was, but she'd eat dirt before telling him. If their friendship couldn't survive this bump in the road, then the whole journey didn't stand much of a chance.

Blythe flung wide the door to her room and opened her mouth to let him have it. She shut her mouth with a snap. What the . . . ? He was gone. His bed was gone, too, and Thrain with it. She peered into every corner just in case. Yep, it was gone.

She looked at the ceiling. No holes. If he thought she'd just meekly let him go, then he didn't know Blythe 56-2310 very well. Quickly she pulled on a dress, then rushed from her room, not bothering to close the door behind her.

Pure anger propelled her up the stairs to his room. She pounded on the door with both fists. "Come out and fight like a man, MacKenzie."

The door swung slowly open, and Darach stared wearily at her. "I'm not a man, so I canna fight like one."

She strode past him, trailing bittyfluffs behind her, and glanced around. Amazing. His bed rested in the middle of the room, and Thrain was still soundly asleep in it. "You said you couldn't move your bed back to your room."

"I lied." Darach shrugged. "Now say what ye must and leave. 'Tis past time I slept." He turned back toward some furs he'd piled in front of the hearth.

Blythe followed him. "Look, I know you're upset about what I did, but I promise you I didn't do it to deceive you. Ecstasy's company policy always demands some kind of hard proof that we completed the job, either a recording or signed affidavit. It's in the contracts clients sign. I thought you'd understand that."

She frowned. He probably didn't care about the legal stuff.

He turned and speared her with his hard gaze. "I signed no contract with Ecstasy. I didna ask ye to make me happy. And if I had signed your affidavit, I would now demand that ye destroy it, because I am no longer happy."

Darach was right, and she was wrong. Somehow knowing that made her even madder. She hated being wrong, but admitting it was the right thing to do. "Fine. So I was wrong." Was that gracious or what? "Here, I'll give you the recorder, and you can stomp on it." She started to remove the charm from around her neck.

He placed his hand over hers, and she drew in her breath at the potency of that simple touch.

"I dinna wish ye to destroy it, Blythe. Ye need it for your job, and I wouldna deny ye that." He rubbed the back of his neck with his hand. "I have ever been logical. It has been a source of pride with me. And my mind tells me that I'm foolish to fash myself over this recording, that I always knew your job must come before all else. Ye told me so." He offered her a smile that never reached his eyes. "But ye did your job too well. Ye taught me to listen to my emotions, and they dinna want to understand. They insist that what we shared was a caring that had nothing to do with Ecstasy. My emotions pay no attention to logic. I must have time to think about this."

"I . . ." What could she say? I care enough to be

thinking about not going back with Ganymede? What place could she have in Darach's life? She didn't really *know* much about his life when he wasn't on duty. They needed to have a long talk, but not now when emotions were running high on both sides.

"Ye need say nothing." Darach guided her toward the door. "I will protect my room today, so ye willna be able to enter." He stopped when they reached the door. "I would like ye to watch . . ." As though thinking better of what he'd been about to say, he shrugged. " 'Tis not important right now."

Blythe stepped into the hall, then turned to him. "We'll talk tonight." She wouldn't phrase it as a question, because that would give him a chance to say no.

He nodded, and she breathed a relieved sigh. At least he wasn't banishing her completely.

Before closing his door, he smiled. This time there was no anger in his smile, but there wasn't much of anything else either. Automatically she scanned his emotions. Nothing. The MacKenzie wall was up again.

"Mayhap ye'll keep the recording. Years from now ye can play it and remember this adventure while your Autotempregulator warms ye." He closed his door as the last bittyfluff made its escape.

The hell with her adventure. She'd remember *him*. Only him. Blythe rushed down the steps to her room before she disgraced herself by bawling in front of his closed door. Once in her room, she threw herself on her bed and did some heavy blinking and rapid breathing to force back the tears.

She hadn't closed her door quickly enough to keep all the bittyfluffs out, but she didn't even look to see where they were. Who cared?

Once she felt calm enough, she took off her dress, washed, and then dressed again. She peered at herself in her makeup mirror. Ach. Red-rimmed eyes and swollen eyelids. She'd better avoid both Textron and Sparkle today. She'd probably haul off and sock Textron just for the joy of it if he asked her what had happened. And Sparkle would probably try to solve Blythe's problem by suggesting she join the Sex-toy-of-the-month club.

As she walked down the tower steps, she tried to keep from tripping over the bittyfluffs. It would not bode well for her day if Ganymede found her broken body at the bottom of the stairs. But then, her day was already a bust. "Okay, guys. I'm going to take you outside so you can do your duty, then we'll see what we can scrounge up to feed you."

The bittyfluffs chittered their joy at hearing her voice.

"Oh, and let's try to keep a low profile. We have to avoid all servants. Hysterical servants are *not* a good thing. Hysterical servants might quit, and then who would cook our 'wondrous' meals?" She paused for thought. "You were introduced to Earth in 2295, so we probably don't want to meet up with a few of the guests who came from an earlier time. I know, I know. Your planet is very proud of your impact on the pet market. But these people?" She made a dismissive gesture. "They wouldn't appreciate you for the national treasures you are."

Once at the bottom of the steps, she slipped out to the courtyard. She was thankful that it was still so early. No one was up yet. Rubbing her arms to keep warm in the chill Scottish morning, she waited for the bittyfluffs to do their thing, then herded them back inside.

"Okay, here's the day's itinerary. Listen up." The bittyfluffs watched her intently. "Feed you. Feed me. Avoid everyone we can. Wait for night. Feed you again. Wait for night. Potty break for all of us. Wait for night. Feed me again." She frowned. "Night should be here by then. Make up with Darach. Have hot sex with Darach. And no, you're not invited to that. Discuss possibility of a future together. Celebrate wildly if answer is yes. Slit throat if answer is no." She stared down at her wide-eyed admirers. "How's that sound to you?"

The bittyfluffs chittered their happiness.

"Yeah, sounds good to me, too."

Chapter Fourteen

"Baby-sitting, Mede?" Sparkle looked down disdainfully from her perch atop the fireplace mantel. "Blythe sure saw you coming."

Ganymede stood beside the mantel, gazing across his room with a bemused expression. Furry pink bodies occupied every surface except the mantel. "Hey, she's a customer, and if you want to stay in business, you keep your customers happy. It's not like I'm stuck with them forever. Blythe said she'd get them on her way up to her room for the night." He turned to glance at the arrow slit. "It's almost dark now, so she should be here any minute."

"Uh-huh. Sure." Sparkle knew she was cynical, but sometimes she thought she understood life and people a lot better than Mede. "The little pink guys do have a wow factor, though. I mean, Blythe told you they were her greatest fear, and Darach was able to make them real. That kind of talent blows me away." She glanced at Mede's sulky expression. "What's your greatest fear, Mede?"

"I'm living it." He waded through the sea of bittyfluffs to slump onto his bed. "I lied to you, Sparkle. I hate being good. I have so much untapped potential for rottenness that I'll never realize. The Big Boss cut me off in mid-career, and it's like I can't get my heart into this goodness crap." A bittyfluff climbed onto his lap, and he absently stroked its pink fur.

Sparkle was touched in spite of herself. Leaping from the mantel, she tiptoed through the bittyfluffs, then jumped up beside Mede. She rubbed her head against his arm. "I hear you talking. What would happen if you eased back into your old life and did a few evil deeds? Nothing really bad, just a testing of the waters kind of thing?"

He shrugged. "Haven't a clue. The Big Boss might just get steamed enough to erase me."

Sparkle thought about that. "Not likely. He has a reputation for being pretty patient." She began to wash her face. "Personally, I don't get the point of all this patience stuff. If I were the Big Boss, I'd just squash anyone who didn't do things my way. That's just me, though."

Mede winced. "Bad versus good is a non-issue right now. I have other problems."

"No kidding." Sparkle felt sorry for Mede. What was his reward for being good? Nothing. Here Mede was working his tail off to do the right thing, and life kept kicking him in the teeth. No one would *ever* catch Sparkle Stardust doing a good deed. There was no payoff.

"All the servants have disappeared. Where the hel . . . Where in tarnation did they go?" He rubbed his eyes. "Dinner was a disaster. We all sat down to eat, and no food. Not only no food, but no cook and no one to serve the food. I couldn't even find anyone to yell at. We all had to cook our own meals."

Sparkle tried to look upbeat. "I'd rack that up in the positive column. I don't know where you got that cook, but I'd bet she moonlights as a consultant for the doggy cuisine industry. Besides, all your guests want to do is grab a bite and get back to their other interests." She offered him a pointed stare. "Thanks to yours truly, food is not their main focus right now." Except for Clara. Sparkle didn't like to fail, but she'd failed with that woman. All Clara seemed interested in was vampires, and the only resident vampire was already taken.

"What about my ghosts? Have they done *anything* besides have sex?" He reached for his last bottle of the pink stuff.

Sparkle shifted her gaze to the hearth. Maybe she was feeling a little bit guilty here. "Uh, no. They wanted to post a complaint, though. They went up to the battlements last night to express their . . . emotional commitment to each other, and discovered that Blythe and Darach had beat them to it. I feel their pain, because the battlements are their thing. They had to do their expressing in Clara's room. Lucky for them, she didn't use it last night." Which was a little weird since Clara hadn't hooked up with anyone.

Mede offered her a weak smile. "There's an upside to this. Things can't get any worse."

Dinner was over, such as it was, and Blythe was the only one still sitting at the table. She stared blankly into the hearth's fire, seeing only the end of her career at Ecstasy. It shouldn't have come as any surprise, because she'd been ready to blow when Textron had sat down next to her and demanded she show proof that she was working hard on the job.

She allowed herself a small smile. Darach would be proud of her when she told him. Blythe had simply turned to Textron and told him where he could stuff his job. Of course, he couldn't, because that place was too tight.

Her decision to leave Ecstasy hadn't been thought out and examined from every angle. It had simply evolved from where she was in her life. Since she no longer believed that she should stay because of her family's ties to the company, she could think about what was right for *her*. Ecstasy Inc. was about making other people happy, but it had never made *her* happy. Blythe could admit that now. Darach had given her the courage to shed her personal hair shirt, Ecstasy Inc., to pursue true happiness. He was right. Finding joy in her life would be the best way to honor her family.

Knowing she was finished with Ecstasy had been freeing. And the look on Textron's face had almost been the highlight of her whole trip. Almost. The real highlight should be awake by now and ready to talk.

Standing, Blythe stretched and started toward the steps leading to Ganymede's room. She'd pick up the bittyfluffs, then go to her room and freshen up before tackling her stubborn vampire.

She'd only taken a few steps when she heard a voice in her head.

"Blythe, come to Darach's room. I need ye."

She stood frozen. Not Darach's or Sparkle's voice. Then who . . . ?

" 'Tis Thrain. The women have taken Darach."

Fear paralyzed Blythe for the moment it took her to understand the horror of what Thrain had said, and then she was racing up the stairs to Darach's room.

By the time she reached the top of the tower, she was breathing hard and her heart was pounding out a terrified rhythm. Darach's door was wide open. He'd never leave it open like that.

Rushing into the room, she looked around, hoping against hope that Thrain was wrong. He wasn't. "What happened?" As she tried to get close to the bed, she slammed up against Darach's protective shield.

Loathing for the women filled Thrain's eyes. "They have found a way to make the bog myrtle into a powder. When they saw that ye were busy eating and wouldna interrupt them, they must have secured a small container of bog myrtle above the door, then moved far enough out of sight so that Darach wouldna sense them when he awoke. Darach removed the protection from across his entry, then opened the door to leave. He was going down to speak with ye. Opening the door caused the powder to fall. There were many of the women, and as soon as the bog myrtle made him helpless, they took him away quickly." Thrain slammed his fist against the headboard. "They would have taken me also, but Darach had protected the bed, so neither they nor their vile powder could reach me."

Blythe closed her eyes, trying to shut out the obvious conclusion. "That means you can't help Darach."

"I dinna have the power to dispel Darach's protection." The words seemed dragged from the depths of his despair. "I tried to speak to his mind, but he didna answer. He is either unable to answer my thoughts, or else he feels that speaking to me would only put others in danger."

"Then how can I help him?" There *had* to be a way. She needed to find a starting point, find someone who could help.

"Darach wouldna wish ye to put yourself in danger to save him. That is why I believe he might be refusing to speak with me. He knows I would tell ye what he said."

No. They couldn't have him. No one she loved would die again while she had breath in her body. *Loved?* The word transfixed her. Yes, she loved Darach MacKenzie, and she was damned well going to tell him so.

She turned to leave the room with Thrain's parting thought touching her. *"Be safe, Blythe."*

This wasn't about being safe. This was about saving the man she loved. And as she closed the door behind her, she hadn't a clue how she was going to do that. But she'd better start by getting the Freeze-frame.

As she was about to push her door open, Clara stumbled up the stairs shouting her name. Blythe didn't have time for whatever Clara wanted. She continued into her room with Clara trailing behind her.

"Blythe, I can help you find Darach." Clara tugged at her sleeve as Blythe slipped the Freeze-frame into her pocket.

Blythe spun to face her. "What do you know about Darach?"

"I really wanted to be in on a vampire hunt. It's what I've always dreamed about. But after Darach saved me last night, I couldn't finish it. So I hid last night and didn't come out until I knew they'd taken Darach away." Tears slipped down her cheeks, and she brushed them away with the back of her hand. "I know I should've come out today and warned somebody, but I was so afraid. They would've killed me if they thought I'd told someone."

Even trade, Clara. I might kill you for not *telling someone.* "What do you know?"

"Come up to the battlements so I can show you

where they are." She hurried to the door as Blythe flung on her cloak.

Once on the battlements, Clara pointed to a ring of fire visible not far from the castle. "They didn't go far because they had to carry him, and he's pretty big. Besides, they have to be finished by dawn. He's no good to them dead."

Blythe clenched her teeth to keep from shrieking at this woman. She made it sound as if Darach were just a disposable item to use, then throw away. "Anything else?"

Clara nodded. "They spent a lot of time planning this, because they didn't want to be interrupted once they'd captured such a powerful vampire. A chance like this might never come again."

"Get to the point." She stared at the ring of fire. How would she reach Darach?

"They chose a rocky spot, then cleared away everything that would burn. Ever since Darach arrived at the castle, they've been busy piling up lots of wood to form a circle, enough to keep the fire going till dawn. Now that they've lit it, no one can get in or out of the ring." Clara bit her lip. "When dawn comes and the fire burns down, they'll just walk away and leave him. As soon as they're gone, we can run in and bring him back to the castle." She looked hopeful.

"That'll be too late." Blythe closed her eyes. She couldn't stand the thought of him suffering. And more than the physical pain, he would hate feeling helpless.

To a man who valued control so highly, being bound would be the true torture. "Much too late." She opened her eyes. "Will you go with me now to help save him?"

Clara's eyes widened. "I can't, Blythe. There're twenty of them, and they're dangerous. They'd kill us. Besides, we couldn't get through the fire now anyway." She looked relieved that she'd thought of a logical excuse not to help Blythe.

"Right." Blythe didn't try to hide the contempt in her gaze. "Thanks for the info, but it would've done a lot more good if you'd said something sooner. Get out of my way."

Blythe pushed past Clara and ran down the steps. She tried to plan as she went, but fear for Darach was making mush of her brain. It would take too long to hunt down someone to help her. Besides, who in this castle would have the guts to face those women? Probably no one. So she'd be wasting precious time.

She could soak her heavy cloak in the loch, then try to beat out enough of the fire to clear a path into the ring. But from what she'd seen from the battlements, the flames would probably be too high for that to work. She had to try, though.

Once inside the ring? She didn't know. Her Freezeframe would get some of the women, but then the rest of them could rush her. And even if she could hold them off, Darach would probably be too weak to escape with her. A horse? Bringing a horse wouldn't do any good if she couldn't get Darach onto the horse.

Blythe was so busy trying to plan that she almost ran over Sparkle, who was standing at the foot of the steps.

"Whoa, girlfriend. You're going in the wrong direction. Turn around and head back to that sexy vampire." Sparkle peered up the steps. *"Have you seen my ghosts? If they're doing it on the battlements, I'm going to kick butt all the way down these stairs. It's time they did some work. No one has decent work ethics anymore. Hell, I'd even settle for indecent ones. The servants aren't working. The ghosts aren't working. The only one working is* moi. *I think—"*

"Shut up, Sparkle."

Sparkle blinked at her.

Probably no one had ever talked to Sparkle that way. "The sexy vampire's been kidnapped. Listen up." Blythe explained the details quickly, then took a deep breath. "I need your help to get him back."

Sparkle looked at her as though Blythe had suggested she never talk about sex again. "You want me to do something *good?"* She'd spoken aloud, proof that she was truly shocked.

"It wouldn't really be good. You'd be saving a vampire, an age-old symbol of darkness and evil. So actually, you'd be doing something bad." Would Sparkle buy into that reasoning?

Sparkle looked doubtful. "Yeah, but I know that Darach is pretty much a good guy, so I'd still be doing something good."

"Sorry. Forget I asked." Blythe sighed. "I guess it

would take a cosmic troublemaker with lots of courage to accept that kind of challenge." She started to go around Sparkle.

"Wait." Sparkle's tail whipped back and forth, evidence of some kind of inner conflict.

Blythe felt a glimmer of hope. "Think about all your wasted effort. You went the extra mile to bring Darach and me together, two completely incompatible people—a vampire and the happiness queen of Casper, Wyoming—and now a bunch of crazy women will ruin what would've been a triumph of wicked meddling." She shook her head. "Too bad."

"They'll kill him?" Sparkle flattened her ears, and her tail whipped back and forth in a frenzy.

"Yes." Just saying the word made Blythe want to scream. "I love him, and they're not going to kill someone I love." This was pitiful. She was pouring out her heart to a self-proclaimed it's-all-about-me . . . woman. Strange, but for the first time, she was looking beyond the cute cat persona and flip sarcasm to accept Sparkle's womanhood.

"Give me a sec. I can justify this." Sparkle padded beside her as Blythe strode to the great-hall door and pulled it open. She followed Blythe out into the courtyard. "The sensual world would suffer a huge hit if Darach died, and it's my duty to protect all that's sensual. How am I doing?"

Blythe stopped to stare at Sparkle. Was she actually

considering helping? "You're doing great." *Please let me say all the right words.*

"And foiling those bitches who think they're so bad would really up my reputation as one cosmic troublemaker that no one messes with." She twitched her whiskers. "I like the sound of that."

"So will you help?" Blythe held her breath.

Sparkle's eyes looked troubled. "Who am I kidding? The bottom line is that I'd be doing a good deed, and I've never set out to do anything good in my whole existence. Look what I did here. I brought couples together who would either annoy Mede, or in the case of Textron and Sandy, each other. I've always been about sex and trouble."

Blythe exhaled sharply and turned from Sparkle. She walked toward the fire and didn't even glance back at the cat. She should've known that getting Sparkle's help was too much to hope for.

Blythe decided to skip the cloak soaking, because she'd already wasted too much time, and a heavy, wet cloak would only slow her down. She didn't even realize that Sparkle was still following her until the cat spoke. "Okay, okay, I'll help."

Thank you! "Why did you change your mind?" Blythe didn't look down at Sparkle.

"What's your plan? I don't have the kind of power Mede has, so I don't know how much help I'll be." Sparkle was good at non-answers.

But Blythe wasn't going to let her get away with it.

"What made you do a good deed, Sparkle? Why're you helping Darach?"

Sparkle's answer was a string of low mumbles and hisses.

"I can't *hear* you."

Sparkle glared at her. "Fine. So I like Darach. But if you ever tell anyone I did something good of my own free will, I'll deny it. Then I'll get even."

Blythe smiled down at her. Funny that she'd never tried to scan Sparkle's emotions. Subconsciously, she must have figured she knew exactly what feelings she'd find. That would teach her not to make assumptions based only on appearances and what people said. If someone had told her ahead of time that Sparkle would be the one to put herself on the line for Darach, she would've laughed out loud.

"My lips are sealed. It might help if you could change into a larger form." Like a fully armed, ten-foot Maedern warrior.

"Uh-uh. Changing is too hard and takes too long. We don't have that kind of time." Sparkle sniffed at the scent of burning wood. "I can't believe I'm going to do something good."

Blythe didn't have time to discuss this one good blot on Sparkle's otherwise bad reputation. They were close to the fire.

"Can you get me through that fire?" Blythe couldn't see what was happening behind the high flames, but she could hear what sounded like angry voices.

"I don't know." Sparkle stared at the flames. "I've never tried my power on something like this." She glanced at Blythe. "Will you hang in there with me?"

Blythe didn't even have to think about her answer. "I'll do whatever it takes to free Darach. If it's a choice between staying here while he dies or taking a chance on your power, I'll trust your power every time."

"Okay, here's the deal. I want you to pick me up and hold me over your head, because I don't have a clue how big a path I can make or how long I can keep it open. So we need to keep together until we pass the fire line." She eyed the flames. "Once we get to the other side, I'll have to stay by the fire and try to keep the path open for our escape." Sparkle shifted her gaze to Blythe. "I won't be able to help you, but I promise I won't run away. I'll be waiting for you and Darach with some kind of fire-free escape outta here."

You're a good person, Sparkle Stardust. Words that Blythe would never dare say aloud for fear of insulting Sparkle. So she settled for, "Thanks. We'll remember you."

Swallowing the rock that seemed to have lodged in her throat, Blythe picked Sparkle up, then raised the cat high above her head.

She walked toward the flames.

Blythe didn't know if a path would open for them, if she'd be able to save Darach, or if she'd even be able to save herself. But if she survived tonight, she'd know one thing. She had walked through hell to save the man she loved.

Heat beat against Blythe, and her arms shook with the effort of holding Sparkle up.

"Stop shaking me. I can't concentrate." Sparkle sounded nervous.

Great. Nervous did *not* make Blythe feel secure. "I'm trying, but you're heavy."

"I knew my butt was too big."

"Stop thinking about your butt and concentrate." The heat was unbearable, searing every inch of exposed skin and sucking the air from her lungs.

Blythe fixed her gaze on the flames, deliberately disconnecting her survival instinct. And just as she could see shapes in the big puffy clouds on a summer day, she could see faces in the leaping flames. Mandor laughing as he taught her how to steer her glide ride when she was ten. Dad grinning with pride when she won a blue ribbon at a local horse show. And Mom smiling gently as she calmed Blythe after pulling her from the container of dreaded bittyfluffs. They all smiled at her, loved her, and somehow she felt sure they were here for her now.

Unconditional love. They'd always given her that. Blythe's memories of that love strengthened her and gave her the courage to go forward. *For love.*

Without warning, the fire parted. The suddenness made Blythe stumble. Afraid that it would close again,

Blythe ran through the opening, still holding Sparkle above her head.

"Whoa. Put me down. I feel seasick."

Blythe put Sparkle on the ground, and started to turn away.

"Don't worry, I'll wait for you here. When I do a good deed, I do it right." Sparkle sat and wrapped her tail around herself. "I'd try to contact Mede to help us, but he's afraid the Big Boss will zap him if he hurts a human, and he'd definitely have to hurt some humans here. He wouldn't be much help." She sounded unhappy with the thought. Distractedly she glanced at her tail. "Is my tail singed? It feels singed."

"Your tail is fine." Drawing in a deep breath of cool air, Blythe walked toward the large group of women gathered around the center of the clearing.

They were so busy arguing that Blythe was in their midst before any of them noticed. As the women turned to confront her, she marveled at how beautiful the face of evil could be. Every one of the women had a face and figure that would ensure any man's undivided attention. And according to Darach, they were wealthy and powerful, too.

The woman who stepped forward to challenge her had long dark hair and gray eyes that glittered with banked emotion. They were the eyes of a huntress—a frustrated huntress, because as Blythe scanned her feelings, the woman's impatient anger washed over Blythe. And just beneath her surface emotions flowed a molten river of ugly greed: bitter and horrifying. Blythe shivered.

"How did you get through the fire?" Even as the woman spoke, she glanced past Blythe to Sparkle and the fire-free path she guarded. The woman'e eyes widened. "You need not answer. I see, but I do not understand."

Blythe gave the woman credit for not backing away from her, but she supposed that women with the nerve to practice the vicious cruelty these women did, would need a certain kind of perverted courage.

"Why are you here? Do you think to save your lover?" The woman's smile was cold and pitiless.

Blythe widened her eyes and hoped she looked sufficiently innocent. "Of course not. Do I look stupid?" Like, yeah. "Clara told me what you guys were planning, and it sounded like fun. I've been doing it with the vampire for thrills, but it looks like you've got a kinky twist on the sex thing. I was hoping to join in." Blythe pasted a hopeful look on her face. She'd be lucky if she got through this whole thing without throwing up.

A woman behind Blythe spoke up. "What about the cat? It's keeping the path open with magic. If you truly wish to take part, make the cat close the path. We want no others joining us." The woman sounded as though a magic cat was nothing to get excited about.

Of course, women who believed that having sex with

a vampire would make them immortal wouldn't even blink at a magic cat.

"You're joking, right?" It was getting hard to maintain a happy face. "No way am I cutting off my escape route. I don't trust you, ladies. So the cat keeps the path open."

They all nodded as though her distrust made perfect sense. Nice, friendly group.

"You and the others in the castle speak strangely." The first woman's suspicions seemed to have eased, and now she was merely curious.

And you act strangely. "We come from far distant lands." Blythe figured she'd better leave it at that. There had to be just so much weirdness these women could accept. Then again, maybe not.

The woman studied Blythe with a calculating stare. "The vampire is not cooperating. Since you have already enjoyed his body, you might be able to offer some suggestions." She nodded, then smiled. "Yes, I think your arrival shows that the fates favor us. If you are able to help us tonight, we will allow you to join us." Her expression suggested that not many were lucky enough to receive that kind of invite.

Blythe was almost ready to scream with her need to reach Darach, to see what they'd done to him. But the mob gathered around her cut off her view of the clearing's center.

"Everyone was arguing when I got here. How can the vampire not be cooperating? From what Clara said, I guessed that he didn't have much choice in the matter. I thought that you'd have everything under control." *Please let me see Darach.*

The woman's expression turned vicious. "Five of us have mounted him, but he refuses to give us his seed. No matter what we do, he defies us. If you can't help, we will hurt him until he cooperates or dies. No vampire has been able to withstand us as long as he has." Her gaze turned almost maniacal. "But he is also the most powerful vampire we have ever captured, and therefore the most valuable to us. He could truly make us immortal. Can you destroy his control?"

Hurt him? Rage coursed through Blythe, giving her the courage to do whatever it took to steal their victim from them. She almost gagged on the words she had to say. "I know all the places to touch and stroke to bring him to the peak of desire. He'll come for me. And once I've broken his defiance, you can use him."

The woman nodded. "It sounds logical."

I'm glad someone thinks it's logical. "Aren't you going to tell me your names? If we're going to work together, I'd like to know what to call you." Blythe offered her best fake friendly smile. She wanted their names so she could personally hunt each one down to make sure none of them ever again enjoyed a moment of happiness.

The woman gave her a sly grin in return. "We don't share real names. Therefore, if one of us is taken, she cannot betray the others. You may call me Margaret."

"Hey, I love it. Phony names. You can call me Vi." Short for Vengeance Inc. What a great idea for a new company. From what she could see of this time, she could make a fortune with a company like that. And she'd start with these women.

"So what about a group name? Something powerful to throw fear into vampires everywhere. I think Immortal Huntresses has a certain panache." *Try Bitches from Hell.*

Margaret shook her head. "We use nothing that could identify us."

"Hey, it's your call, but I think every team needs a name to pull it together. It bonds people and affirms their common purpose." It would also help anyone tracking the group to find and destroy its members, but it seemed Margaret already knew that.

"Tell me what you've done to the vampire so far." She had to know, but at the same time she didn't want to hear it, didn't want to feel the sick rage coursing through her.

Margaret nodded and sighed. "We had to draw some of his blood to weaken him once the bog myrtle wore off or else he could have used his power to free himself. Then when he defied us, we disciplined him in hopes that the pain would make him comply. All has failed."

Through a growing haze of fury, Blythe recognized that Margaret was capable of almost anything.

"We did all that we had done with the others. While the bog myrtle still held him in its grip, we forced him to drink blood mixed with opium, thorn apple, and various potent herbs. The man who made the potion swore that it would never fail. It would produce a massive erection and uncontrollable sexual hunger. The vampire's erection is indeed huge, but he refuses to give in to the sexual hunger."

Blythe knew Darach's power to control his emotions and his body. She couldn't even think about the pain he was enduring. If she didn't say something fast, she'd probably launch herself at Margaret and do some serious facial damage. That wouldn't help Darach, but it would sure give Blythe a lot of satisfaction. *It would also blow away any chance you have of rescuing him.*

"Maybe you need to go back to that man and get a new potion." She started pushing her way through the women.

"We can't. We killed him as soon as we had it. There was always a chance he might speak of us to someone." Margaret's tone said that the man's death was of no importance. "I hope we did not weaken the vampire so much that he cannot perform."

Blythe's fear for Darach was almost enough to bring her to her knees. Even before these animals had bled him, Darach's strength had been diminished because of the blood he'd given Thrain. Would he have enough strength to leave here under his own power?

She had to see him *now*.

There must have been something scary in her expression, because the crowd of women parted in front of her. She got her first look at Darach.

And knew that if she had a lethal weapon in her hand, she would kill all of these soulless predators without even a twinge of conscience.

Chapter Fifteen

They had stretched Darach naked on an X-shaped platform that was about knee high, then bound him to it. His wrists and ankles were bloody from his struggle to free himself.

The women hadn't stopped there. They'd cut deep gashes in his torso and thighs. The bloody ground around the platform was a testament to their effectiveness in weakening him.

The horror they'd visited on his body continued. Someone had whipped him. Bloody welts crisscrossed his chest and stomach. She assumed this was punishment for his refusal to service them.

They hadn't bloodied his erection. Of course, they wouldn't want to damage the instrument of their immortality. But whatever they had forced him to drink had made him so large and hard that Blythe had no idea how he had held back his orgasm while each of the five women rode him.

Blythe looked around the circle of women until she found the one holding a whip. She might not be able to defeat all twenty of them, but Blythe promised herself that if she went down tonight, she'd take this woman with her.

Blythe closed her eyes for a moment. Nothing in her safe world had prepared her for this kind of savagery or the searing hatred flooding her body, her soul. But she had to push aside her horror and concentrate only on helping Darach.

She glanced at the women crowding close to her. "Back off. I can't do this right with you breathing down my neck."

The women seemed to think this was a reasonable request, because they backed away. They could still see what she did, but Blythe knew that with the fire's loud crackling, they were too far away to hear anything she said to Darach.

Drawing in a deep breath, she walked toward him. Darach was in vampire form, his lips drawn back to expose his sharp canines, and his glittering gaze was fixed on the women. Fear shivered down Blythe's spine. When he finally looked at her, would it be with deadly rage and loathing?

He shifted his gaze to her. What was he thinking? Did he believe that she'd betrayed him? She knew that with his sensitive hearing he would've heard everything she'd said to Margaret. And after his reaction to the recording she'd made for Ecstasy, he might have difficulty trusting her now.

Blythe held his gaze as she drew closer, and for once she wished that he would enter her thoughts so he'd know how she truly felt. He had shown the women his hatred, but he showed her nothing. His face was a mask—expressionless, cold.

Finally, she stood looking down at him. His biceps and shoulder muscles bulged with the strain of his spread arms pulled tight by the ropes at his wrists. Chest and stomach muscles also showed the strain, and Blythe had to look away from the bloody evidence of what they'd done to him. Her gaze slid down to his thighs, spread in obscene invitation to any who wanted to use him. Ropes at his ankles kept his legs apart, exposing him in a way that mocked his helplessness, that said he was nothing more than a virile animal meant to serve them. They offered him no human respect, no pity. And Blythe promised herself that when the time came, she would offer them none either.

She breathed a silent prayer to whatever god watched over vampires and the women who loved them. Darach had to trust her. Without his trust, she didn't stand a chance of getting them out of here alive.

"Don't you think you've lain around here doing nothing long enough, vampire? How about we get our butts back to the castle?" She tried to smile at him, but it didn't quite come off.

"Leave, Blythe. Ye canna free me. If ye try, they'll kill ye. Tell them ye've changed your mind and wish to go back to the castle." Even though his voice gave no hint of his feelings, emotion shone in his eyes.

"Uh-uh. Can't do that for you. Sparkle and I are sort of committed to this rescue thing." Blythe felt almost limp with relief that he hadn't bought into the lies she'd told Margaret.

"I wouldna have thought Sparkle would put herself in danger for another." He speared Blythe with a hard stare. "Ye'll take Sparkle and leave as I told ye to."

"You never know about people until the chips are down. And no, we're not leaving." She tapped him on his chest. "And in case you haven't noticed, you can't make us leave."

Suddenly the mask was gone, as though he could no longer maintain his usual rigid control over his emotions. Fear flooded his eyes. "I have accepted my own death. No matter what they do, they will get nothing from me this night. And when the dawn comes, my life will end. But I canna watch *ye* die, Blythe. Dinna ask it of me." He made no effort to hide the desperation in his voice.

"Then help me, Darach, because no matter what happens, we leave here together." She held his gaze as she lifted the Ecstasy charm from around her neck, dropped it to the ground, then ground it beneath her heel. "That's what's left of my career. I'm leaving it here to rot. But I won't be leaving you here. Count on it."

His eyes widened, and Blythe figured she'd finally gotten through to him. "Are you ready to listen to my plan?"

"I willna see ye die."

"I'll take that as a yes." She reached down and touched his erection. He winced. "This must be painful by now. They have a lot to answer for." Blythe pushed the anger away. Saving him was all that mattered. "How weak are you?"

"I wouldna be able to walk even if I could release my bonds. Loss of blood and the vile drink they forced on me have taken all of my power. I canna even enter your mind." Darach's gaze riveted her. "Ye canna save me. I dinna know why ye try."

Sure you do. Think about it, vampire. "Here's what we're going to do. We'll make love, and while that's happening you can feed from me. Once you're strong enough to remove the ropes, I'll try to hold the women off with my Freeze-frame while we escape. Sparkle will close the ring of fire as soon as we're out of it."

"No!" His shout of denial was loud enough to make the women murmur their excitement.

They'd be murmuring a different tune if they knew what he was objecting to.

"I knew you'd love it." Reaching beneath her dress, she slipped off her panties.

"Ye dinna understand." Darach fought his bonds, then lay still. And Blythe knew he was gathering his control, the only thing he had left to fight with. "I love ye, Blythe. My love combined with my great need would prove too strong for me. Once I started to feed, I wouldna be able to stop. Would ye have me die, knowing that I destroyed ye?"

I love ye. Not even the threat of death could dampen her wild spurt of joy. At this moment, she could defeat a thousand evil wackos because Darach loved her.

She placed her finger over his lips. "You'll stop *because* you love me. I believe in you, Darach MacKenzie, and nothing you say will change my mind."

Blythe watched his eyes and saw the exact moment he accepted what he couldn't change. "I will open my emotions to ye so that ye may use your power if I lose control." He clenched his fists, and she knew he was gathering the remains of that great control around him.

The impatient muttering of the crowd reached Blythe, and she knew they wouldn't wait much longer. She dropped her cloak to the ground; then, lifting her dress, she straddled his hips.

" 'Twould be safer if ye did this without truly mounting me. Your gown will cover all, and none need know. 'Twill be easier for me to control my feeding if I dinna enter ye."

"*Mounting?* I mount a horse. I make love to you. Don't try to depersonalize this. We're going to make hot, exciting love right here, because I know that if you don't lose control you'll never bite me." Blythe leaned over him, her hair trailing across his bare stomach and chest. Pushing aside damp strands of his hair, she whispered in his ear. "I didn't ever think these words would come out of my mouth." She nipped his earlobe. "Bite me, vampire."

She placed her hand over his heart and felt its wild pounding as her words shuddered through him. He lifted his lips away from his fangs in a silent snarl.

"I love it when you snarl at me." She straightened. He probably thought she was a cruel bitch, but she understood how weak he was. He had to have her blood, and he would take it only if she could push him to an orgasm. Only then would he lose his damned control.

The bottom line? She would have to seduce him.

"I willna make it easy." His narrowed gaze promised he'd fight her every inch of the way.

"You're already making it hard." She reached under her dress to run the tip of her finger around the head of his erection. "Sorry, I couldn't resist that." Her voice sounded a little breathless.

Then, miracle of miracles, the corners of his mouth lifted in the beginning of a smile. "I must not smile overmuch because yon creatures would grow suspicious, but ye're the only woman who could make me smile in the midst of such danger." His smile faded. "And such fear." He looked away from her. "Ye never asked me what my greatest fear was, a fear such as ye had for the bittyfluffs."

"I didn't ask because I didn't think you had one." Blythe couldn't conceive of this strong man fearing anything the way she had feared the bittyfluffs.

"But I do, Blythe." He met her gaze again. "I have always feared being bound and helpless. Other than my fear for ye, 'tis my greatest horror. The fear doesna reason, it simply exists. I have never told this to another."

"Then we'll have to do something about setting you free." Darach had just given her a gift worth more than all the promotions she could have ever earned from Ecstasy. "Too bad I didn't bring my copy of the best-selling how-to manual, *A Thousand Ways to Seduce a Vampire*. Guess I'll have to bumble along on my own."

He rewarded her with another twitch of his lips. "When I first met ye, I wished to know what it felt like to have your hair slide across my bared body. I didna think ye would grant my wish in this way."

"You'll live to have a lot more wishes granted." Time for some serious seducing. The women wouldn't wait forever.

Blythe lowered herself until she could feel the head of his erection prodding between her spread thighs. The urge to settle onto him and feel all that male sex stretching her wide, filling her, was an almost unbearable temptation. She resisted.

Leaning forward, she purposely trailed her hair across his body and watched his muscles ripple in response before covering his mouth with hers. He allowed her to be the aggressor, probably hoarding his almighty control.

Blythe slid her tongue across his bottom lip, nipping and teasing until, with a groan of surrender, he opened his mouth to her. She took full advantage, exploring all his heat and need, tracing the shape and texture of his tongue with demanding strokes, and indulging her fascination with his two most dangerous teeth.

When she finally released his lips, she kissed a path across his jaw and down the side of his neck. She paused at the base of his throat and slowly, lingeringly slid her tongue across the spot where his pulse beat a frantic rhythm. "Your heart is still beating strong. We have to make sure you escape tonight, otherwise your heart will die with you. And your heart belongs to me, Darach. You don't mess with my property." She knew her voice was thick with growing need. The heat of his skin beneath her lips, the male taste of him, were taking their toll. But she wasn't finished just yet.

He moved his head back and forth restlessly. His low moan told Blythe that her seduction was gaining momentum.

She'd originally thought she could simply remain straddling his hips until she was ready to settle onto his erection. But she'd have to change her plans. He was going to resist allowing himself to climax for fear of losing control and killing her. She'd have to drive him into such a sexual frenzy that he lost his control. Blythe only hoped she was up to the sexual frenzy challenge.

She slid off of his erection and changed position. Standing between his spread legs, she could see the damp proof of her own excitement on the head of his arousal.

He watched her out of eyes hot with his growing desire. "Ye plan to torture me further?"

"Of course. You doubted?" Leaning over, she allowed her hair to slide across his erection.

He shuddered, and she could almost see him tensing himself to resist. "Dinna go further. Ye have no idea what ye'll unleash on yourself."

"Promises, promises." She cupped him in her palms, but did nothing more. "I'm not going to touch you with my mouth, Darach. The mob of crazies over there would enjoy it too much."

She could see the tension leave him. He thought he'd won.

"Instead, I'm going to tell you all the things I intend to do to your body once we're out of here." She rubbed a rhythmic pattern with her thumbs across the tightly stretched skin of his sacs.

"We'll have hours and hours of foreplay." She thought about that. "Okay, so we'll have minutes and minutes of foreplay."

"I dinna think—"

"Deep thought is not necessary here, MacKenzie." She watched his hips lift slightly in response to what she was doing with her thumbs. "You'll lie down on my relaxation mat in front of your hearth, and I'll slowly massage heated oil into every inch of your naked body: your inner thighs, your buttocks, your chest and stomach. I'll warm my hands, then spread the oil over your sacs like this." She slid her fingers around his sacs and gently squeezed.

He groaned in response and raised his hips in a silent plea.

"I'll smooth my fingers up and down your erection and enjoy the warm glide of the oil making you slick and ready. Then I'll rub all that gleaming oil over the head of—"

His low growl warned her that she'd probably gone far enough. Good thing too, because her body was busily clenching, and the moisture between her thighs was a surefire signal that she was way beyond ready.

Once more she straddled his hips, lowering herself until his head nudged her open. She bit her lip to keep from screaming and locked her legs in place to keep from slamming down on his erection.

When she raised her gaze to Darach's face, she couldn't control her swift intake of breath. His lips were curled back from his sharp canines; his eyes were feral and heated with sexual hunger.

"Ye shouldna have done this, Blythe."

His voice was still that of the man she loved, but everything else radiated animal heat.

"How long should I wait before trying to stop you?"

He didn't pretend to misunderstand. "When ye start to feel dizzy, ye must stop me. If I willna stop, ye must use your Freeze-frame on me. Dinna hesitate, because once ye grow weak from loss of blood, 'twill mean I've taken too much from ye. We will both be doomed."

Blythe nodded as she slowly started to lower herself onto him.

"Look at me." His guttural command demanded her attention.

She met his gaze.

"No matter what happens, know that I have never loved anyone as much as I love ye, woman from another time."

Blythe nodded. *Do not throw yourself on top of him and cry*. She wouldn't say "I love you." Not now. But soon, when life and death hung in the balance. At that moment, those three small words could tip the balance toward life.

Around her she could hear the voices of the women urging her on. Like a pack of hyenas, they waited for her to finish so that they could take what was left. *Not this time, you bitches.*

She settled smoothly onto his sex, feeling her body stretch to accept his size, and whimpering at the incredible sensation of the man she loved filling her. Blythe waited until she knew she couldn't wait another second, then lifted herself from him, only to lower herself again. She gloried in the sensation of his sex sliding out of her only to fill her once again.

Her tempo quickened, her breathing came in quick gasps, and her heart pounded faster and faster. She could feel Darach trying to lift himself to meet her, but he was too weak and the ropes didn't allow for much movement.

Blythe had to pick exactly the right moment. She had to be the one in control tonight. Gritting her teeth, she forced back her building orgasm. Her body, deprived of what it wanted, *needed,* continued to clench around him, and the heaviness low in her belly continued to grow with wanting.

She felt him shudder as he uttered a harsh cry of denial. His orgasm was only seconds away.

Leaning forward, she allowed her hair to form a curtain around their faces. Lifting his head until his lips touched her throat where blood flowed strong beneath her skin, she spoke quietly to him. "Drink from me, vampire. Share the life that flows through me." She closed her eyes. "Do it *now.*"

His lips moved against her throat, and for a moment she thought he'd still resist. Then she felt the slide of his fangs against her neck and the sudden shock of penetration.

Blythe had no time to think if there'd been pain, because the sexual sensations flooding her washed away all thought. *This* was the supreme erotic experience. His sex was buried deep inside her while she shared her life's essence with every beat of her heart.

Unspeakable pleasure sizzled and burned through her body. Nothing would stop her climax now. With a wild cry of fulfillment, her muscles clenched around him as if she could squeeze every last moment of ecstasy from him.

Spasm after spasm rocked her, and as if from a distance she heard his cry join hers. She felt his release deep inside her.

As she tried to slow her breathing, Blythe could only think of their love tonight as a circle of giving. Darach and she had truly put their lives in each other's hands.

When the first wave of dizziness hit her, she was still wrapped up in the afterglow of love. The second wave made her numb with fear.

With hands that shook, she ran her fingers through his hair. "You've had enough. Stop, Darach."

He didn't respond. She couldn't say that he hadn't warned her. She tried to push his head away, but his returning strength made it impossible. If she didn't stop him now, they would both be dead.

Blythe played her ace. "I love you." She whispered her three-word message and felt a slight lightening of pressure against her skin. "Stop, Darach." She continued to stroke his hair. "When you learn to fly in a hundred years, I want to fly with you. Seems to me we talked about what it would be like to make love in midair. I want to find out. And when you look in that mirror and see your face for the first time, I want you to see my face beside yours." The dizziness was growing worse and she closed her eyes. "Let me go. Please, Darach."

Suddenly the pressure on her neck was gone. She

pushed herself away from him with arms that shook. Touching her neck with shaking fingers, she found no blood, no puncture wounds. "How did you do that?"

Darach didn't answer her question. "Ye said ye loved me." He gazed at her with eyes wide and disbelieving.

"You noticed." She offered him a quivery smile.

"We'll speak more of this loving once we've returned to the castle."

Blythe's relief was soul deep. Once again he sounded like her in-control lover. She climbed off of him, then stood nervously by his side. "Can you get rid of the ropes?"

"Aye, but I dinna have the strength to do more. I am still weak." His gaze touched her with warmth and . . . love. "I have never known a woman as brave as ye were this night."

Blythe didn't have a chance to answer.

The women were closing in on them. "He gave you his seed, didn't he? I couldn't tell because your gown was covering his organ."

Darach lifted his lips in a snarl as the woman named Margaret talked to Blythe. Every protective instinct passed down through his clan demanded he keep these creatures away from the woman he loved.

In one motion, he freed his arms and legs, but when he stood, his legs felt as though they wouldn't support him. Darach clenched his teeth and moved toward the women. He hoped they didn't notice his unsteady gait.

Startled, they fell back.

Blythe quickly pulled out her Freeze-frame. "Fun's over, ladies. Guess your immortality will have to wait for another night, because Darach and I are leaving here together."

He kept his hand on Blythe's shoulder as he guided her around the women and toward the opening in the fire where Sparkle waited. When he passed the spot where they had flung his clothing, he scooped up his shirt and pulled it over his head. He winced as the material scraped over the cuts on his body.

They almost made it.

"Don't let the vampire get away!" Margaret pulled a knife from her cloak. "They only have one weapon, and the vampire is still too weak to hurt us. See how he walks?"

Suddenly all twenty women charged toward them, shouting and waving knives. Some paused to pick up rocks.

Blythe aimed the Freeze-frame and fired. She stopped four women before Darach grabbed her arm and pulled her through the break in the fire. Sparkle scampered through behind them.

"Run!" Darach had strength for only the one word as he clasped Blythe's hand and tried to flee. Freyja help him, for he had never felt this weak in his life. "Ye and Sparkle must leave me and return to the castle, Blythe. I will only hold ye back."

"You're joking, right? I have a lot of effort invested

in your life, and I protect my investments." She turned around to glance behind her. "Sparkle!"

Darach turned to follow her gaze. He had believed that Sparkle was with them. She was not. She still stood by the fire.

"What're you doing?" Blythe's cry was a wail of terror.

"I'm trying to close the frickin' fire path. But I can't concentrate. Someone tell those women to shut up so that I can do some focusing here." Darach widened his eyes. Sparkle must be truly upset if she had forgotten to speak to their minds.

The women had heard Sparkle also. A cat that talked made even them pause for a moment. They stood just inside the ring of fire muttering among themselves and casting wary glances at Sparkle. Some turned back to stare at the four women who stood frozen in place by the Freeze-frame.

Darach knew these things would not stop them for long. The women were mad with their obsession, and their pursuit of him would only end with his recapture or their deaths.

"Run, Sparkle!" Blythe's shout rose above the crackling fire and muttering women.

Sparkle looked at the women and made her choice. She ran, coming toward Darach and Blythe in great flying leaps.

Her flight seemed to free the women from their indecision. With wild shouts, they poured through the opening in the fire. They flung knives and heaved stones as they came. Sparkle was the only one within their range, and suddenly she screamed and went down. Almost immediately she staggered to her feet and tried to continue running, but her limping gait wouldn't keep her in front of the mob long.

Darach's training as a warrior took over. His clan never left fellow warriors behind. And even though Sparkle did not look like one, she was a fellow warrior in every sense of the word.

He ran to Sparkle, scooped her into his arms, then stumbled back to where Blythe stood firing her Freeze-frame at the women. She managed to hit a few more, but nervousness was affecting her aim.

After only a few strides, Darach knew they would not make it. He was not the only one weakened by loss of blood. Blythe looked pale, and she was breathing hard as she tried to run. The women were gaining on them. He must plead for help from one he had hoped never to need.

He bent his head to where Sparkle crouched in his arms. "Ye must call Ganymede. I canna reach his mind, but ye can. If he does not help us, we will die."

Sparkle stared up at him with frightened orange eyes, and for the first time since Darach had met her, she had no words.

She turned her gaze toward the castle, and Darach knew she spoke to Ganymede.

* * *

Ganymede raged through the castle with the bittyfluffs trailing behind him. Could anything else go wrong? Everyone was disappearing. First all the servants had gone, and now Darach, Blythe, and Sparkle had disappeared. What the heck was going on?

Sparkle. He hadn't formed many friendships in his thousands of years, and he liked it that way. Attachments to other living beings slowed you down, made you less effective. But Sparkle was different. She'd wormed her way into his . . . heart? Nope, no heart. She'd wormed her way into his affections.

As he charged up to the battlements to see if he could spot her somewhere around the outside of the castle, a strange emotion touched him.

Fear. *True* fear. He'd experienced many emotions in his existence, but fear wasn't one of them. The most powerful cosmic troublemaker in the universe had nothing to fear. Except the Big Boss. But even when the Big Boss had handed down his thou-shalt-be-good edict, Ganymede hadn't been really afraid. Just frustrated.

Now he was afraid. He looked into the darkness, searching for her. Darkness had no power to keep him from seeing what he needed to see.

Suddenly her voice touched his mind. It was frightened and quivery, but still her voice. *"There're some crazy women chasing us, Mede. One of them threw a rock at me, and I think she broke my leg. Darach came back to save me, but the women are gaining on us.*

They hurt Darach, and he's too weak to save us. Help!"

A familiar coldness settled over Ganymede. For thousands of years he'd laid waste to the universe and felt no regrets. The Big Boss had shut him down, but the old Ganymede still waited patiently, or *not* so patiently, just below all that goodness and light. Some bitch had hurt Sparkle. She would pay for it, and to hell with goodness and light.

"Ask Darach what these women fear the most." As he spoke to Sparkle, he searched the darkness for her. When he finally found her, what he saw filled him with fury such as he hadn't felt in centuries. Hatred and the need for violence rose in a red haze that shook the whole castle with its power. The bittyfluffs scurried away from him, chittering in terror.

Then he smiled. No one in the castle would recognize that smile. No longer was he the bluff and bumbling lord of the castle. He was once again Ganymede, the lord of chaos, and now the dispenser of vengeance. Nothing could save those women.

"This sounds weird to me, Mede, but here's what both Darach and Blythe say you should do."

Ganymede listened, nodded, then focused his immense power on the women who dared to hurt Sparkle.

Darach still struggled forward with Sparkle held tight against his body and Blythe's hand clasped in his. If Ganymede didn't do something fast, Darach would have to make a stand against the women.

Blythe's weapon had refused to fire the last few times she tried it, and she had mumbled something about cheap off-planet products. The women were now almost close enough to do damage with their knives and stones. But they would have to go through him to reach Blythe and Sparkle.

A knife flew past his head and buried itself in a nearby tree. It was time to make a stand. He would hand Sparkle to Blythe and face the women. They wanted him; no one else mattered to them. Mayhap while he struggled, Blythe could make her escape. Surely she would realize that she must run, not only to save her own life, but Sparkle's as well.

Stopping, he shoved Sparkle into Blythe's arms. "Run."

"I won't leave you." Her eyes were wide with fear.

"Would ye condemn Sparkle to death as well as yourself? If ye stay, three will die instead of only one."

The argument got no further, because suddenly a startling flash of light enveloped the advancing women. Darach threw his arm across his eyes to keep from being blinded. Then as quickly as the light came it was gone.

It left behind shocked silence.

Darach lowered his arm and looked toward what had once been a mob of vicious women. What was left behind was a mob of doddering old men.

He couldn't help it—he smiled. " 'Tis justice."

The old men looked at each other, then down at themselves with horror. They cried out their terror and disbelief in shaky old voices. Then they scattered, as though they thought they could outrun their fate. One of them staggered their way, and Darach could see the mindless panic in the old man's eyes. Both Blythe and Sparkle looked as though they would enjoy reaching out and swatting the man, but they controlled the urge. Silently they watched him totter past them on creaky ancient legs.

Blythe nodded. "They had nothing but contempt for men, so it's only fitting that they end their short lives as males. And at their age, mating isn't an option. So they can forget about their dreams of immortality. It would take a space-bus filled with sex potency regeneration implants to do them any good." She looked up at Darach, and her smile lit up his future. "We can look forward to a peaceful life together without having to worry about wacko women." She seemed to think about that. "Okay, so maybe not quite peaceful. Things tend to happen around you, but at least I'll never be bored."

The sound of sobbing drew Darach's attention to Sparkle. Cats could not cry, but Sparkle would never let details stop her from what she wished to do.

Blythe clutched Sparkle tighter. "Hey, it's okay. You're safe now. You don't have to be upset."

"Upset? I'm not upset. I'm happy. I haven't been this

happy since I turned a meeting of Citizens Against Sexual Excess into an orgy."

Sparkle gazed up at Darach and Blythe with teary eyes. "Mede defied the Big Boss for me." When they stared at her blankly, she tried to make it clearer. "Mede wasn't supposed to harm a human. Ever. Tonight he did, for *me*."

She gazed toward the castle with what Darach could only describe as a mixture of love and lust. With Sparkle, *everything* included sex in the mixture.

"The old Mede is back. And since it looks like you two are in it together for the long haul, I have to talk to my big bad troublemaker about paying up on a bet." She offered them a sly watery cat smile. "I lust after a golden god. Preferably naked."

Darach looked at Blythe, then shrugged. " 'Tis time we went home." His gaze softened as he let the horror of this night go, and embraced the true wonder of what Blythe had given him. "I must release Thrain from my bed. Then we can explore this loving ye spoke of." Even as he talked, he could feel himself tightening, his need returning. "Methinks the vile potion the women gave me is still strong. I grow hard again. What do ye think Ecstasy would prescribe to help me?"

Blythe leaned into him and laughed. "I don't know what Ecstasy would prescribe, but Dr. Blythe prescribes her never-fail sensual solution."

Epilogue

Blythe pressed close to Darach as they stood in the great hall watching the tour group prepare for their return trip through time. Textron was ignoring Sandy, so Blythe guessed the underwear deal was off. And Clara refused to meet Blythe's gaze. Blythe felt righteous satisfaction. Clara *should* feel guilty.

"Look at number ten on this list, Blythe. Mayhap we can try it tonight. There is honey in the kitchen." Darach was engrossed in Sparkle's list of *The Top Fifty Things to Do with a Naked Man.*

"Let me look at that list."

He handed it to her and she scanned the suggestions. "Number fifteen sounds better."

He glanced at number fifteen and his eyes widened. "Aye."

Blythe noticed Ganymede heading their way. Sparkle rested in the crook of his arm, and the bittyfluffs faithfully crowded around him. For some strange reason, the tiny fur balls had transferred their adoration to Ganymede. Blythe smiled. She had a feeling Ganymede was responsible for the transfer.

Ganymede stopped in front of them, shifted from foot to foot, then coughed nervously.

"Just say it, Mede." Sparkle cast Blythe an all-suffering look. *"Men. What would they do without women to help them express their emotions?"* She glanced toward the rest of the tour group. *"And I'm back to the silent cat routine. I have to play the quiet kitty part until we get rid of Mede's customers."*

Sparkle licked her mouth with a small pink tongue. *"Then we're off to an exotic island for some rest and relaxation. Now that Mede's stopped worrying about whether the Big Boss is going to zap him every time he falls off the goodness-and-light wagon, he's a lot more open to my sensual suggestions."* Her gaze slid to Ganymede. *"I have a date with a naked golden god. For a whole month."*

Blythe had to bite her lip to keep from laughing out loud. Since Sparkle's close call, Ganymede had carried her everywhere so that she wouldn't have to walk on her injured leg. She was a tiny tyrant, but Ganymede never complained about her bossiness. He claimed they were just good friends. Right.

Ganymede drew in a deep breath of courage. "Look, blood-su . . . I mean Darach. If it wasn't for you, Sparkle would be Scottish roadkill by now."

Sparkle cast him a disgusted look. *"Does he have a way with words or what?"*

Ganymede frowned. "Of course, if it wasn't for you, she wouldn't have been there in the first place. But I'll let that slide." He shoved out his hand. "Thanks for saving her. If I'm ever in the area with a tour group, you and Blythe can do some time-hopping free." His pained expression suggested that the word "free" was tough to say.

Darach clasped his hand and nodded. "I thank ye for saving all of us, Ganymede. In appreciation, I offer ye the use of the MacKenzie castle for one of your tours each year." He grinned. "Free."

Ganymede brightened immediately. "Really? That's great." He cuffed Darach across the shoulder. Darach winced. "We're almost ready to go. Hey, Blythe, do you mind if I take the bittyfluffs home with me? They've sort of grown attached." He looked hopeful.

Blythe knew exactly who had grown attached. "Sure, take all of them. I want them to be happy."

As Ganymede turned to walk away, Sparkle climbed up to peer over the top of his shoulder. *"Blythe, if there're any girl things you find you can't live without, make a list and get it to Ganymede next year. I'll see that he brings them to you."* Her eyes gleamed with wicked glee. *"Don't forget to have lots and lots of hot delicious sex. Oh, and if you see my ghosts, tell them they're fired."*

Darach waited until Ganymede was out of hearing

range. "Are ye sure ye wish to remain in this time with me, Blythe?" His gaze held hers. "Once we are married, I will stay with ye always. Always can be overlong if ye're not sure." He raked his fingers through his long hair. His hands shook. "If ye wish to live in your time, ye could return now with Ganymede, and I could join ye next year when Ganymede brings another tour group here. I need only return once every twenty years to fulfill my duty."

Blythe wanted to wrap her arms around this big gorgeous man who had no idea how much she loved him. He would have to pry her fingers from his body to get rid of her.

"Odin's wrath." Darach's expression was a mixture of frustration and disgust. "What I am trying to say is that I love ye more than I love any time or place. I care only that I am with ye." He speared her with his intent gaze. "Forever."

Blythe smiled up at him. "Good thing, vampire, because you'll never be rid of me." She stood on tiptoe and kissed him softly on the lips.

He seemed to steel himself for what he needed to say next. "I can give ye no bairns."

"Get something straight, Darach." She cupped his face between her hands. "I'm not marrying you for children. In 2339, Earth is so overpopulated that many women never have babies. I had already decided years ago that if I ever wanted a child, I'd adopt one. And once and for all, understand that I love *you*, not a particular time or place."

Blythe watched the tension drain from him. Leaning down, he returned her kiss, then grinned and held up Sparkle's list. "I canna wait to start on number one."

Darach wrapped his arm around her waist, and they waved goodbye as the time travelers disappeared. Blythe stared into the empty great hall. This, then, was love. She was walking away from all her possessions and all the people she'd ever known. Ganymede had agreed to deliver a few messages from her to friends and relatives. Yes, she'd miss the conveniences of her time, but *things* couldn't compare to the emotion she felt every time she looked at Darach. She was starting an exciting new life with the man she loved at her side. Nothing else mattered.

"I'm feeling kind of hungry." Blythe smiled up at Darach. "Come to the kitchen and help me find something to eat. And we can get that honey while we're at it."

She was still thinking about the honey when Thrain stepped out of the shadows.

"I leave tonight, Darach." He clasped Darach's shoulders, then released him. "Thank ye for my life."

"Ye're welcome to stay." Darach's gaze was troubled. "We have much to talk about."

Thrain grinned, and Blythe realized how much Sparkle's "golden god" description fit him. But Blythe hadn't exactly seen him at his best before this.

"I still need much rest, and I would get none with sounds of lust keeping me awake." He turned his smile on Blythe, and she blinked at the pure power of that smile. She'd just bet he mowed women down by the hundreds wherever he went.

Thrain returned his attention to Darach. "Pride and hurt feelings kept me away from ye all these years. But when death neared, I realized how much our friendship meant to me. I know where your London home is and will visit ye there."

Darach nodded. "Ye were the only friend I ever truly regretted losing. The words I said at our last meeting were cruel and untrue. Aesa should never have come between us."

Blythe started toward the kitchen to give the two men a few minutes alone. Once there, she rooted around for something to eat while she waited for Darach to join her.

By the time he entered the kitchen, Blythe had discovered something important. "Everything here is raw, and I don't know how to cook."

Darach offered her an indulgent smile. "It doesna matter if ye canna prepare a meal well, because ye'll soon have a cook to do that."

"Uh, you don't understand. I've never cooked a thing in my life. I don't even know what some of these things are." She swept her arm over the strange array of *things* she'd found in the kitchen.

Darach looked startled.

"Okay, here's the scoop on food in my time. I pay a yearly fee to a local food preparation service. Each day I choose what I want to eat from an online menu, and the service delivers the fully cooked meals at the time I specify. I won't go into the how of it, but the meals simply appear in a delivery cubicle built into my dining area wall." Blythe held up her hands. "Nobody cooks anymore. Why would they?"

"Why indeed?" He looked resigned.

She watched silently while he left to get water, then returned.

"I dinna eat, but I've seen others cook. After I wash the vegetables and cut them into pieces, ye may put them into a pot." He paused to offer her a thoughtful glance. "Ye *do* know what a pot looks like?"

"Smart-ass." She grinned and went in search of a suitable pot while he washed the vegetables. By the time she returned, he was starting to cut them up.

He glanced at her pot and smiled. "Unless ye're a witch in need of a cauldron, ye might find something smaller."

With a humph of disgust, she went to look for another pot. "So when do you think you'll be able to see yourself in a mirror?"

He was silent for a moment. "I have already gained my newest power."

Surprised, Blythe turned to stare at him. "Well, why didn't you say something?"

Darach shrugged. "I wished to save it until we were alone."

Blythe was touched. "As soon as I eat, let's go up to our room. I'll dig out my makeup mirror, then you can take a good look at that 'wondrous' face."

She frowned. He didn't act overly excited at the prospect. Blythe chose a smaller pot and walked back to the table where Darach was still cutting vegetables. She put the ones he'd already cut into the pot. "What's that big thing you're cutting up now?"

He chuckled, but didn't look at her. " 'Tis called an onion, Blythe."

"Oh. Well, how was I to know? I've never seen a whole one before. It's huge." Genetically engineered veggies in her time were pretty small, and scientists had created designer colors for them. No wonder she hadn't recognized this one. But she still felt defensive about her ignorance. When they settled down in their home, she'd have to spend some time with the cook.

"Ye'd know it verra well if ye had to cut up one this potent." He sounded strange, sort of clogged up.

"Never doubt my love, Blythe, because only one who loved ye beyond reason would submit to so unmanly a thing." He sounded really cranky.

"Unmanly?" What was he talking about? "Okay, so I know that cutting up an onion wouldn't be at the top of your superhero résumé, but I don't think it threatens your masculinity."

He made an impatient sound. "I dinna speak of cutting up the onion."

"Then what?"

He looked at her.

And Blythe knew that she had truly found her forever love as she watched the tears slide down his face.